Praise fo... ...rey

"A fast-paced, thrilling ride. Readers of Lynette Eason and Colleen Coble will enjoy this first novel in the JEOPARDY FALLS series from Pettrey."

—*Library Journal* starred review of *One Wrong Move*

"Pettrey launches her new JEOPARDY FALLS romantic suspense series with this gripping tale.... Fans of series that follow investigative teams, such as Lynn H. Blackburn's DEFEND AND PROTECT, will be hooked by Pettrey's latest."

—*Booklist* on *One Wrong Move*

"This action-packed thriller is sure to please."

—Irene Hannon, bestselling and award-winning author, on *The Deadly Shallows*

"Another fantastic suspense by Dani Pettrey! I fell in love with Christian and Andi's sweet romance, and the plot kept me on the edge of my seat all the way to the end. Excellent!"

—Susan May Warren, *USA Today* bestselling author, on *One Wrong Move*

"I love Dani's writing, and *The Deadly Shallows* is one of her best! Tightly written and dripping with tension. I couldn't turn the pages fast enough."

—Carrie Stuart Parks, bestselling and award-winning author of *Relative Silence*

"Pulse-pounding.... Pettrey masterfully balances Noah and Brooke's burgeoning relationship with the unraveling of the tightly plotted mystery. Fans of Lynette Eason and DiAnn Mills will enjoy this."

—*Publishers Weekly* on *The Deadly Shallows*

TWO
SECONDS
TOO LATE

BOOKS BY DANI PETTREY

ALASKAN COURAGE

Submerged
Shattered
Stranded
Silenced
Sabotaged

CHESAPEAKE VALOR

Cold Shot
Still Life
Blind Spot
Dead Drift

COASTAL GUARDIANS

The Killing Tide
The Crushing Depths
The Deadly Shallows
The Shifting Current: A COASTAL GUARDIAN *Novella*

JEOPARDY FALLS

One Wrong Move
Two Seconds Too Late

Shadowed: An ALASKAN COURAGE *Novella from Sins of the Past: A Romantic Suspense Novella Collection*

Deadly Isle from *The Cost of Betrayal: Three Romantic Suspense Novellas*

TWO SECONDS TOO LATE

DANI PETTREY

BETHANYHOUSE
a division of Baker Publishing Group
Minneapolis, Minnesota

Published by Bethany House Publishers
Minneapolis, Minnesota
BethanyHouse.com

Bethany House Publishers is a division of
Baker Publishing Group, Grand Rapids, Michigan

Printed in the United States of America

Library of Congress Cataloging-in-Publication Data
Names: Pettrey, Dani, author.
Title: Two seconds too late / Dani Pettrey.
Description: Minneapolis, Minnesota : Bethany House Publishers, a division
    of Baker Publishing Group, 2025. | Series: Jeopardy Falls ; 2
Identifiers: LCCN 2024059582 | ISBN 9780764238499 (paper) | ISBN
    9780764244599 (casebound) | ISBN 9781493448982 (ebook)
Subjects: LCGFT: Christian fiction. | Detective and mystery fiction. | Novels.
Classification: LCC PS3616.E89 T86 2025 | DDC 813/.6—dc23/eng/20241217
LC record available at https://lccn.loc.gov/2024059582

Cover design by Jennifer Parker

Published in association with Books & Such Literary Management, BooksAnd Such.com.

Baker Publishing Group publications use paper produced from sustainable forestry practices and postconsumer waste whenever possible.

25   26   27   28   29   30   31   7   6   5   4   3   2   1

This book was written during an extremely difficult time for our family. We moved from Maryland to Florida, and three weeks later, our house was flooded with four feet of water from Hurricane Helene. With the recent move, most of our belongings were still in boxes on the floor, and we lost ninety-five percent of our belongings, including two cars. But dear readers and writer friends blessed us beyond measure in more ways than we could have imagined. This book is dedicated to all my readers, my friends, and especially my dear writer friends. Thank you for being the hands and feet of God's provision.

PROLOGUE

THWACK. The bullet collided with the car at Riley's back a moment before a retort echoed in the stale air of the junkyard.

As she ducked beneath the heap of twisted metal that once was a sleek Porsche, a second shot shattered the driver's window. She covered her head, but it was no use. Glass shards rained down, clinging to her hair as a sliver sliced her cheek.

Her heart raged in her chest, stealing her breath.

She gripped the SIG, her finger on the trigger.

Sweat slithered down her brow, clouding her eyes.

Greyson was right. This had been an awful idea. If only she'd listened to him—at least this once.

"You're going to die," Pete Scarletto said with a lilt of laughter.

Please come. Why was it taking the police so long? She exhaled. *Don't let this end in death.* She'd never taken a life, and she didn't want to start now. She knew how to shoot, but a man was far different from bottles on a fence post.

"You hear me? You're dead," he roared, his anger vibrating in her chest.

She shifted, the sharp edge of the bumper cutting through her jacket, lashing her back. She smothered a cry. She couldn't give away her position.

A sharp, splitting pain burned across the top of her ear seconds before the report. He'd found her. She was as good as dead. Her full hope rested on the police to stop this before she had to pull the trigger.

Please turn the corner. Please. I don't want to do this. But he was giving her no choice. It was him or her.

Hot tears streaked down her cheeks, her heart racing, adrenaline burning her limbs.

Footsteps sounded.

Closer.

Closer.

She held her breath.

Pete's extended arm stretched into her line of sight, his Beretta visible past the edge of the twisted pile of metal, his finger on the trigger. He rounded the heap, and she fired.

ONE

THREE CLICKS RIGHT and . . .

The lock disengaged. Triumph shot through Kelly Frazier. They'd finally done it.

Jared squeezed her shoulder. This was it. The moment they'd worked so hard for. Without a word, he raised his arm.

Her gaze flicked to his lit watch face.

Three minutes and their window shut.

She cranked the handle, and the thick safe door opened. She shined her pencil flashlight inside, and a smile curled on her lips at the stack of money. *Retribution.* It had been the only way.

Without hesitation, he scooped the safe's contents—black velvet bags, passports, and cold, hard cash—into the hard-sided case.

Snapping the case shut, he held up his arm and indicated his watch, the second hand ticking away.

Less than a minute.

Shutting the safe door, she swung the cliché picture-in-front-of-the-wall-safe back into place.

Voices carried down the hallway.

She shut her eyes for the blink of a second. They were coming.

An hour and a half later, she checked her rearview mirror for the umpteenth time. Surely someone had been sent after her. It was a given, but where was *he*? Had he already found her and was toying with her? Or, worse yet, was he waiting and watching? She prayed she had just enough lead to make the drops, and not enough to hang herself.

She rushed down 84 South, her chest tightening, her breathing shallow.

Calm down and stick to the plan.

One drop for the case on her passenger seat and one drop at Riley MacLeod's.

Riley jolted upright in bed. Sweat drenched, she blinked, panic shaking her limbs.

Not again. It'd been a month and still the nightmares came.

Deep breath. Take one.

Only shallow spurts wheezed out.

She yanked off the smothering covers and ran a trembling hand through her damp hair.

Her soul and body weary, she planted her feet on the cold winter floor as Pete's glazed-over eyes haunted her waking dreams.

Rising from bed, she hurried to the hook on the wall and slipped into her robe, then walk-hopped for her fluffy slippers against the far wall. It'd been the coldest December on record for she didn't know how many years.

Half awake, she shuffled into the kitchen situated at the rear of her house, the windows overlooking the mountains stretching to the sky. She yawned, hoping she'd remembered to program the coffeepot. Her gaze darted to the red machine, aromatic coffee dripping into the carafe. Thank goodness.

Sleep had eluded her again. She'd had no choice with Pete. It was either him or her. No question about it. So why did hot guilt continue to saturate her soul? Why wouldn't her heart heal? She leaned against the counter and grabbed a cup of steaming coffee.

Speaking of her heart . . . her gaze shifted to the photo of their PI firm. She smiled at the ragtag bunch. All ragtag save Greyson Chadwick, who always wore well-tailored suits that fit him oh-so-right.

She smiled at the soft hint of a smile on his lips. If she could just transport forward an hour, she'd be with him at the office, and that strange sense of peace that filled her whenever she was in his presence would settle her mind—at least for a time. Seeing him was the best part of her day. She sighed. If only the reverse were true.

The soft purr of a motor hummed in the distance. *Odd.* It wasn't the rumble of her brother Deckard's SUV nor her brother Christian's new Bronco. It rolled away from her house, heading east. Even odder. No one but the three of them used the back way off the ranch.

Setting down her coffee mug, she moved for the front of the house, curious who was visiting so early. Gravel crunched on the drive leading away from the main house at the top of the hill, where Deckard lived, and faded away.

Sun slit through the glass panes on either side of the front door. She opened it and reached for the screen door when something jabbed into the sole of her foot.

Taking a step back, she peered down. A white envelope lay wedged between the two doors. Bending, she picked it up, examining the protruding shape.

She flipped it over.

Keep it safe at all costs. I'm trusting you.

The eerie sensation of being watched crawled along her skin as the words scrolled across the envelope sunk in. Who was trusting her, and with what?

Scanning the ranch and finding it still, she turned her attention back to the envelope. She studied the handwriting, hoping it would identify the sender but . . . nothing. Although, it did seem somewhat familiar, but she couldn't place why.

Slipping her finger beneath the fold, she tore it open and pulled out a locker key. She frowned. *What on earth?*

She studied the gold key and the *315* written in white across the blue plastic on top. The strong sensation of someone's presence again washed over her, sending a shiver rippling up her back and along her arms.

Scanning the property once more, her gaze halted on the large copse of pinion trees across the way. A shadow shifted—the silhouette of a man slipping through the trees. She dashed inside to grab her gun, then raced for the door, only to collide into something hard and solid. "Oomph."

She lifted her SIG, her gaze tracking up.

"Don't shoot the messenger," Greyson said, his hands raised.

"Move! There's someone in the trees." She rushed headlong for them, Grey on her heels. Reaching the copse, she and Grey cleared it from either end. Whoever had been there was gone.

"What is going on?" he asked.

"I don't know. That's what I was trying to figure out when I ran into you." She squinted against the morning sun, shielding her eyes with her free hand. "What are you doing here?" The sudden remembrance of being in her nightgown and a robe brought heat rushing to her cheeks.

"Deck invited me over for some coffee before work. When I got here, he said he'd heard a vehicle and asked me to check on you because you didn't answer your phone. He's out looking for whoever was on the property because they didn't park at the main house like a known visitor to the ranch would."

"Oh . . ." She bit her bottom lip. "I'm pretty sure I left my phone in the bedroom."

He ducked his head, gazing at her, his eyes—a mix of gray and green like the sky in a July storm—held her still. "You all right?" he asked, concern lacing his deep tone.

"I heard a car engine, and then saw a shadow, the outline of a man, in the trees."

"I heard the cars too," Deck said, walking up, shotgun in hand. Her brother was tall, a heck of a shot, and entirely too handsome for his own good—women fell at his feet. All but one.

"Cars? As in plural?" Had one passed by before she'd awoken? What were two unexpected vehicles doing on their ranch at sunrise?

"I heard them too," her brother Christian said, striding up from the opposite direction, his house the farthest out. Three properties for three siblings. The fourth still living the life they'd left. Riley winced. She didn't like to set her mind on *her*. Not after everything. Not after so much pain.

"I saw tire treads up past the house," Deck said.

Greyson headed back toward the trees.

Deck lifted his chin as Greyson passed him. "What's up?"

"Ri saw someone over here. Just checking it out."

"I can handle it." Despite her attire, she was more than capable of scanning for remnants of someone's presence. She was the skip tracer and tracker of the family and their PI firm. Joining Grey in the shadowed copse, she studied the boot prints. Larger size than her brothers', which was saying something given Christian's size twelve shoe. This had to be a thirteen.

Grey followed the tire treads leading toward the rear exit of the ranch.

"Whoever it was is gone." She lowered the gun by her side.

"You weren't expecting anyone?" Deck asked Christian.

He shook his head, and they both turned to her.

"No, but someone left this." She fished out the envelope she'd shoved into her robe pocket.

"What's that?" Grey asked, arching a brow.

She handed it to him. "I'm going to get changed."

"There's no signature," he called after her.

"Nope."

"Any idea who it's from?" he asked, catching up to her stride far too easily.

"Not a clue." She shrugged, reaching her front porch while her brothers followed the tire treads in either direction to see how far they went.

Grey cleared his throat. "Doesn't sound good."

"Can't imagine it is." She stepped over her threshold.

"I don't like it."

"I imagine you don't." Circumstances aside, vexing the man brought a warm smile to her lips.

"It could be dangerous."

"That would be my guess."

Greyson leaned against the doorframe, arms crossed. "It appears that trouble has come looking for you again."

Maybe this time she should heed his warnings rather than rushing headlong into whatever this was. But her stubborn streak held firm. At least for now. As long as it didn't end up like Pete Scarletto.

Her chest squeezed at the very thought of him.

Greyson narrowed his eyes. "What's wrong?"

"Huh?" *Great comeback, Ri.*

"Something is wrong. I can see it on your brow."

She tried smoothing it.

"That's not going to help," he said, following her inside as she left the door open for him.

She lifted her cup of now-cold coffee and topped it off. "Help yourself." She gestured to the mug rack.

"Thanks." He lifted one off a hook and flipped it over, filling it until steam swirled from the rim. "So what is it?"

The fact that Pete Scarletto came to mind every time a new case came in. Every case wouldn't end that way. She *knew* it, but her feelings taunted her otherwise.

Stupid witch ditched a key at some chick's house—an armed chick with three armed men on a ranch. It looked like a locker key, best he could tell, but what did it go to? She could have stashed the safe's contents anywhere along the way to the ranch while he chased to catch up. He'd nearly gotten her. *Nearly.* He gritted his teeth.

Why that ranch? That chick? In the end, it mattered not—as long as he retrieved the key.

He studied the house with his long-range binoculars. The woman had to leave the ranch sometime, and when she did, he'd get it. If she didn't leave, he'd wait until the cover of nightfall, hike in on foot, and take it by force.

TWO

RILEY PULLED INTO THE LOT of MIS at a quarter till nine. *MacLeod Investigation and Security.* She loved the new sign in bronzed, streamlined letters. Hopefully the guys liked her choice, but knowing them, they'd probably forgotten she'd even ordered a new sign.

She shifted her car into Park and smiled, despite everyone still being on edge over the mystery envelope when she'd left the ranch. Greyson's Range Rover had shimmered in her rearview mirror in the full rising sun as she'd made her way down the long drive leading away from her home. He'd been a breath behind her, but there was no sign of him now. Only Deckard's truck sat in the parking lot.

She exited her car, and her smile spread. *Finally.* She'd finally beaten him. It had taken a winding snake of back roads, but she'd beaten him from the ranch. It was a silly competition, but it was a competition all the same, and she didn't like losing. Though neither did Grey. She walked through the fluttering snow and rubbed her arms as she entered the building, glancing back at the angry, charcoal sky. Worse was on its way.

Shaking off a shiver still tingling along her arms, she strode to the elevator and pushed the Up button. The doors slid open, and she swiped her key card for their floor. Every day the realization of where they were and what they did still shocked her when she considered the pit they'd clawed their way out of.

The elevator dinged and jerked to stop.

She bounded to the office door, key card in hand, and punched in her code. She opened the door to find Greyson sitting at his desk. Her shoulders dropped. "How . . . what . . . are you doing here?"

Greyson reclined in his office chair, hands interlocked behind his head and the charming smile that did funny things to her legs on his lips. "I work here."

"Your car isn't in the parking lot." She swiped snowflakes off her jade overcoat and slipped off her fluffy white scarf and mittens.

"The Rover is being serviced around the corner." His smile widened, his handsome eyes creasing. Such depths resided in those soulful eyes. Depths she'd love to sink into. "Thought you had me, didn't you?" He rocked forward, planting his Edward Greens on the plush gray carpeting.

"Oh, come on." Deckard sighed as he emerged from the back hall, folder in hand. "Please tell me you're not sparring over who got here first?" He shook his head. "The minute Greyson raced in here, I knew this was coming."

"Oh." She arched her brows. "So you raced in?"

"Walked briskly." He winked, and her heart fluttered.

Deck tapped the folder in his hand. "When you two chuckle-nuts are through sparring, I'll be in the conference room." He walked down the hall, leaving her and Grey alone, at least until Christian showed. Though he was stopping by his girlfriend's to bring her coffee and a cinnamon roll, so who knew how long he'd be.

Greyson stood and gestured to the back hall Deck had just walked down. "After you."

Still smarting over the loss *again*, she made her way to what they referred to as the round room.

Entering, Greyson pulled out a chair for her.

"Thank you." She sat at the circular table the room had been named for. Grabbing a butterscotch from the bowl in the center of the table, she popped one into her mouth, praying her racing heart would settle. How did Greyson affect her so? A simple wink brought heat rushing to her cheeks.

Greyson frowned. "You hot? I can turn down the heat."

She lifted one of the blank steno pads off the table and fanned herself. "Yep." It was better than sharing the reason for her blush. Though, in truth, her cheeks were warm, so technically she wasn't lying.

Grey moved for the thermostat as Christian rushed in. He gave his lopsided, apologetic smile. "Sorry I'm late."

Deckard lifted his chin with a teasing grin. "Finally manage to stop canoodling with Andi?"

Riley crossed one booted foot over the other and shook her head. Since he and Andi met on a heist case months ago, they'd been nearly inseparable. Not surprising. Christian had met his match in her.

He took a seat and swiveled in the chair. "When you have a girl, I'm going to josh you just as bad."

Deckard harrumphed. "That'll be the day."

"Probably not as far away as you think," she murmured under her breath. She liked Harper Grace, who'd left on a humanitarian trip right after working a corruption case with Deckard. It'd been three months, and regardless of what Deck claimed, he'd been missing her ever since.

"And I wasn't canoodling," Christian protested. He shrugged a broad shoulder on a smile. "Well, not the whole time."

"Uh-huh." Deckard leaned forward. "Can we focus on work now?"

"Please," Christian said.

"To start," Deck began, "the Todd Miller case is a wrap. He's facing trial for two counts of fraud."

"Let's hope he doesn't get off with just a fine to pay and time served," she said, resting her arms on the table. Men like Todd Miller had a way of skirting the law. But she prayed that wouldn't be the case this time.

Deckard exhaled a whistle. "We can hope, but that's the

direction most fraud cases go, especially for the rich with their fancy lawyers."

Frustration rattled inside. Riley popped another butterscotch into her mouth, setting her wrapper on the table until she could throw it away, though she had a habit of forgetting, which drove Grey nuts. He was always finding them crumpled somewhere. At times she did it just to mess with him, and she could swear she'd seen a smile grace his handsome face while he shook his head.

"Brown Eyed Girl" trilled on her phone, and she shimmied it from her jean pocket. "Sorry, but I think I should take this." The last time Veronica Gaiman—soon to be Melling—called, Christian and Andi had been whisked away on the heist case.

"All good," Deck said.

"Veronica," Riley said, wondering if the woman might've dialed the wrong number by mistake. They had been talking more of late, building more of a relationship as they had a mutual friend in Kelly Frazier. "What's up?"

"Kelly's missing," Veronica rushed out.

THREE

"HANG ON. I'm putting you on speaker," Riley said. "The gang is here."

"Okay," Roni said, her breath coming in short spurts.

"How long has Kelly been missing?"

"Kelly, your new friend?" Greyson asked with furrowed brow.

She nodded, and he shifted beside her, his knees brushing hers. A sense of security rushed through her. How did a simple movement evoke such a reaction? But it did—*always*.

"I saw her around eleven last night," Roni said. "When I woke this morning, she was gone. She and Tate had a terrible blowout last night."

Riley flipped open the cover of her steno pad and jotted down the info. "Her boyfriend?" She'd heard of Tate but never met him.

"Yes. Kelly was all spooked when we talked, and now she's gone."

"Spooked about what?" Riley tapped the notepad with her pen.

Veronica huffed and puffed. "Her fight with Tate."

"What's up?" Deck asked. "You sound out of breath."

"I'm hiking."

"Okay . . ." Riley frowned. Why call from a hike of all places? She shook off the thought and focused back on the relayed

21

information. "Spooked is an odd reaction for a fight." Anger. Tears. Far more common.

"I assumed she was worried how he was going to react."

Riley shifted. "Are you saying she was worried Tate might harm her?"

"I don't know." Veronica's striving breaths ceased. "Finally." She sighed in relief.

"Finally?" Deck quirked his head.

"Finally reached the top." Roni sneezed. "Excuse me. Tree pollen."

"I gotta ask," Deck said. "Why call from hiking? Did you just learn she was missing on the hike?"

"No, but I wanted to be away from gossipy ears, and housekeeping is in my room."

"Gossipy ears?" Riley asked.

"I'm at a high-brow retreat, and the women present are like a gossip factory."

"Got it." Riley shifted gears. "Let's backpedal a bit. Have you tried calling Kelly?"

"Of course," Veronica snapped. "Sorry," she said. "I'm just all out of sorts worried about her."

"You weren't able to reach her?"

"No. My calls just went to voice mail, which isn't set up, so I can't even leave a message. I've texted, too, a handful of times, but nothing."

Not like Kelly at all. Riley tapped the exquisite roller ball pen Greyson had gifted her last Christmas against her steno pad. Clearly, Roni was at a retreat, so Riley knew the answer to this, but she had to ask anyway. "Have you been by her place?"

"I'm at a retreat."

"I figured. I'll go by her place. See if she's home and just not answering the phone."

"We'll go," Deck said. "You finish the call."

"You sure?" she asked as her brothers stood.

"Positive." Deck lifted his chin in that good-bye gesture of his.

"Thanks, guys. She's in 3C at the Mountain Range Apartments."

"Got it." Deck popped out the door, Christian following.

"I doubt he'll find her there," Roni said after Deck left.

"Why do you say that?"

"Because I'm sure something happened to her."

"Why, exactly?" What did Veronica believe happened?

"Kelly was *here* with me at the retreat. We were set to have breakfast together, and she never showed."

Definitely not like Kelly. "So she disappeared from the retreat?" Riley asked, just to clarify.

"Yes." Veronica huffed.

Riley ignored Veronica's impatience.

"What retreat are you at?"

"Expressive Wellness Retreat and Spa. It's up near Tierra Amarilla."

Riley jotted it down.

"She wouldn't leave without saying good-bye," Veronica reiterated. "Come on, you know Kelly."

"Yeah, I do." It really would be out of character for Kelly to take off without saying good-bye. "Maybe she left early and didn't want to wake you, or really late last night. What did Tate say? I'm assuming you spoke with him."

"Of course. He said he got a separate room after their fight and didn't realize she was gone until I asked him to check their room."

"What about her luggage?" Greyson chimed in. "Is it still in the room?"

"No," Roni said. "But I'm telling you something is wrong. I can feel it."

"Did you speak to the staff? Perhaps someone saw her leave."

"The director said Kelly came to her early this morning to say good-bye and thank her for the stay."

"So she said Kelly left of her own accord this morning?"

"Yes." Roni sighed. "It appears that way."

"You said she left early. How early are we talking?" She resumed tapping her pen against the notepad.

Grey looked over, and she stopped. Her tapping nonstop while thinking drove him nuts. Just as his nonstop bouncing knee did her. She swore he liked vexing her just as much as she did him.

"Julie, the director, said she left around six a.m."

"I'd say she just didn't want to wake you," Riley began. "But—"

"I'm up at four thirty every day," Veronica cut in. "Kelly knew that."

Everyone in town knew it after Roni started a petition to get Maggie's Coffee Corner to open an hour earlier to suit her. It'd failed, but Roni had still tried.

"Did she have her car, or did she ride with Tate?" Greyson asked.

"She had her own car. So does Tate. Due to work hours or something, they met here."

"Is Kelly's car gone?" Grey asked.

"Yes." *Clickity-clack.* Nails tapped along a hard surface. Riley guessed it was Veronica's phone case. Always long red nails with Roni.

"I really do wonder if she left and her cell died," Riley said, but it wasn't like Kelly to just pick up and leave. She had to know Roni would be worried.

A withering sigh escaped Roni's lips. "You sound like the police."

"I was going to ask if you had called them," Greyson said.

"What did they have to say?" Though Riley could already guess.

"They said there's no cause for panic, and it's too soon to file a missing person's report. As far as they know, Kelly left of her own accord since there's nothing to suggest otherwise, which is why I want to hire you, Riley."

Riley tucked her chin in. "Hire me?"

"Yes, I need you here," Roni said, her tone resolute.

"There?" She met Grey's confused gaze.

"Yes. At the retreat because, first, Tate's here, and I want you to question him before he leaves. He says he's not staying at a couples' retreat alone, so he's going to take off on some trip just like he thinks Kelly has, but he won't say where he's going or for how long. It's very suspicious, if you ask me."

Perhaps. It at least bordered on suspicious. Riley sat forward, resting her forearms on the table.

"And second?" Greyson prompted, pulling a butterscotch wrapper from his lap. He held it up and gave her that dipped-chin, eyebrows-lifted look.

Oops. *Sorry,* she mouthed.

"Second," Roni continued, "she disappeared from *here,* and I want you to interview the guests."

"Why? I doubt that retreat center would be happy with us questioning their clientele," Greyson said, sitting back.

"That's why you two need to come undercover."

"Two?" Riley scrunched her nose.

"It's a couples' retreat. You need to bring your better half. And given I seriously doubt you want to play couple with one of your brothers . . ."

"Ewww . . ." Absolutely not.

"Right," Roni said, and Riley could practically hear her smile. "You'll need to partner with that tall glass of water."

Greyson? She was suggesting Riley have a fake relationship with Grey? Tingles shot through her—a combination of *yes, please* and *no way.*

She'd enjoy the time with the man she secretly loved—a true love that simmered inside, not the teenage crush she used to have. But while he spent a lot of time with her, and she occasionally caught him staring, he'd certainly never made a move or comment in that direction.

Besides, he went about things completely opposite than she did. Methodical logic versus her by-the-gut feelings. The combination worked in the office, but would it in the field? Besides, Greyson hadn't worked in the field in years.

Greyson cleared his throat and shifted his gaze away.

Was that a blush on his cheeks?

"Hello?" Roni said at the silence.

"Sorry," Riley jumped in. "Just thinking . . . I don't know if—"

"Oh, please, you know you want to." Roni chuckled.

Roni! Mortification sifted through her. Was she that obvious?

"Who wouldn't?" Roni added.

Okay. That sounded better. Mortification abated.

"You and hotty pack and get out here. I'll get you registered as my guests."

"Let's back up just a little. You think someone saw what? Why do you want us questioning everyone?"

"As far as I'm concerned, everyone here is a suspect, with Tate leading the list. So pack your bags. I'll pay you whatever it costs to find her and make sure she's safe."

"Let's wait until we hear from Deck. Make sure she's not at her apartment or work."

"You might as well get packing in the meantime, because I know she's not at either place. My gut is never wrong."

Riley couldn't knock her. She worked by instinct, too, which killed Mr. Plotter and Planner. He respected her talent and skill set—much of which she'd learned from him—and he'd said as much. But he insisted she took too many risks from following her gut, and after Pete Scarletto, maybe he was right.

"What names should I put you under when I register you?" Roni asked.

"I don't know if fake names are necessary."

"Why? Has Tate seen you before? Can he identify you?"

"No. We've never met, but—" This was all going too fast. What was happening, and why wouldn't her heart stop racing? She knew why. He was sitting right beside her.

"Look, Roni, if Kelly's missing, there's a protocol to the way I work cases. An order. Once places she could be are all ruled out, I run down information on her—learn everything I can that might help find her. If I still can't locate her, then I'll head out into the field and start searching."

"I can't say I like the delay." Roni tapped her nails again.

"If nothing pops up . . ." She looked at Greyson, and he nodded. "We'll head out for the retreat first thing tomorrow morning."

Roni exhaled. "Very well. So back to the aliases you want me to register you under?"

"I don't know," she began.

"Fake names can't hurt," Greyson said.

Emotion riddled through Riley. The thought of playing a couple with Greyson was both exhilarating and terrifying. "Okay," she said, trying to force herself to relax, her shoulders taut as a strung rubber band. "If we're coming . . . I'll be Allie Bennet."

"Nice. *The Notebook* and *Pride and Prejudice*. Good combo."

She wouldn't have expected Roni to get it so quick.

"And you, hotty?" Roni's voice held teasing pleasure.

"John Smith," he said.

"Too vanilla . . . How about Noah Hunt? Yes, that's it." Roni snapped. "I'll text you the details."

Before Grey could respond, Roni ended the call.

His brow furrowed as his gaze fixed on Riley. "Noah Hunt?"

"Noah from *The Notebook* and Hunt for Ethan Hunt from *Mission: Impossible*, I'm guessing."

"Oh." A smiled tugged at the corner of his lips, then faded as fast as it came.

Her stomach sloshed. Did he not want to go with her? Was he dreading the couple thing? "What's wrong?" she couldn't help but ask.

He shifted on a stiff inhale. "If Kelly *is* missing, then we probably know who left you that key."

Had it been Kelly? And, if so, what kind of trouble was her friend in? Concern swelled in her stomach. She prayed Kelly was all right, but her gut, like Roni's, said otherwise.

He sat in the parking lot of a two-story brick building, the thick falling snow obscuring his view of the office window.

He shifted in his seat, the leather creaking beneath his weight.

PIs. He exhaled. Complications could arise if he didn't deal with things in an expedient manner. He needed the witch, but he also needed the key she'd left. Needed the contents attached to it.

He tapped the wheel with gloved hands. He'd never missed achieving a primary objective, and he wouldn't start now.

Riley MacLeod had been easy enough to track down. He stared at the picture on his phone. Her portrait on the company website didn't do her justice. She was captivating. Hopefully she'd left the key behind so she could keep that pretty face. Torture never looked good on anyone, but if he needed to pry the information from her, pry he would.

FOUR

"YOU WANT TO RUN KELLY while I run Tate?" Greyson asked, treasuring the alone time with Riley now that the office was empty save the two of them. He loved when they partnered together, working late into the night, running down people who needed finding or needed help. They had it down to an art form.

"Let's go with our usual areas," she said.

He slid his laptop to the left side of his desk. "Why don't you join me in here? It'll be easier to share information, and I've got plenty of room." He prayed she said yes. Just sitting beside her brought him joy, and he needed it after the last month. After the anniversaries of . . . He took a solid, slow exhale. The anniversaries of his losses. The thought of both brought a recurring pain swelling in, dipping his mood, and he hated it. He hated his emotions for not listening to his head. And Riley . . . His chest squeezed. He'd nearly lost her. If she hadn't shot Pete . . . He stiffened, cutting off the thought of her not being in his life—even if it wasn't in the way he longed for.

"Sounds good," she said, shifting his thoughts back to her. She was the light in his darkness. Even if it could never be more.

"I'll go grab my stuff." She headed down the back hall for her office.

"Need any help carrying things?" he asked.

"Sure. That'd be great. Thanks."

"Of course." He fell in step beside her.

She turned, moving to her dorm-size fridge. Kneeling down, she grabbed a large Monster drink and a Coke. Straightening, she snagged a bag of pretzels and handful of butterscotch candies from the bowl on top.

"Not the butterscotch . . ." he teased, standing in the doorway, his sleeves rolled up on his sinewy arms. That subtle yet charming smile that tickled her senses crossed his lips.

"It's the best," she managed to say, juggling the items in her arms to pop one in her mouth. She inclined her head toward her laptop. "Do you mind grabbing it?"

"No problem." He pushed off the doorframe.

Her phone buzzed. Once again juggling the items in her arms as they strode back to his desk, she managed to slide her phone from her back jean pocket. "It's Deck."

"And?" He hoped Kelly was home safe and sound.

Riley read the text and released a rushed exhale. "She's not there, so they're on the way to her work."

Moments later, they were situated side-by-side at his desk. Now if he could only concentrate on the case.

■ ■

Deck pulled up to a tavern not far from the base of the Pajarito Ski resort in Los Alamos after Kelly's apartment was a bust. Why she worked so far from Jeopardy Falls was curious, but it was close to her boyfriend's place, so perhaps that was the reason. Nothing at Kelly's apartment stood out other than her eclectic collection of books—varying from poker and blackjack to outdoor adventure and survival skills. So the lady was into card games, outdoor adventures, solar panels, and composting. It was a combination he hadn't seen before.

He shifted his truck into Park and studied his surroundings—occupational hazard.

Several couples walked through the parking lot. Evergreens dotted the landscape, powdered snow bowing their limbs.

"Evermore Lodge," Christian said beside him. "This is it."

Deck shifted his gaze to the log-cabin-style tavern with Bavarian scrollwork running across the lintel over the thick brown door with oversized bronze handles. "Let's do this." He climbed from the car, and Christian followed suit.

Entering, Deck wiped the soles of his winter boots on the mat.

"Ain't No Mountain High Enough" ironically played from the jukebox in the corner. "Ages since I've seen one of those," he noted.

"Ditto."

"All right. Riley said Kelly had mentioned her coworker Becky several times, so we should look for her first."

"Got it." Christian nodded.

The hostess greeted them. "Table for two?"

"Sure," Deck said. He could eat, and it would give them more time in the place. More coworkers to chat with. "Is Kelly working today?"

The hostess grabbed two menus and two bundles of silverware wrapped in napkins. "Nope. She's on vacation for a couple weeks." She swiped a strand of hair from her eyes. "Wish I could afford a two-week vacay." She crossed off their table with a black *X* on the seating chart. "You can follow me." Leading the way into the dining area, she stopped at the first bench. "This work?"

"Actually, could we be closer to the bar? There's a hockey game I'd like to watch." Deck smiled.

"Sure thing." She smiled back. "You a Golden Knights fan?"

Not on your life. "I'm rooting for Caps." Anyone but Vegas.

"You don't hear that around here a lot, Vegas being the local favorite," she said, leading them to another table. She glanced over her shoulder, running her gaze up and down him.

Deck slid onto the bench she indicated, choosing the side facing the bar. "What can I say?" He shrugged. "I'm different."

"I can see that," she said as Christian took the bench seat opposite him. She handed them their silverware bundles, holding his a bit longer than necessary. She seemed nice enough but not his type. Though he wasn't sure what was. Not true. He knew exactly his type, and she was overseas.

The hostess handed them their menus, then stepped back with a smile. "Cara will be right with you."

"Thank you . . ." He leaned forward. "Tamela." He smiled, and pink covered her cheeks.

"Let me know if I can get you anything at all." She backed away, her smile still dimpling her cheeks.

Christian shook his head. "You're ridiculous."

"What?" Deck shrugged.

"You just wink or give a smile, and women fall at your feet."

"Not true." Harper hadn't. Probably part of why he liked her so much. *She* was different—strong, capable, determined. A woman unto her own. Albeit a very independent one who wasn't looking for any sort of relationship—not that he really did those. Date, sure. But relationship? That was a level of commitment he had no desire to make, even for someone as wonderful as Harper Grace.

"It is, and you know it." Christian looked over his shoulder, his head high above the bench privacy wall. "We've got two bartenders. Kelly bartends, right?"

"Yep, and so does Becky, according to Ri."

"They're both females. Let's hope one is Becky," Christian said.

Deck slid out of the bench. "Order me a root beer and a bacon cheeseburger. I'll be back."

"Got it. I'd say good luck, but we both know you don't need it." Reaching the bar, he pulled out the only open seat available.

"Scooooore Vegaaaas!" the TV announcer drew out in an enthused call.

The crowd cheered.

Deck rubbed the back of his neck. He loathed everything to do with their childhood home. If living in casino hotels could be called home.

"What can I get you?"

He looked up to find a brunette standing in front of him.

"I'll take a Shirley Temple."

She chuckled. "Really?"

"Yep." He shifted forward on the barstool, resting his elbows on the bar. "I love those little umbrellas."

"We put those in other drinks too." She chuckled.

"Nah. I'll stick with Shirley, but thanks."

"You got it. One Shirley Temple with an umbrella." Amusement lit her brown eyes. "Any color preference?"

"Surprise me." He winked.

Pink flushed her cheeks.

"Oh, hey," he said as she moved for the silver counter laden with bottles.

"Yeah?" She paused, spinning back around to face him.

"Is Becky working?"

She rested her hand on her hip. "Harder than I should be."

"Gotcha. I'm Deckard." He extended his hand.

"Becky." She shook it, wariness in her eyes.

"I was wondering if I could talk to you for a sec?"

She gestured to the full bar. "We're kinda busy with the game crowd."

"You have a break coming up?"

"Look, I'm flattered you want to chat. You're quite charming and all, but I've got a boyfriend."

"Oh, it's nothing like that." He pulled out his PI license. "I'm looking for Kelly. She's gone missing, and I heard you two are friends."

Becky narrowed her eyes. "Missing? As in really missing?"

"I'm afraid so. We're talking to everyone in her life just in case they know where she is or even where she might be."

"I don't know that I can help, but I'm happy to try. Give me five, and I'll take my break."

"Thanks. I appreciate it."

With fresh mugs of steaming coffee in front of them, thanks to their waitress, and his half-drunk Shirley Temple, they waited.

33

Five minutes on the dot later, Becky approached their table, sipping a soda.

"Hey." Deck stood and let her in the bench, then squeezed in by his hulking tree of a brother so she had space. "Thanks for taking the time to talk with us. This is my brother Christian, also a PI."

They exchanged nods.

She fidgeted with her straw. "I can't believe she's missing." She shook her head with disbelief. "How can I help?"

"When was the last time you saw Kelly?" he asked.

"A week ago. Right before she went on vacation."

"Did she tell you where she was going?" Christian asked.

She shrugged. "Someplace with Tate."

"Speaking of Tate," he continued, "do you know him?"

"Not really." She bobbed her straw in her glass. "He only came by once or twice."

"Seem like a nice guy?" Christian shifted beside him, almost elbowing him. The dude was too broad to be sharing a bench seat with.

"Not so nice." Becky twirled her straw.

Deck arched his brow. "Not so nice how?"

She looked over her shoulder, then fixed her gaze back on him with an exhale. "The first time Tate came in, he seemed nice enough. The second time he was in here, he was a jerk. Bossing Kelly all around."

"Oh?" Christian leaned forward again, resting his forearms on the table.

"Yeah. And she doesn't take junk from anyone, which made it so weird she let him get away with it." Becky took a sip of soda.

Deck took a shot. "Was he ever rough with her?"

"Not in front of us." She fiddled with her straw, swirling the ice and little remaining soda in her cup. "But we heard rumors."

Rumors often gave the best clues. "What kind of rumors?"

"Bethany, who used to work here, knew Tate's last girlfriend, and word is there was a domestic disturbance between the two."

"He get arrested?" Surely Riley would have found that when

she ran him through public records, but she hadn't said anything yet. Maybe she hadn't gotten that far.

"Not that I heard. I don't think any charges were filed, or I got that impression when I asked Kelly about it."

"How'd Kelly respond?" Christian ran his finger around the rim of his mug.

"She tried to breeze past it, but she seemed tense."

"Any chance he'd hurt her?" Christian probed again, his brows furrowed.

Becky nibbled her bottom lip. "I really don't know for sure."

"But do you *think* he did?" he nudged.

"Yeah," she said after moment's pause, "but that's just my theory."

Christian shifted his attention to Deck. "So maybe she's running from an abusive boyfriend?"

They both turned to Becky.

"Could be, I suppose." Her jaw tightened. "I sure hope not."

Deck rubbed the back of his neck. That didn't explain the key. What would she need to hide from her boyfriend? He shifted, the pleather cushion crinkling beneath him. "Is there anyone else close with Kelly we should talk to?"

"Kelly kept things close to the vest, for the most part. But I remember her mentioning a lady in Jeopardy Falls she shared coffee with weekly. Someone with an *R* name. Randy . . . Riley . . ."

"Riley's our sister." Christian shifted, the pleather squeaking beneath him.

"Gotcha." She folded a piece of gum in her mouth and glanced at her watch. "Not to rush you guys. I want to help all I can, but I've only got a couple minutes left, and we're still slammed."

Deck nodded. "We'll hurry."

"Thanks." She blew a bubble of grape Bubblicious.

"Anyone else you can think of?" he asked.

"She heads out on weekend adventures with a couple friends. I think it's Amy and Guy or Gus—something like that. Oh, and her poker club friends."

Deck cocked his head. "Her poker club?"

"Yeah, she takes lessons on Wednesday evenings, and then plays on the nights she's not working."

Interesting. That would explain the handful of poker and blackjack books they'd seen in her apartment—all highlighted with sticky notes popping out the page edges.

"You know the name of the club?" Christian pulled a small notebook and pen from his shirt pocket and poised himself to jot down the information.

"Players' Den," she said with a lift of her chin. "It's not far from here. The guy in charge, his name is Tony. I went with Kelly one time. He's a nice guy."

"Thanks," Deck said.

"Glad I could be of some help." She slid out of the booth and stood.

"You've been a big help."

"I'm glad. Please keep me posted. I hope he hasn't done anything to her."

FIVE

"HOW'S IT GOING, DARLIN'?" Greyson asked several hours into their work.

She loved when he called her that. Just the sound of it on his lips . . . Though it was said by pretty much every cowboy in town, so it wasn't said in the connotation she hoped for. She exhaled and chastised herself. She should be focusing on the case and not on the stellar man beside her.

"Ri?" He nudged her.

"Right." She cleared her throat. "I got all the basics on Kelly running public records—full name, current and former addresses, phone number, lack of arrest record, no bankruptcy."

"She's only been in Jeopardy Falls a little while, if I recall correctly. Where did she live before here?"

She stiffened, loathing to even utter the name. "Vegas."

An apologetic expression shifted on his face, dancing across his five-o'clock shadow. "I'm sorry." Weight hung in his words.

"It's fine." She shrugged. "It's just an address." Not like they had to go there. Praise God! She hadn't been back since they'd fled Big Max in the middle of the night, and she never planned to return. Just being there would bring a swarm of brutal memories back—ones she'd been trying to bury ever since.

He dipped his dimpled chin. "You okay?"

"Fine." She shook it off and propelled forward. "I discovered a lot more."

"Let's hear it." He scooted his chair closer, his woodsy scent lingering in the air.

Great. Him smelling fabulous would make concentrating oh-so-easy, but she tried her best to pin her focus on analyzing the data she'd mined.

"Kelly Frazier looks like your average person. As I mentioned, no criminal record. But in the preceding months she paid off her car, paid off and canceled her three credit cards, closed her local bank account, and I can't find where she switched it to, and the oddities go on." She reclined, tossing her pen on top of her notebook. "It's a lot of change, and I can't help but wonder why."

A sexy smile curled on his lips.

She shifted under his gaze, but the tenderness in his storm-brewed eyes only warmed her. "What is it?"

His smile widened. "I'm just trying to figure out if there's ever a time when you aren't wondering why."

She fought to simmer the smirk tugging at her lips. He had her there. "The *why* and the *how* are what intrigue me on a case, and once I figure those out, I find my mark." She hadn't missed finding one yet. But with what happened with Scarletto . . . she feared she'd pull back in the face of danger in a way she never had before.

"Agreed," he said. "I just find your constant curiosity . . . impressive."

She blinked. Not the expected answer, especially after she'd ignored his advice when it came to Scarletto.

"You okay?" he asked, eyes narrowed.

"Yep." She nodded. "And I'll take that compliment."

He chuckled under his breath as she kept a smile fixed on her lips. "I figured you would. Now, what's next?" He leaned back in his swivel chair and interlocked his fingers behind his head. His sleeves rolled above his elbows revealed his sinewy forearms.

Warmth rushed up her neck. She swallowed, then cleared her throat. "The question of why she paid things off, closed them up. It's like she was preparing to run, but I can't see Kelly doing that . . . unless she's in danger as Roni believes. But she made the changes months ago so it couldn't be a result of the fight she had with Tate there."

"Yeah." He exhaled. "My first thought was she didn't want any debt with the car loan or credit cards. Or she may have wanted to deal with only cash. Without legal means we can't see her bank statements."

"Speaking of authorities," she began, "Deck texted that he was going to run the case by Joel after their hockey game." Sheriff Joel Brunswick was a great investigator, and even though there wasn't physical evidence to support Kelly being in danger, it was wise of Deckard to loop him in.

"Smart," Grey said. "I think we have to work on the presumption that she could have left on her own as the retreat director explained to Roni."

"True . . . but there are enough factors that make me curious."

He chuckled. "There you go again with that curiosity of yours."

She tried to exude an unamused expression, but a traitorous grin ruined the attempt. How did he always make her smile? Shaking off the thought of Greyson and her deepening—well, bottom-of-the-ocean-floor deep—feelings for him, she forced herself back to the case *again*.

She rocked back in her chair, crossing one leg over the other. "Let's look at the big picture and zero in on Kelly's actions for the last six months. She had a lot of changes between the accounts closing and the move to Jeopardy Falls from Vegas."

"So what are you thinking?"

"It feels like she was setting something in motion."

"Such as?"

"It kind of looks like she was preparing to disappear."

Greyson's brows furrowed. "But why?"

"Maybe fleeing an abusive boyfriend. Questions about Tate harming her have risen twice. First Roni's concern and then the coworker the guys talked with before calling in." She shook her head. "And the way she went about things . . . those are specific steps I take when I help people disappear."

"I'll dig deeper into Tate Matthews," Grey said, swiveling back to his computer. "It's definitely not looking good for him."

She exhaled. Not good at all.

SIX

KELLY SEARCHED the Las Cruces bus depot overflow lot. Her knee bounced, nearly hitting the steering wheel. Where was he?

Her heart hammering in her throat, she tapped the wheel. *Come on. There aren't that many rows.* She eased down the first one and started her systematic search again. He had to be here. He'd left directly for Cruces while she made the drops, but his cobalt blue 4Runner would have stood out.

She blinked back tears. *I hope they didn't get to you.* Just before she broke into a worried sob, Jared's car entered the parking lot. Relief and questions swirled inside her. She released her death grip on the steering wheel, her palms moist. She drove toward the row he parked in and found a spot two down from his.

She climbed from her car, her heart still thumping in her chest, and strode on shaking legs toward him. "What took you so long?"

"I had to get the tickets, and I also stopped at a friend's to get a little insurance on the way." Jared opened his coat and flashed a glimpse of a gun in a side holster.

"A gun?" That had never been part of the plan, but it definitely couldn't hurt if he knew how to use it. She hadn't fired one a day in her life.

"We know the men coming after us will be armed. Figured we'd better be too."

"Speaking of tails, I lost mine." She scanned the restaurant lot across the street and the buildings around it. He could be lurking anywhere.

"Great. I think I lost mine too."

"*Think*? This isn't a time for guessing."

"I lost him on the pass into Truth or Consequences, where my friend who gave me this lives."

Snow filtered down in small flakes, not bothering to stick to the asphalt. Where they were headed would be quite the opposite.

"You ready?" she asked.

He nodded. "Grab what you need from your car. I've got all the supplies ready."

She nodded, and, in a flash, grabbed her duffel and gear bag from her trunk and tossed them into his 4Runner. She just prayed Roni didn't do anything rash and report her missing to the police or to Riley MacLeod. She needed Riley protecting the key, not tracking them. She was the best tracker, and if she got on their trail, it would take them to the brink of their limits to avoid being found.

"Ready?" he asked, opening the passenger side door for her.

"More than ready. We've got a long drive ahead of us, and time's a-wasting."

He nodded, his brow creasing. Good. Jared needed a little worry. He was too casual and cocky in thinking they could outsmart whoever was sent after them.

He turned the ignition and flipped on the wipers for the flakes that melted as soon as they hit the windshield. He shifted into gear, and they reversed out of the spot, leaving her car behind.

"You think they'll buy that we're headed for the border?"

"We have two bus tickets saying so, plus your car left in the lot. I still say it should throw them off our trail for a while."

She held her hands in front of the heat register, rubbing them together. "I sure hope you're right."

He reached for her hand, and she slipped hers in his. "Me too."

She cleared her throat, the antsiness in her quite unbearable. "What do you think about the velvet pouches?" She shifted sideways, managing to stay buckled. "I mean, I get the cash and the passports, which now gives us a handful of his aliases, but why the stuff in the pouches?"

"I have no idea but I'm glad they're safe," he said, tapping the wheel as they pulled out of the bus depot lot, heading back north on 25 but only until 60, then they'd take the back roads west and then hit 191 to continue their northern trek.

She hoped all the backtracking they'd planned would pay off and the men would concentrate their search south, while they headed in the opposite direction. Their path, though farther west, passed not far from the retreat center. The thought of being within a hundred miles of the place squeezed her lungs. But he was convinced it was the best route, so she'd go with it. Just as he'd go with her to their next stop, where they'd disappear into the mountains. If anyone figured out they weren't on the bus, surely trekking through the San Juan Mountains would knock them off their trail. Wouldn't it?

His gaze flashed to the rearview mirror, then he looked over his shoulder.

She stilled. "What is it?"

"I thought I saw the black SUV that was following me a few cars back."

She stiffened as she looked over her shoulder. "Are you sure?" She scanned the cars, not seeing it. Then a white car with a roof rack filled with kayaks exited the freeway, clearing her line of sight to the SUV. "Gun it!"

SEVEN

AFTER CHANGING into his hockey uniform and grabbing his gear bag, Deckard stopped in his kitchen, where Christian was still munching away on the tray of enchiladas he'd left on the stove.

He chuckled. "Think you got enough?"

"It's good," Christian said between bites.

He chuckled again. At six-four and two hundred pounds, there was a lot to feed.

"I'm going to FaceTime Ri and Greyson quick before I leave and catch them up."

Christian set down his fork. "Sounds like a plan." He dragged his laptop he'd been working on over and started pulling things up.

Deck moved to sit by him, and the call was already going before he settled in.

Ri answered, Grey coming into view beside her. "What's up?"

"Just wanted to fill you in some more from our earlier call."

"Great," she said, lifting her pen and sliding her notepad in front of her. "Shoot."

He ran back through the basics, then focused on the immediate.

"Becky said Tate was moody," Christian said. "And it sounds like he has trouble controlling his temper. At least with his last girlfriend."

"We're tracking the girlfriend down," Deck said before taking a sip of soda. "Want to hear from her what happened."

"Good. Let me know what she says when you get ahold of her," Grey said, his jaw tight.

They all loathed women being abused. Unfortunately, it was one of the ugly things they saw on the job. But Riley had helped more than one abused woman disappear when the system let her down.

"We also learned from the guy that runs the poker club where Kelly plays that she is quite into gambling," Christian said between bites, his plate almost bare. "Which explains the poker books we saw in her apartment."

"According to the guy at the club, Tony, she came in to learn poker but has switched over to learning blackjack from a woman in the club named Marybeth," Deck said. "We're planning to go back to interview her. Then we're going to hit the Horseshoe and the Wolves Bane casinos, where she'd been playing for more than poker chips."

"Interesting." Riley tapped her lip with the tip of the pen.

"It gets more so," Christian said, setting his empty plate aside.

"Oh?" Grey asked.

Deck rested his arms on the table. "Tony said she'd been asking about how to count cards."

"Really?" Grey frowned. "I didn't think that was allowed."

"It's not illegal," Riley explained, "but the casinos will toss you out if they catch you doing it."

Christian leaned forward, placing his tree branch–like forearms on the table—nearly knocking Deck's off.

Deck looked over at his bro. "Personal bubble invasion, man."

Christian moved his arm, but not before pegging him in the rib.

"Really, dude?" Deck said, hands lifted.

"What?" Christian shrugged.

Deck shook his head. "I—"

"Hello." Riley snapped her fingers. "Focus, guys."

Grey cleared his throat. "Circling back to the ex-girlfriend. We didn't find any listing of a domestic disturbance on Tate's record."

"According to Becky, Kelly passed it off as 'no charges were filed,' like it was a big misunderstanding, but Becky said she seemed nervous while sharing about it."

Riley lifted her arms in disgust. "So he got away with it with the girlfriend?"

"Yep. Looks like it." Deck nodded. "We'll track her down." He glanced at his watch. "Gotta go. Have a game to be at."

"Thanks, guys," Ri said as the FaceTime call ended.

"Good luck today," Christian said.

"Thanks," Deck said, heading for the front door, his gear bag across his shoulder. The law-enforcement indoor hockey league definitely brought a lot of characters together on the ice, and it would be the perfect opportunity to talk over the case with his good friend Sheriff Joel Brunswick. Joel excelled at his job, and Deck prayed he'd have some helpful insight into a case that had no shape yet—just a mysterious key and Roni's concern to fuel it.

EIGHT

HER LIMBS BURNING with the waning adrenaline, Kelly looked back again, searching the road for the black SUV they'd lost. It wasn't the man who'd been tailing her. He'd been tailing Jared, and despite his valiant attempts to lose him before the meetup, he'd found them.

Jared looked over his shoulder and sighed out a big exhale. "I lost him again." His taut shoulders relaxed.

Despite his belief they were safe, that was the last thing she felt. Rather, on the brink of careening off a circus wire a hundred feet in the air hit closer to the emotions roiling through her. She flicked her fingers in and out of making a fist. "He's never going to stop sending someone after us. He'll make certain of that. We lose the tail, and he'll come back." She hated to acknowledge the truth, but she knew it. He'd unrelentingly hunt them down.

"I know." Jared gripped the wheel, snow slashing at their windshield, driving right at them in white streaks. "Hopefully, this"—he pointed at the thick white flakes—"will help us lose our tracker."

Speaking of trackers . . . Kelly sighed. Riley was a talented tracker too. If Roni got her on their trail out of concern, she wouldn't stop. But they needed to do this alone. Needed to execute their well-laid-out plan a year in the making. She just prayed they lived long enough to see it out.

Riley headed up the mountain pass leading from Santa Fe to Jeopardy Falls. The road was steep and full of switchbacks. Normally, that wasn't a problem, but with the drenching snow, visibility was fewer than five feet ahead in the beam of her headlights. Having made the final decision to attend the retreat in the morning, she and Grey planned to question Tate and anyone else who seemed pertinent to chat with. Playing a couple with Grey still had her nerves tingling in the best possible way.

His woodsy scent lingered on her coat from hugging him goodnight. It was a rare hug, but he'd leaned in. Surely it was a move to hug her, but as soon as she was in his arms, he'd stiffened. *Stiffened.* Was it so uncomfortable to hold her?

She bit her bottom lip, struggling to settle the feelings racing through her. The thought of working in the field with him elated her. She couldn't wait to see him in action. Deck swore he was a level above. But despite seeing him daily, there was still so much she didn't know. He kept a guard in place, and she couldn't figure out why—at least not yet.

Focus on the road and not him. She exhaled. Like that was possible.

Halfway up the mountain pass, her headlights swept over a car on the side of the road, its hood jacked up, a man leaning over, working on something inside.

Tension racked through her. Never stop—both her brothers had drilled that into her. It was good advice, but this poor guy was stranded in the middle of a massive snowstorm. She couldn't in good conscience pass on by. She pulled to a stop behind him on the right-hand shoulder and rolled down her window a couple of inches, being cognizant enough to grab her tire thumper in her left hand, holding it just below the window. "Can I call Triple A or a tow truck for you?" she yelled, fearing the wind whisking through the canyon would drown out her words.

He straightened and cupped his hand by his ear.

She tried yelling louder, but it was no good.

He walked closer.

Alertness seized her, her body steeling. In her headlight beams, all she could make out was a hooded figure. He broke into a run. Before she could close the window, he raised a gun through the opening. On reflex, she batted it away with the tire thumper.

He cussed and raced to retrieve it. She floored it, her tires sliding on the thick snow.

Please go. Please. Please. Please.

The tires finally gained traction, and she looked back to see the man race for his truck, drop the propped-up hood, and climb inside.

She took stock of where she was. Only a quarter of a mile to the side roads that wound back to Jeopardy Falls. She took a deep inhale and streamed it out as his headlights bounced across her rearview mirror in the distance—faint in the heavy snow.

"Okay," she whispered. She could do this. *Please, Father, keep me safe.*

With a deep breath, she switched off her headlights and floored it for the secluded side road.

Banking right at the evergreen-shadowed entrance, she tore down the back road, bumping over high slopes and gaining air before dropping to the leveled part of the road below. She flicked her gaze to the rearview mirror. No sign of him. Either he'd turned off his headlights, too, or she'd managed to lose him. Not willing to risk assuming the latter, she plowed ahead.

"Call Deck," she said to Siri.

The phone rang.

Come on. Pick up.

"How was the game?" Greyson asked when Deck called to catch him up on the conversation with Joel.

"We won," Deck said.

"Great—"

"Hang on, Ri's calling. I'll call you back."

"Sounds good." Grey disconnected the call.

"Hey, Ri," Deck answered. "What's up?"

"I was nearly attacked, and I think the man is still following me." Panic seared adrenaline through his limbs. "What?"

"He's out there somewhere. It's too dark, and the snow too thick to see how far back."

"Where are you?" He jumped to his feet and grabbed his keys.

"On the back roads running alongside the Keller property."

"How far in?"

"I'd guess I'm near the wildflower patch."

"I'm on the way." He raced out to his car and turned the ignition. Snow crunched beneath his tires as he backed up. "Christian is on his way home from Andi's. He might intercept you first depending on how close he is. We'll be there." He pushed the accelerator flush with the floorboard. "Stay safe."

Please, Lord, keep her safe. Don't let anything happen to Cool Whip.

"My headlights are off," she said, clearly trying to temper the concern in her voice, but a hint of it laced her words.

"Smart."

"Call when you're close, and I'll turn them on so you can see me."

"Roger that." He tore down the road. "Hold tight."

"I see headlights." This time she didn't try to mask the panic in her voice. "He found me."

Deckard slammed the wheel. "I'm five minutes out. Hang on, kid."

He hung up and called Christian, apprising him of the situation, his heart in his throat. Barreling down the winding, snow-covered road, he raced toward his sister, his entire body rigid.

His tires slid out. He course corrected and continued on—a battle raging between him and the blizzard.

Wind whipped blankets of snow across his windshield, the gusts rattling his SUV.

He feared for Riley on these back roads, though when 4-wheel-ing, she was the most daring of them all. Always taking the biggest risks. But that was Ri, and she *knew* these roads. He prayed that got her through.

His heart pounding, he flew over a high slope and dropped to the dip below, his car bouncing.

"Call Riley," he said to Siri.

The call went straight to voice mail.

"No!" He slammed the dash with his fist. He tried again. Voice mail.

Please let her be all right.

"Call Christian."

"Calling Christian," Siri replied.

It took a moment, but the phone rang. *Thank you, Lord.*

"Yeah?" Christian asked in a flurry.

"Have you found her?"

"Not yet, but I'm closing in. I see a truck ahead."

"It's gotta be the car after her."

"I'll handle it," Christian said. "You find Ri."

"Her phone is going straight to voice mail. I can't get through to tell her to turn her headlights on and I can't risk running right into her."

"She'll see your lights coming."

"I hope so." The snow was so thick it was like being in an ice cave surrounded by unending white.

He shifted off-road, racing through the snow-blanketed, hilly pastures running parallel to the road.

After another mile, fear for his sister sent a shiver racing up his spine. Where was she?

NINE

RILEY DIDN'T HAVE TO LOOK in the rearview mirror to know he was behind her. Small white globes of light streaked through the snowy night, bouncing off her dash. He was close. Very close. She had to do something, but what?

Think. And think fast.

The cleft. It was suicide in this snow. It was flat-out dangerous in perfect conditions, but he was leaving her no choice.

Taking a steeling breath, she broke right, praying she wouldn't hit the embankment that ran part of the trek.

She caught air on a hill. Her heart whooshing in her ears, she pressed on. Unwilling to look anywhere other than straight ahead. Even though she was driving blind, she couldn't risk looking back.

Her muscles taut nearly to the point of pain, she prayed with all her might she wouldn't go over the edge. She hit a familiar hill on the trail and caught air again. Next came the snake—her nickname for the winding passage.

You can do this. You've done it a few dozen times. Just settle and run the course.

No headlights shone behind her now. She'd lost him, and in perfect time; the passage stopped twenty feet ahead. She prayed he wouldn't be on the main road waiting for her, but it was the path she had to take from here. Swerving out on the branch that shot off the back trail to the main one, she nearly collided with a pair of headlights.

＊

◼ ◼

He banged the steering wheel with the palm of his hand, the hit vibrating up his arm. He had her, but those men had to get on their trail, whisking in to save her. No doubt her brothers. The PI family. He'd run them. Tracked them. Knew enough about them to match their moves. Now with both closing in the route from either end, he had to disappear. But he'd be back. He'd watch for an opportunity to get the blasted woman away from the protection of her brothers and the third guy who worked at MIS. He needed to get her alone and get the location of the key out of her. Although he suspected it was on her, which meant taking it by force, or taking her with it. *Yes.* He liked the latter. She was a pretty thing. He wouldn't mind some one-on-one time with her—as long as she didn't see his face, but he could manage that.

Reversing into the trees with his lights off, he sank back into the darkness and watched the brothers sweeping in to rescue his target. He grunted. He'd leave for now, but he'd be back.

◼ ◼

Forty minutes later, Riley's heart was still lodged in her throat, the blinding headlights flashing again before her eyes—the moment cemented in her brain. Thankfully, she'd swerved in time, and the car turned out to be Deckard's SUV. Once she was safe with him, Christian took time to sweep the full trail with no sighting of the truck. She'd lost the attacker, but tension still gripped her limbs in a vise. Given the ambush and presence of two people—*at least* two, given the two vehicles' tire treads—on their property, her sense of security teetered on the edge.

She ambled down the lane to her house after insisting she was fine and didn't need one of her brothers to escort her the short distance to her home. But with the odd sensation of being watched raking over her anew. She studied the tree line, searching for shadows, but given the snowfall, the world appeared white. She exhaled. She'd spent the past half hour convincing Deck she didn't need to stay at his house. She was fine. Or maybe she would be if she kept telling herself that. Wind lashed her back as snow rained down in sheets, covering her boot prints a second after she'd made them. The storm had blown in hard and fast, so Deck had to see to the horses in rapid fashion. Each stood with their blanket on near the lean-tos, except Rambler, who was as stubborn and unruly as her, according to her brothers' teasing.

Reaching her door, she fumbled with her keys in her mittened hands. She yanked one mitten off with her teeth and wrapped her chilling fingers around it. Finally getting the key in the lock, she turned it, and relief shot through her as she stepped inside her warm house and flipped on the lights, then with one glance around, it died.

Her sofa cushions lay tossed about the floor, her baskets of blankets and mail upheaved—the items strewn across the terracotta tiles. Reaching for her SIG, she stepped through the living room, clearing the space. She moved as quietly as possible to the kitchen, and with a solid intake of breath, she spun around the arched opening into the dark room. Her eyes taking a moment to adjust, she blinked and scanned the shadows. The pantry door lay cracked open. She moved for it, her breath tight in her chest. She carefully opened the door. Flour, sugar, and coffee lay strewn on the floor, baskets knocked over, containers shoved to the side. Stepping out of the pantry, she moved for the bedrooms. Clearing the guest room first, then heading for hers. A creak sounded, and she froze.

You've got this.

Images of her and Pete's shootout flashed before her eyes.

This wasn't that.

The creaking echoed again—coming from her bathroom.

She moved through her room, her throat narrowing and breath coming in shallow spurts. She stepped to the cracked door.

Creak.

She should have called Deck but hadn't wanted to risk giving away her position in case someone was inside. She had this.

On a mental count of three, she opened the door with the muzzle of her SIG, letting it lead her into the room.

The night-light cast just enough light for her to see. Empty. Relief swelled as she took in the curtains and the window frame creaking in the rattling wind.

TEN

DECK SAT AT HIS DESK, combing through files of a cold case that had become a borderline obsession for him. Anything to keep his mind off what was happening with his baby sister and off *her*.

Spending every night waiting for Harper Grace to text was ridiculous. He barely knew the lady. They'd only spent a short time together while Christian and Andi worked a recent heist case, and he and Harper—Andi's best friend and former FBI colleague— paired up to investigate corruption claims for Andi. It'd been a matter of a couple of weeks, and then Harper was gone. Off to Africa on a humanitarian trip for months.

He raked a hand through his hair. Why couldn't he stop thinking about her?

He stalked to the kitchen for a glass of water, and his cell vibrated in his lounge pants pocket. Retrieving it, he glanced at the number. "Hey, Grey," he said, struggling to keep worry from his voice.

"What's wrong?"

So much for trying. His mind was a mishmash of great concern for his sister and warm thoughts of Harper, which irritated the heck out of him.

"Deck?" Grey said. "What's going on?"

He exhaled, the panic that swept through him at his sister's distress call sweeping over him anew. "Someone attempted to ambush Riley on her way home from work."

"What?" Grey asked, his voice tight, strained.

Deck explained most of it, but was cut short by another call. He checked the screen. "Hey, Grey. It's Riley. Hang on just a sec, or I can call you back?"

"I'll hold." Concern held thick in Grey's voice.

"Hey, kid," Deck said, switching to her call.

"Again with the kid?" she said, clearly attempting irritation, but her voice quivered.

He stiffened. "What's wrong?" Was she still shaken up from the ambush?

She cleared her throat. "I'm fine, and the place is clear, but someone broke into my house and trashed it."

Anger and protectiveness washed over him, and he headed for the door without thinking, calling Christian on the way.

"What's up, man?" Christian's voice held slumber.

"Someone broke into Ri's."

"Coming."

Racing there, Deck realized Grey was still on hold. He clicked over, and in the barest of words caught him up to speed. Grey dropped the call before Deck could.

Reaching Riley's open door, he burst inside. The floor was covered with the contents of her house.

She walked out of the kitchen, her arms wrapped tight around her. Fire burned in her eyes, yet weariness radiated there too.

He rushed forward, engulfing her petite frame in his arms, and she leaned into him.

"You okay, kid?" he asked, hands on her shoulders.

"Yep." She nodded but bit her bottom lip. Nervousness tracked through her gaze and stiff smile. He stepped back, and she straightened, then exhaled. "Furious at this mess more than anything else."

He scanned the room, better this time. Lamps knocked over,

couch cushions tossed about the floor, everything upturned. "You know what they were looking for?"

"It has to be the key."

"Where is it?" he asked, shifting his attention to the heart of the matter.

She pulled it from her pocket.

"Why don't you give it to me?" he offered, not wanting anyone to have a reason to come after Riley again. Whoever had left the key left her in a heap of danger.

Hot fury rushed through Greyson as he raced for his Rover.

He shifted the SUV into Reverse and skidded out of the snow-covered drive.

His headlights cast beams through the thick snow driving at his windshield.

He accelerated, praying the road was empty, and time passed in warped fashion.

His heart thumping in his chest, the feel of Riley in his arms invaded his thoughts again. Rather, *still* invaded. He'd gone in for the hug without thinking, the feel of her in his arms amazing, but the realization of what he was doing hit him, and he'd awkwardly pulled away. He was never awkward. Not for years. Not since going into the military what seemed like a lifetime ago. That had shaken it out of him in a good way. But around Riley . . . he lost all his cool. He flicked his wipers higher as the snow drove in waves, wind lashing the Rover, shaking it as he made his way up to Jeopardy Falls from his home in Santa Fe.

"Come on!" He pushed the gas pedal and shifted again, going with the slide, then managing to pull out of it. Finally, hitting the long dirt driveway covered in a thick blanket of white, he streamed down it, all the way to Riley's door.

Wind whirling in his ears, he raced inside.

Riley, Deck, and Christian each held various belongings in their hands. His gaze fixed on Riley.

She turned to Deck. "You called Grey?"

"He was on the phone with me when you called."

"Oh."

Grey stiffened. She didn't want him there? Ouch.

She looked up at him, fatigue in her eyes. Evidence of tears shed mixed with her furious expression. "Thanks for being here. But you didn't need to come all the way out here."

He swallowed. *It's you. Of course I came.* "I wanted to make sure you were safe. See if there's anything I can do." He wanted so much more. Wanted to wrap her in his arms and tell her he'd die before he ever let anything happen to her.

"Jump on in," Christian said, pulling Grey from his thoughts and tossing him a blanket. He gestured to the tumbled basket, throw blankets strewn about the floor nearby.

"Of course." He started folding blankets.

Two hours later, Ri's place was back to normal—or at least the stuff in it was. But having been breached, the normalcy and safety of home on the ranch had to be anything but for Riley.

"I think that just about does it. Thank you so much," she said, broom in hand, its bristles tipped white with flour. "I'll handle the mopping and such in the morning."

"I can mop for you," Grey said, moving toward her kitchen, where she kept her supplies.

"It's not necessary," she said, once again pulling him from the tumble of his thoughts. "But thanks. I appreciate you all helping me put things back together." She looked around. "Now I can sleep." She set the broom aside and moved to hug Deck goodnight.

"Whoa!" Deck said.

"What?" She frowned.

"You're not thinking of sleeping here, are you?"

Her nose scrunched in that adorable way it did when she was about to argue. "Why wouldn't I at this point?"

"Seriously? Your home was just broken into," Deck said. "Not to mention the ambush on the road."

"He's right." Christian ran a hand through his hair. "You should definitely stay with one of us." Grey so wished it was with him. Not with him in that way, but under his watch and care. He needed to do something practical or he'd pace the floor with concern all night.

"I don't think that's necessary." Riley shrugged a shoulder. "Whoever did this didn't find the key here, so why come back?"

"Because they know you either stashed the key, in which case they need the information from you—" Deck began.

"Or they know you have it on you, and they take you," Greyson said, his stomach bottoming out. "Either way, you need to get rid of that key. Let one of us keep it. We'll protect it."

"I'll take it away from here," Riley said. "Take it to the retreat tomorrow morning."

"I like *you* away from here. That's a fantastic idea, but the key . . ." Deck said.

She rested her hands on her curvy hips. "You guys can keep going, but I've made up my mind. I'm not letting it out of my sight."

"We don't even know what it goes to," Christian said.

"I stopped in town during my lunch break on the ranch. I tried it at the bus depot, but no luck. And Clyde's gym—again no luck."

Greyson took a stiff inhale, his rib cage gripping his lungs. "Are you sure there's no way to talk you out of this?"

"Positive. Where I go, the key goes."

Which terrified him.

ELEVEN

GREY PACED DECK'S GUEST ROOM. Having already packed for the trip to the retreat center before he learned of the break-in, he'd stashed his bag in his car and raced over. Now that things had settled and Riley was asleep in the room next door, he reclined on the bed, thankful to be near her. He was even more thankful for a trip that would get her away until the guys could catch whoever was after her.

Please, Father, continue to keep Riley safe. My soul can't take losing another person I care so deeply about.

A soft cry broke the silence. *Riley.*

Without bothering to think, he raced into her room, gun in hand. He found her upright in bed, hair clinging to her cheeks and neck.

He cleared the room, relief sweeping over him. "It's clear."

"No one was here," she said, shaking her head.

"I heard you cry," he said, striding to sit on the side of her bed—again without thinking it through. His leg rubbed against hers as she shifted, and comfort and warmth eased inside.

Fear radiated in her eyes. It was the first time he'd seen it there, except for after the shooting of Pete Scarletto.

"What's wrong, Ri?"

"It's silly," she said, swiping her hair back behind her shoulders. "I just had a bad dream, that's all."

"It doesn't look like that's all," he said with quiet confidence that more was going on than a random bad dream. Was it the events of tonight or was Pete still haunting her? "Ri?" he whispered.

She scooched up, propping the pillows behind her back. "It's nothing."

He dipped his chin, gazing into her frightened eyes. "Please tell me." *Please let me help you.* Ironic, given the demons that haunted him.

"Would you mind?" she asked, reaching out her trembling hand. "I just need something steady."

"Of course." He took hold of her hand. He'd given her the occasional squeeze of confidence when they were goofing off but had never held her hand like this, and despite the circumstances, it felt like home. Like they belonged like this.

Her warm, moist fingers slipped in between his. "Sorry. My hands are clammy. If you'd rather not . . ."

"I'm good." Better than good. He'd hold her hand no matter what. He leaned into her almost involuntarily, rubbing his thumb along her index finger—caressing it in smooth strokes—hoping to settle her. "Do you want to talk about it?"

She swallowed and brought her knees to her chest.

"Talking about it helps. Holding things inside only lets them fester and grow." Easy for him to say. If only he practiced what he preached. He rarely talked about David or his mother, it was too painful, but it continued to corrode away a hole inside that would not heal.

She shifted, leaning deeper into the pillows behind her. "I . . ."

"Whatever you say stays between us."

"I don't want to worry Deck or Christian over nothing."

Definitely not nothing, given her shaken demeanor and tear-filled eyes. "I won't say a word." He was just thankful she was willing to share with him. To be of some measure of comfort to her filled him with gratitude. "So what is it?" he prompted, his voice soft.

She bit her bottom lip, and he prayed she didn't clam up. She took a long inhale, then exhaled in a stream. "It's Pete."

He was right. That shootout haunted her, and she was still clutching it.

"I'm so sorry. But you know you had no choice. It was him or you." The resurgence of emotions that nearly drowned him when he got the call about the shootout, when he got on site and saw how close she'd come to dying . . . he'd nearly died himself. What would he do without the bright light of Riley in his life?

"I know." She straightened her legs, brushing his in the process. "My brain knows that, but my heart . . ."

"Doesn't feel it?" He knew that feeling only too well.

She nodded. "It's like my body is betraying me. Overriding my head knowledge. It's taking on a life of its own."

He understood that better than anybody. "It'll take time, but you just have to convince yourself of the truth of the situation. Let it sink in. Focus on it whenever the nightmares come. You have to combat them with your thoughts, and your heart will follow." At least it did for most people, himself excluded. "You have to learn to let go." *Hypocrite.* He clung tighter than a monkey swinging on a high branch overhead. But not her. He didn't want that pain to consume Riley, to hold her hostage.

She bit her bottom lip again. "What if it doesn't? What if my heart never heals?"

"It will."

"How do you know that?"

"Because you're the strongest woman I know. *You* can beat anything." She already had beaten the worst of circumstances to come out of the family life she'd grown up in before being put in a foster home alone—separated from her siblings until Deck came of age and could adopt her. She'd already risen out of the ashes once; he had no doubt she could do so again.

"I don't know about that." She shrugged a shoulder.

"It's true. You just keep telling yourself that. Fight the urge to let it consume you."

Tears brimmed in her eyes.

"You did what you had to do. If you hadn't shot, it'd be you in the grave."

She nodded, tears streaming down her sweet cheeks.

"Shh." He brushed them away with the pad of his thumb.

She leaned into his hand, and he cupped her face, caressing her cheek. She leaned deeper in, resting her cheek in his palm.

He could stay like this forever.

"Stay with me?" she said, looking up at him with those big, innocent blue eyes.

"Stay—" He choked out a cough. "Stay with you?"

"Sit with me," she said. "Just until I fall back asleep. Would that be okay?"

Any time with her was okay, but being here for her now was priceless to him. "Of course, I'll stay. You sleep, and I'll be right here."

"Thank you." She slid back down so her head rested on the stack of two pillows, her hair fanning out across the navy sheets.

She rolled over on her side, curling up, her knees resting against his thigh. He held still, very still.

"Is that okay? I just want to feel you're here. Want to feel safe."

He nodded. She felt safe with him. Warmth filled him.

Her eyes closed and her breathing grew even as she drifted off to sleep.

Snow gushed down in droves, the wind slapping at Kelly's chapped cheeks, her lips cracked despite the ChapStick she had been slathering on.

"We need to stop and sleep a few hours," Jared said from behind her, his voice echoing off the canyon below.

There was a five-hundred-foot drop fewer than a dozen feet to their right according to her hiking GPS, but how much longer would the signal hold in this blizzard? Her compass skills could come into play, but if she was off by even a foot, they'd be at the bottom of the canyon, and nothing would be made right—other than that Lance was out the money. But . . . "Why do you think he had the other items in the safe?" she called over her shoulder, her words competing with the rush of wind blowing the snow at a forty-five-degree angle at her face.

"What?" he called back.

She stopped. Just for a breath. Regret sifted through her.

"Finally," he said, stopping beside her.

With the thick snow and his white winter gear, he blended in with their surroundings. Good. Maybe that would keep them safe from whoever was coming. Because someone was definitely coming. She knew Lance too well. She'd studied him all these years. "We need to get going." They'd talk later. What had she been thinking? She'd been thinking about the contents of the safe.

Jared tugged her arm. "Hey," he said, giving it a shake. "It's not going to do us any good if we're exhausted. We'll naturally slow down, and you know it. Besides, so far, we haven't seen anybody in that scope of yours. We can rest a few hours and let this blizzard settle some."

He was right, but she didn't have it in her. They had to press on. "The falling snow will cover our tracks."

"We're leaving knee-high tracks. It's not falling that fast. Find us a cave and we'll sleep for two hours. That's it. Just two."

She relented against her better judgment, and soon they were snuggled in a cave, using body heat and their thin Mylar blanket for warmth. A fire was far too risky, much to Jared's chagrin. How did he not understand the depth of the threat against them?

She cringed.

"What's wrong?" He held up his flashlight, studying her. "You just tensed big time."

She bit her bottom lip, and it drew blood. *Oww*. Dang chapped lips.

"Kel?"

"I just wonder . . . I hope I didn't bring danger to Riley."

"If you did, she can handle it. It's why you chose her."

"No, I chose her because I knew she'd keep it safe at all costs, but I'd barely lost my tail when I dropped it. I don't think anyone saw me leave it for her, but what if they did?"

"Then she's in as much danger as us."

Her jaw tightened. "That's what I'm afraid of."

TWELVE

RILEY EASED HER EYES OPEN. Sun streamed through the slit in the curtain. A sliver of the pink-hued mountains, glowing in the sunrise and slated with thick areas of snow, which still fell, peeked through the opening.

She stretched, feeling the warmth of a hand on her arm—a soft, tender touch. She blinked, then her eyes shot wide open as she took in the sight of Greyson lying facedown on the pillow beside her. Shock abating, she studied him. He looked so peaceful. Poor thing must've kept watch too long and fallen asleep. Grey was in her bed, and he looked gorgeous—his rugged jawline smattered with more than a five-o'clock shadow, which only added to his handsomeness. She longed to reach out and touch it—curious how it would feel. Coarse? Soft? Her gaze shifted to his arms bent out at his sides and the sinewy muscles of his forearms. She continued up along his upper arms until she reached the edge of his white T-shirt.

She bit her bottom lip. He looked too sweet to wake, but his hand lay on her arm. Could she move without waking him?

He murmured, and she rubbed her arm, then his eyes opened. He looked over, half-asleep, and smiled. Then his eyes widened, and he yanked his hand back. "I'm sorry. I was—"

"You don't have to apologize. I'm just glad you rested well. We've got a busy day ahead."

He nodded and pulled himself up, resting his back against the headboard. "You take the bathroom first."

"Will do." She hopped from the bed and headed for the shower.

The time with Greyson continued to dance through Riley's mind an hour later as they headed for his Range Rover.

Supporting each other and providing comfort, being married and waking up beside him . . . but it was just a pipe dream. Grey didn't feel that away about her, though she could swear she'd seen passion and longing in his eyes last night. But she was probably just fooling herself. Seeing what she needed rather than what was there.

Her brothers and Andi stood in a row outside by the car, waiting to see them off for the retreat center. They'd done the recon work, so now it was time to head into the field, and the best place to start was the last place Kelly had been seen.

Grey took her bag and placed it in the back of his Rover.

Andi gave her a hug and whispered in her ear, "Have fun." She was the one person who'd astutely figured out Riley's feelings for Grey. It was nice having someone else to talk to about it, and she trusted Andi with her secret. She would hold it tight. Just as Riley would hold the key tight.

Deck stepped forward to put his arms around her and pat her back. He smiled. "Can't say I'm not glad you're getting away from here for a few days."

"I know."

Christian moved in to hug her next. He engulfed her, making her feel the size of Tinker Bell in his big embrace. "I second Deck. Maybe take time to enjoy the spa stuff there while you're questioning people. But be careful."

"Yep, though it does sound like Kelly left of her own accord thus far. The question is why," she said as Christian stepped back to Andi's side.

"And," Deck said, slouching his hands in his Wrangler pockets, "most importantly, why she left you that message and key."

"We should get going," Grey said, opening the passenger door for her.

He offered his hand, and she took hold as she climbed up and in. One simple touch and she warmed all over again, security and tenderness filling her.

"You guys be safe," Deck said before Grey could shut her door.

"We will be," he said.

"Seriously, Ri," Christian added. "No big risks."

"Not promising that."

"Come on, Ri. Please be safe," Deck said.

She nodded. "I'll do my best." That apparently sufficed because her brothers let it drop.

"One more hug," Andi said, stepping to the car.

Riley leaned out, and Andi wrapped her in a gentle hug. "You've got this," she whispered.

Riley smiled.

Andi straightened and gave her a wink before shutting the door for her.

Greyson climbed into the driver's seat and clicked on the ignition. "It heats fast."

"I'm okay."

"Your hand was shivering."

Trembling from his touch was more like it, but saying that aloud would be mortifying.

Grey gave her a sideways glance.

"I'm fine," she said, knowing what was on the tip of his tongue.

He tapped the wheel. "That's what you always say."

"Because I am." Eventually the nightmares would cease. They had to. She couldn't live the rest of her life exhausted and saturated to the bone with remorse.

"Ri?" he said in that tone that cut right through her defenses.

"I appreciate your concern."

He shook his head with that sideways smile she loved. "No, you don't."

"Okay." A smile curled on her own lips. "Fair enough. I don't."

She rifled through her mini-backpack purse for her sunglasses, the sun blinding off the snow.

He glanced over at her while they waited at the one light on Main Street. "Given your nightmares, I worry you're carrying around false guilt over what happened."

"False guilt?" She *was* guilty. She'd had no choice, but she'd ended a man's life. Even though her head knew it was either her or him, her heart still wrestled with the consequences.

"I understand what you're going through," Greyson said as the light turned green and he accelerated.

She shifted. "You do?"

"I went through a time . . ." He took a sharp inhale, then released it as they drove down the remainder of Main Street and through the heart of town.

The brisk wind and lower-than-normal temperatures kept the streets nearly empty. Odd for their bustling little town. It was like Jeopardy Falls was frozen in time, with icicles hanging from the gutters and awnings of the shops lining the street.

He banked right on Brighton, leaving the town behind. Their adventure had begun. The idea of working with Greyson in the field excited her, but for now she was focused on what he was about to tell her. And despite his long pause, she wasn't letting him off the hook. "Grey?" she nudged. "You were saying?"

His jaw twitched. "I had a . . . difficult situation. It set me back for a long while." He gripped the steering wheel, his knuckles turning white.

"But it eventually went away?" Was that where this story was going?

He glanced over, compassion thick in his stormy gray-green eyes. The color of winter waves. "It eased . . . some."

"But didn't leave?" She frowned. If Greyson, the most logical and rational man she knew, couldn't fully move past something, how was she—emotionally driven and passionate—supposed to?

"Not fully."

"That's not great to hear," she said with utter honesty.

"True, but there's a significant difference between our circumstances."

"Oh?"

He cleared his throat. "I made a mistake," he exhaled the words.

"You didn't."

"Wh—" "Brown Eyed Girl" played. *Not now.* She lifted her cell. "It's Roni."

"You'd best pick up."

She released a stream of air. The man was right, bad as the timing was. "Hey, Roni. What's going on?"

"You on your way yet? Tate is looking squirrely, as if he could dash any minute."

"We're on the way." She leaned toward Greyson and glanced at the GPS mounted on the dash just to the right of him. "ETA two hours."

"Okay. Hurry. Oh, and I put your reservation under the names you requested, Noah Hunt and Allie Bennet. You're all set to check in."

"Thanks, Roni. We'll see you soon."

"Good. I have a bad feeling, and whenever I get vibes like these, I'm almost always right."

"She sounds like you," Grey said when Riley hung up the phone.

"True." She worked by instinct too. So very different from Grey. It's why they worked well together—at least in the office. Now they'd see how well they worked in the field.

A thought ran through her mind. Had Greyson's mistake happened before he stopped working in the field? Was it *why* he stopped working in it? "You were saying . . . ?"

He gave a sad chuckle. "You're not going to let this go, are you?"

"Nope. You know the rules. You started, now you need to finish." No dropped stories.

"It was before I sold Deck the practice. I was working in the field . . ." His voice faded off again.

"Gotcha." She forced herself not to lead with questions. To let him take his time despite the rabid curiosity running through her.

Pain etched on his face.

She bit her bottom lip. *What on earth happened?*

His shoulders dropped on a sigh. "There was a missing woman. Three, actually, before it was over. One of the families hired me when the police ran out of leads. I tracked the perp to the Jicarilla reservation. The tribal police worked the case, but Phillip Longshaw—the lead on the case—kept me on it, which he took flak for, but we worked well together."

She was afraid to ask based on the deep furrow in his brow, but the words slipped out all the same. "And the women?"

The muscle in his jaw flickered. "We found two bodies shoved into shallow cave dwellings. They'd been raped, and I won't go into the rest, but his method for killing was beyond cruel."

"Oh, I'm so sorry. That had to be terrible to work."

"The terrible part," he said, gripping the wheel, his knuckles white, "is that *I* could have stopped the third. I could have, should have, saved her life." He ground his teeth, and Riley winced at the crunching.

"I don't understand." She yearned to pull him into her arms, to make the pain so brutally apparent on his face evaporate.

He swallowed, his Adam's apple bobbing. "I made a mistake."

It took everything in her to remain silent, but she did—giving him time and space.

After a brief pause, he continued, "We had interviewed the guy, and I didn't think it was him. He didn't fit the profile. Had a wife and a kid. Was prominent in the community. Very outgoing. I just didn't see it, and he killed again."

The agony Grey's voice held shot through her. "Oh, honey . . ." The term of affection slipped from her lips unbidden, and she reached for his hand.

He glanced over, pain pooling in his eyes. Without a word, he slipped his hand into hers, intertwining their fingers.

"I'm so sorry," she breathed, the words whispering past her lips.

He stared straight ahead, his gaze pinned on the road, his jaw stiff. "I'm the sorry one. A woman is dead because of me."

She caressed his hand with the pad of her thumb. "You didn't know. And I'm guessing Phillip didn't know either?"

"No, but I still should have seen it. I mistook his good-guy act for just that. I didn't see the evil in him." He shook his head on a deep, guttural sigh. "I don't understand how I missed it."

"He must have hidden it well. They often do. Even Satan masquerades as an angel of light."

"I should have bowed out of the case at that point." He looked over at her for the briefest of seconds, and she absorbed his pain—the sorrow raw and at the surface. She longed for him to stop the car so she could wrap him in her arms.

"So that's why you stopped?" He'd ceased doing something he loved—it was so clear seeing him shine working in the field on this investigation.

He hesitated, then released a long exhale. "It's part of why."

"Part?"

"That's a conversation for another day."

She bit her bottom lip. "Okay, but can I just say I think you're being far too hard on yourself?"

The muscle in his jaw twitched, his carriage growing taut. "Cassie Williams would be alive today if it weren't for me."

She gripped his hand tighter. "Phillip made the same call as you."

"Yes, but—"

"No *but*s. You both made the same call. The perp was clearly a master of disguise—the truly evil ones usually are—and in our line of work, we have to make judgment calls all the time." She'd pulled the trigger. He'd misjudged a man. She looked down, her jaw shifting. "Sometimes we get it wrong."

He glanced over at her and frowned. "That sounded personal."

Her muscles tensed and she remained silent. He didn't need to know how personal, though given how he'd bared his heart, she needed to be open with him. She hesitated, struggling to gather her courage to share the ugly truth.

His gaze held longer on her than it should, given the road ahead.

"You didn't make a mistake," he said before she'd mustered her courage.

Her head said the same thing, but her heart couldn't accept that, and she didn't understand the disconnect.

"Ri?" He jiggled her hand at the silence. "You had no choice."

She exhaled in a whoosh, the words in her head surging to be released. "Then why does it keep haunting me?" she said, being fully transparent as guilt riddled through her.

"Because it's never easy to end a life, but sometimes we have no choice. It's either us or them."

She furrowed her brow. "That sounded personal." She used his words back on him rather than shining a mirror on the turbulent feelings eating away at her. "Have you been in that situation?" she asked, longing to know. If he had, then maybe he could help her in her battle between logic and emotion.

"Yes," his words held an edge, "in the military." He stared at the road ahead.

She shifted in her seat. "But that's different. You were in a war."

"Ending a life"—his free hand tightened on the wheel—"is ending a life."

They sat in the silence until he broke it several heavy moments later. "He would have killed you." Raw concern radiated in his flash of a glance before he returned his attention to the road. "You understand that, right?" His hand squeezed tighter. "You would have been killed." He squeezed tighter still. "We . . ." he said, voice quavering, "we could have lost you."

That sounded even more personal.

He held way back, letting the tracker do its job. Just the size of a coin and it provided so much information—time and speed in addition to location. He had them, and they didn't even know it.

He smiled as they fled the little town, curious where they thought it safe to run to. He had followed the MacLeod woman back to her house last night. Zooming in with his binoculars from a thousand meters away, he'd been close enough to see her startled and borderline-frightened expression when she discovered he'd trashed her place. She played it off as mad when her brothers arrived, but he saw through her. He was coming to like her. Watching her had become a pleasure, but he couldn't get too close. Not after the close call on the road with those idiots swooping in to save her. Now it was down to one, who'd be easy enough to knock off. He needed to get the girl and that blasted key—wherever it led.

THIRTEEN

AN HOUR OF RIDING in silence later, Grey shifted, the hardness of his brow easing. His gaze flicked to the dash clock. "We really ought to get to work, or we're going to run out of time before we get to the retreat."

"Right." Riley had distanced herself from the purpose of their drive, her mind so wrapped up in his pain and her own. "The retreat."

He gave her a sideways glance, assessing her before looking back at the road. "We should go over our relationship."

Our relationship—how she wished that were true in the romantic sense.

"You said we had to go over things we should know about each other, so why don't you start. I have no clue."

"Men rarely do," she said, bringing a soft chuckle to her lips. The mood lightened—easing off the indwelling pain. "Okay . . ." She shifted in her seat to face him better, resting her back against the locked passenger door. "Let's start with how we met."

"Perhaps at a gallery showing in town?"

"That works. Maybe the Gaiman Gallery, which would tie us to Veronica now that she and Brad are running it."

"Great. One down. What's next?"

"How long have we been together?"

He tapped the wheel with his free hand, his other still entwined with hers. She wondered how long that would last, not that she was complaining. She was more than content to hold it all the way there. Speaking of there, she wondered what exactly they were walking into—the environment, the people. What would it take to pull off her and Grey as a couple?

"I'm thinking a year," he said.

"A year?" She dipped her chin. "We should be engaged, then."

He coughed. "Engaged?"

"Yes. If two people our age are together that long, why not be engaged?"

He arched a brow. "Our age?"

"So you're slightly older than me."

"Slightly? I'd hardly call a decade slightly older."

"At our age, a difference like that doesn't matter." At least it didn't to her. "Unless . . . you view me as too young for you?" She was being outright bold, but now was the time to discover how he really felt about her under the guise of a fake relationship. At least that happened in novels all the time, so why not in real life? "Grey?" she nudged at his silence. "Do you view me as too young for you?"

"No," he said, and her heart leapt. "But I do believe I'm too old for you."

She frowned. "That doesn't make sense."

"You should be with someone younger, someone . . . with less baggage."

"Baggage?"

With tenderness, he eased his hand from hers, clamping onto the wheel. "I think we're getting off track. If a year is too long, how is nine months?"

She didn't like the apparent change in subject, but after all he'd shared, she wasn't going to force him to keep going down that path. It was time for some lightheartedness. "Nine months works. It's long enough to be serious, but not too long people will wonder why we haven't taken the next step."

"Okay. Nine months it is. What's next?"

They ran through a slew of get-to-know-you questions—favorite color, favorite foods, how they spent their time together. She liked building a life with him, even if it wasn't real—though that part stung.

"Is that enough?" Grey asked, turning onto the last stretch of road leading to the retreat.

She glanced at the clock. Twenty minutes left. "Nope. We have a few more." A few more minutes for a few deeper relationship questions. "Whose house do we spend more time at?"

"Yours," he answered on a dime.

She tilted her head. "Why mine?"

"Because that's where we usually hang out."

"In real life, yes, but in a relationship, I should be well acquainted with your home, and I can count on one hand the times I've been there. So tell me about it. What is your favorite part of your house? How do we spend time there?"

"Favorite part?" He tapped the wheel. "I haven't thought about it, but I suppose my inner courtyard."

"Really?" She pulled her bent leg in tighter. "Same with mine. I love the open space and the sun beaming into the heart of my home, bringing light on all four sides through the sliding glass."

He smiled but there was tentativeness there.

"What?" she nudged.

"It probably sounds silly . . ." He shrugged. "But I love to garden."

Garden? She never would have guessed, but with his meticulous attention to detail and orderliness, she could picture him taking fastidious care of his plants.

"That's cool." She loved learning more about him. "And how do we spend our time there?"

"Out on the patio most of the time with a fire going in a chiminea, wrapped up in blankets on the couch, looking at the stars."

"Sounds perfect," she said without thinking. "I mean for our cover story."

"Right," he said, "for our made-up story."

Why was there a tinge of disappointment in his tone? Did he want things to be real too? Or was she reading too much into it? Playing a couple . . . she was going to have to walk a fine line between the game and her real feelings and not let the two mix. As if that were possible. She just prayed she didn't come out of this scorched.

"Almost there," Grey said. "What's next?"

"Hmm. Okay, now the more personal questions."

"*More* personal?"

Riley rubbed her hands together. "Time to get to the nitty-gritty. When was our first kiss?"

He arched a brow. "You really think someone will ask that?"

"It's good to cover all the bases just in case. Hmm . . ." She tapped her chin. "I think you first kissed me at your place under the stars."

"Sounds good." Beyond good.

She shifted to face him better. "How did each of us know the other was the one?"

He choked, then smothered it with a cough. Could she see right through him, or was it a harmless question? "The one?" he managed.

"The one you want to marry someday."

A smile curled on his lips, but he kept his gaze averted and fixed on the falling snow. If she saw his face, the happiness he struggled to contain, she'd know the truth of how he longed for things to be. She was the one. The one he wanted, the one he loved, but she could never know that. It wouldn't be fair, so he'd keep up the masquerade and enjoy their blissful time together, even if it was pretending on her part.

"Oh, and speaking of kissing, we'll be expected to show public affection."

"Agreed." Wholeheartedly.

"And they're going to put us in the same room."

He coughed. "Same room?"

"It's a couples' retreat. Roni said they'd booked *a* room for us. Is that going to be a problem?"

"No." He could handle it. Rein in his feelings and play the part, couldn't he?

"Great. So rolling with that, what side of the bed do you sleep on?"

He choked. Surely, she wasn't suggesting they'd actually share a bed. Not Riley. "You really think they'll ask that?"

"When women get talking, all kinds of things come up in chit-chat. If he steals the covers, hogs the bed, is always on my side, and so on."

"I see. Okay, so theoretically let's go with me taking the right side of the bed."

"Right. Theoretically."

"You're not suggesting . . . ?"

"No, of course not." She laughed.

He forced a laugh. "I'll sleep on the floor or find a suitable place."

"With us sharing a room, they're going to assume . . ."

"Assume . . . ?"

She dipped her head. "You know, that we're . . ."

"Oh. Right." Clearly not happening. Neither would do such a thing, but they could pretend in public.

"We should keep up the ruse."

He tapped the wheel. "How?"

"Lots of public affection."

He cleared his throat. "Not a problem." Not a problem at all.

FOURTEEN

GREYSON PULLED ONTO the paved drive leading up to the Expressive Wellness Retreat and Spa. Twisting cyclones of snow whipped across the road in the burgeoning wind.

Riley tapped her foot, nervousness tracking through her. "You feel we're ready as a couple?" she asked, not at all prepared for what was to come. How would she keep her true feelings from coming out?

"I do." He smiled, but there was tension—or was it restraint?—in his expression. Was he not looking forward to this? He hadn't been given a choice. It was him or her brothers. What if he was dreading it?

"Ready?" he asked.

No. She nodded.

He got out of the car and strode around the SUV to get her door, but a man in a white puffy vest, matching white pants, and a bright-blue long-sleeve shirt beat him to it.

"Welcome," the man greeted them as he opened Riley's door.

"Thank you," she said, stepping out into the blustering wind that swirled her hair about her face. She managed to corral it by grasping it in one hand and sliding the hair band she always kept on her wrist around it with the other hand, pulling it into a low, sideways ponytail.

"I'm Alvin, a crew member here at Expressive Wellness. Welcome to the crew. I'm at your service."

"Crew member?" Riley said. "I've only heard that at Disney World." She smiled.

He offered a thin smile. "Once you enter those gates, you're part of our crew too. Allow me to get your bags." He moved for the rear hatch of the Rover.

"Thank you." Greyson opened it with his key fob and moved to help.

"Thank you, sir, but I've got it." Alvin slung both duffels over his arms. "You two pack light."

Greyson refrained from commenting, and so did she. Alvin didn't need to know this was a last-minute trip, though she bet he already did—their reservation having come in just last night. What he really didn't need to know was how short of a stay it might be, depending on where the investigation led them and whether Kelly showed up, which was still a viable possibility—or at least Riley prayed so.

⸻ ■ ■ ⸻

He tapped the wheel as their car pulled to a stop outside of the retreat.

Now he knew where they'd be and where he'd sit back and watch. He grabbed the long-range binoculars on his passenger seat.

The problem was how he would reach them while they were surrounded by other people.

He'd keep a good eye on them and pounce when the opportunity presented itself. Even if he found the key, he needed the woman to tell him what it belonged to, which meant taking her. The question was what he did with her after he got what he needed.

⸻ ■ ■ ⸻

"This way," Alvin said, leading them toward a black wrought-iron fence with two ornate doors. He pulled them open and gestured them inside. They entered an expansive garden adorned with beautiful poinsettias in red, pink, and white in what looked like handmade pottery containers.

Wrought-iron chairs faced the elaborate stone fountain that was no doubt lovely with its water flowing in the warmer months. Wind chimes of agate, quartz, and topaz clanged in the lonesome wind.

A wooden pagoda stretched overhead with twisty vines wrapping around it, devoid of flowers or fruit, but Riley could only imagine how beautiful a canopy it would be to walk under in the springtime.

Alvin led them through the garden and into a vast open area with a series of adobe buildings surrounding it. "This is the main courtyard, or square, if you will, of our retreat center. We spend a lot of time out here on warm days. There is our lap pool." He pointed to the right at the covered pool. "Our hot tubs are still open, though. They are in our grotto past the gym facility. Oh, and here comes our director, Miss Chase." He indicated the thirty-something woman with short blond hair cut above the ear, striding toward them. She was dressed in the same colors as Alvin, though she wore white linen pants, a blue cashmere sweater, and, to Riley's surprise, white heels. Sensible, two-inch ones, but still heels on snow-covered terra-cotta tiles.

"You must be Allie and Noah. Welcome to our crew."

"We're thrilled to be here," Greyson said.

"Yes," Riley said. "We're very excited to be here. It sounds wonderful."

"Well, I don't like to brag, but it is a truly transforming experience. You won't leave here the same." She extended her hand to Riley. "I'm Julie Chase, the director."

Riley shook her hand. "How nice of you to greet us personally."

"My pleasure." She shook Greyson's hand. "And you have perfect timing. We're just preparing for brunch." She checked the gold watch on her left wrist. "It'll begin in twenty minutes, and it's a delicious spread if I do say so myself. It's also a wonderful time to get to know the other visiting crew members. Ready for the experience to begin?"

Greyson slipped his arm around her waist and tugged her close against his solid frame. "Of course we are. Right, luv?"

Luv? That sounded amazing on his lips, pretend as it was. "Absolutely, honey."

"Wonderful." Julie smiled with shiny, white teeth.

Someone used whitening strips.

"Allow me to show you to your room so you can get settled in, and then you will meet us in that building." She pointed to the far end of the courtyard, catty-corner from them. "That's our dining room, where all our meals are served."

Greyson nodded.

"Follow me," she said, striding across the open space.

They hurried to keep up with the peppy director.

"That is our sports facility." She pointed at the building on their right. "We have group classes but also offer personal training and free gym time, and we have a luxurious spa. Annabelle gives the best massage. Let me know if you'd like me to arrange a couple's massage."

Heat rushed Riley's face, and she prayed the red didn't show. "Thank you. We might take you up on that."

Greyson glanced at her, eyes wide. Thank goodness Julie's back was to them as shock registered on his face.

Between the flush on her face and him obviously taken aback, they weren't off to a great start as a couple. More practice was required.

"We also have a ballroom in that building." Julie indicated the building with floor-to-ceiling glass windows.

"A ballroom, really?" Riley asked.

"Of course. We only have the best here, and we find dancing is a wonderful way for couples to grow closer, and that's our mission. To bring couples closer together and to help them grow as human beings by expanding their minds through their time here. Strong relationships and strong minds is our crew motto."

"Very nice," Riley said, reaching for Greyson's hand. It took him a moment, then he slipped his fingers through hers, and she relished the simple touch. "Did you hear that, honey?" she said, leaning her head against his arm. His six-two stature dwarfed her five-six one, making his shoulder awkwardly out of reach to rest her head on.

"Yes, luv. I very much look forward to dancing with you."

Such sincerity in his tone. She almost believed it was real.

"It sounds like a wonderful place," Greyson said.

"It's much more than a *place*. It's—" Julie began.

A coyote howled in the distance. Once, then a second time, the sound echoing on the wind..

"Don't worry," Julie said. "They never bother us. Now, as I was saying. Expressive Wellness is much more than a place. It's an experience." She smiled again. "You won't leave the same."

"These are the crew quarters," Julie said, stopping at the adobe building with a terra-cotta roof at the end of the path. She opened the carved wooden door, gesturing them inside. A small inner courtyard greeted them.

Julie strode at a fast clip down the long passageway ahead. "Here we are," she said, stopping before a door with a wooden sign hanging where a peephole should be. It read *Lovers' Nest*.

"Interesting," Riley said, warmth rushing her cheeks, and again she prayed the blush settled before Julie spotted it. "I've never seen a hotel room with a name rather than a number."

"Crew quarters," Julie said with that same smile. "We feel numbers are impersonal, and we want you to experience the warmth and comfort of our accommodations during your time with us."

What was with the cultish vibe? Okay, maybe that was reaching too far, but the crew bit bothered Riley, and a vibe was a vibe.

Julie reached into her pocket and pulled out three old-fashioned, ornate keys. She slipped two off the ring and handed them to Riley and Greyson. "One for each of you, though I doubt you'll be apart. Our couples are always very close together, and I'm sure you'll be the same, given the way you look at each other."

Greyson tugged her to him. "Well, we are desperately in love," he said, then pressed a kiss to her head.

Tingles shot through her.

"How sweet," Julie said. "I think you'll both fit in our little crew beautifully."

Julie unlocked the door with her key and opened it for them, gesturing them inside with a sweep of her arm.

Riley cocked her head. Julie had a master key to their room? Though that wasn't truly a surprise. It's how things worked at hotels, and she figured this was a hotel of sorts, just a fancy one filled with activities.

They stepped inside what would be *their* room. The entryway opened up into a gorgeous, oversized room. A king canopy bed made out of hewn pine sat against the wall to their right. She took in the matching pine dresser on the side wall, then her gaze shifted to an adorable seating area. "It's lovely."

"Isn't it?" Julie said. "It's one of our best rooms. I'm so glad we had it available for you. And," she said, moving for the oversized windows, "you have a view of our grotto."

Grottos indicated plants, but Riley wondered what could possibly bloom this time of year. She stepped to the windows and gazed out at the lavish winterberries and rows of poinsettias artfully displayed. "It's breathtaking."

"It is," Julie agreed. "We keep the hot tub water nice and steamy, so you'll be warm and cozy no matter the weather. It's the perfect place for couples to relax or meditate. Now," she said, stepping back, "I'll let you two lovebirds be. Brunch starts in"—she looked at her watch—"eleven minutes sharp. Don't be late."

"We'll see you then," Riley said as Julie popped out the door.

"Brunch provides a great opportunity to talk with Tate," Greyson said, stepping to the window beside her, the light silhouetting his masculine form.

Case. Focus on the case. "Hopefully he holds the answers we need."

FIFTEEN

RILEY FOLLOWED GREYSON into the dining hall, though the name was deceiving. This was nothing like the college dining halls that had come to mind when Julie mentioned it. Instead of the typical fluorescent lights and plain walls, chandeliers hung from the beamed cathedral ceiling, and the walls were a rich burgundy. She gazed around at the tables adorned with fine linen tablecloths and formally arranged place settings.

"Welcome," Julie said, walking over to greet them.

"Thank you." Riley smiled, scanning the room for Tate. She'd found his picture on Kelly's Facebook page, though for a boyfriend, his presence on the page was quite lacking.

"Are you two looking for someone?" Julie inquired.

"Our friends Roni and Brad," Grey said.

"Of course." Julie smiled—that same Barbie smile every time. "They're at the far table in the back." She gestured toward them.

"Thank you." Riley reached over and took Greyson's hand. "Come on, honey."

"Absolutely, luv."

"Enjoy," Julie said as they headed for the table.

"The person with them is Tate." Riley rose on her tiptoes and whispered in his ear.

He gave a nod, his fingers caressing hers.

She allowed her lips to smile at the tenderness of his touch.

Playing a couple was proving to be more fun and more dangerous than she'd imagined, and they'd just begun.

"Allie and Noah." Roni waved them over.

"Hi there." Riley gave Roni a hug while Greyson shook Brad's hand.

"So glad you could join us. And this is Tate Matthews." Roni gestured to him. Curly brown hair, matching brown eyes, and a slim smile.

"Nice to meet you," Riley said as Greyson pulled out her chair and scooted her in.

Tate nodded in reply.

Why did she have the feeling this was going to be a tough interview?

"So, Tate, what do you do?" Greyson asked as their meals were served.

"I'm an accountant. How about you two?" He pushed his hash-browns around with his fork.

"I'm a lawyer," Greyson said, "and Allie is a reporter."

"Reporter, really?"

"Yes."

"For a newspaper?"

"A small one. We primarily cover community events. That sort of thing." She shrugged.

"I see. So I should be careful what I say." Tate laughed.

"Aww, I'm not that kind of reporter," she said before taking a bite.

"Good to know." Tate smiled.

"I take it you're not a fan of reporters," Greyson said.

"Who is?" Tate laughed again.

Roni forced a laugh in reply.

"Roni mentioned you're Kelly's boyfriend," Riley said.

"Yes." He wiped his mouth with a napkin. "You know Kelly?"

"Yes. We hang out now and again."

"Funny. I don't recall her mentioning an Allie."

"We're recent acquaintances."

"I see," Tate said before taking a sip of lemonade.

"I was surprised not to find her here. She was so excited when she told me about it." She took a slow sip of iced tea.

"She left."

"Left?" She crinkled her nose. "I'm surprised she'd leave mid-retreat."

"I have to say I agree with you." Tate set his glass down. "It's ludicrous to leave a ten-thousand-dollar retreat halfway through, but that's what she chose to do."

"Ten thousand dollars?" Riley nearly choked.

"Yes." His eyes narrowed. "What? Did you get a discount? I asked about specials, and they told me they never offered those."

"No," Greyson jumped in. "I paid, so Allie didn't know how much it cost." He clasped her hand and pressed a kiss to her knuckles. "It was a treat for my love." He smiled at her, and for an instant it all seemed so real.

"I paid too." Tate stiffened. "And I really don't appreciate Kel taking off midway through. Especially after she was the one all gung ho about this place." The waiter refilled his glass. "She made us take this second trip here and then just took off."

"Took off where?" She kept her voice calm, even.

"Who knows." He shrugged. "Kelly has a habit of taking off for weeks at a time on whatever adventure."

"Really? I didn't get that vibe from her."

"Well, like you said, you just met her. I think I know my long-time girlfriend better."

"Of course." Riley lifted her napkin and swiped her mouth. "Is that what she said when she left? That she was going on an adventure?"

"You really are a reporter with all the questions, butting in other people's business." His jaw tightened. "If you'll excuse me. I've lost my appetite." He skidded the chair backward and strode away without so much as a good-bye.

Roni inhaled. "Well, that went about how I thought it would."

"Definitely didn't cross him off our list," Riley said.

"If anything, it added him in permanent marker," Grey said, setting his salad fork down on his plate. Then he dabbed his mouth with the corner of his napkin.

Riley smiled. He fit in well with the proper crowd. Her not so much, but she was okay with that. She leaned closer to Roni. "I do have something I want to ask you."

"Shoot, dear girl." Roni took a sip of her mimosa.

Riley eased the key out of her bag. "Did you see Kelly with this?"

"No." Roni shook her head.

"Are you positive?"

"Positive. But it looks like the keys to the gym lockers here."

She'd be making a stop there. She turned to Greyson.

"There's that look again . . ."

"Everyone," Julie said, cutting off Riley's retort. The lady lifted her hands head-level and clapped at them like they were children. "Eyes up here." She gave a firm smile, reminding Ri more of a school mistress than a retreat director. "Wonderful. Our afternoon activity is going to be just breathtaking. Kevin will be taking you to the nearby Carson National Forest for some refreshing cross-country skiing. The shuttle leaves promptly at one thirty. Please don't be tardy, or you'll miss the ride. Now, go enjoy. Kevin will be waiting for you at the shuttle."

Riley's gaze flicked over to Alvin, the employee who'd greeted them upon arrival. He stood against the far wall, his legs shoulder-width apart, arms bent, hands behind his rear—military stance. Interesting job choice if he had been military. From solider to spa employ seemed an odd transition. She'd have to dig deeper on the man. His gaze fixed on hers and held. She didn't look away, and neither did he.

"Shall we go?" Greyson asked, standing and reaching for her seat back.

She turned her attention to him and smiled. "Yes, please."

Walking from the dining hall, Riley sensed Alvin's penetrating gaze, and it sent a shiver up her arms.

SIXTEEN

"SO WHAT DO YOU THINK?" Riley flopped on the bed in their luxurious room—the fluffy down comforter a cloud beneath her.

"Tate was quite defensive, and I'm not buying the 'took off on an adventure' claim," Grey said with air quotes, "but I'm solely basing that on his body language. You know Kelly. Is she the type to just take off?"

"She is really into outside activities, but as far as I know, she only went for the weekends. Most often with friends down in Camp Verde."

Grey frowned. "Did Tate go along?"

She shook her head. "Not as far as I can tell. She never mentioned him joining her, and nearly all the adventure pics on her Facebook page were of her with friends, Gus and Amy Stanton."

"Interesting. Any chance she took off on an adventure with them?"

"I wondered the same thing, so I tracked down their cell phone numbers. Called them, but both go directly to voice mail saying they are overseas and will return calls after they're back in the States."

"And that wouldn't explain the note and the key."

"Yeah." She sat down on the end of the bed with a sigh. "We've got to keep coming back to that key. It makes sense it was Kelly, but what if it has nothing to do with Tate or the retreat? Maybe someone else is after her and she fled the retreat to go on the run before they found her?"

"Good theory, but who are *they*?"

"Deck found a few people from her poker club and the managers at the casinos who were none-too-happy with her counting cards and winning big under questionable methods."

"They never proved anything."

"Sometimes you just know, even if you don't catch them in the act."

Riley rolled onto her stomach, bracing her weight on her elbows and kicking her feet up, crisscrossing them in the air. "We'll have to have Deck stay on that angle while we work on Tate."

"Seems Kelly had a list of people angry with her."

"Angry enough to leave a desperate note and this . . ." She twirled the locker key in her hand. "I'm beyond curious what the locker this key belongs to is hiding."

Evergreen branches covered Kelly from head to toe, tickling her neck and sticking in the hair that escaped her winter cap. Ignoring the annoying sensation, she lay prone and still—the ground frigid beneath her but her serious winter gear keeping it from penetrating too deep.

She zeroed in with her binoculars, searching the landscape in the valley below—the long stretch of level trail they'd left behind. He was still out there ready to lunge the second he caught up.

Where are you?

Taking a slow, nearly silent inhale, she released it, her shoulders easing with the movement.

There. Eight hundred yards out in the lower clearing. *Brent.*

She studied his gear, including the shotgun, its strap slung across his shoulder. She was no expert, but given the scope on it, she was betting he had long-range capability.

Easing out from her cover, her white snowsuit camouflaging

her, she ran in a crouched position behind the trees, where Jared awaited her intel.

"Well?"

"We've got to move. He's closer than we anticipated."

SEVENTEEN

RILEY SMILED as Greyson slipped his hand into hers on the way to the shuttle. Cross-country skis lined the top of the white Mercedes extended van.

Tingling shot from his touch all the way up her arm. At some point she'd get used to holding his hand—surely it wouldn't send a zap through her every time—but it was quite addictive in the meantime.

"After you," Greyson said, halting by the shuttle door and guiding her up the steps. She looked up to find Kevin in the driver's seat. Relief swept over her. Alvin gave her the creeps.

"Welcome," Kevin said. "There are four seats left in the back."

"Thanks." She ticked off the eleven seats leading to the back four. She settled in, Greyson beside her. Veronica turned around, resting her arm on the seat back separating them.

She leaned in, signaling Riley to do the same with the flick of her red nails. Not the most subtle move. "Tate's gone," she hissed.

Riley frowned. "He left the retreat?"

"Yes. I saw him heading out after brunch." Roni shifted, and Brad joined her in turning around.

Riley scooched to the edge of the seat. "Did you speak with him?"

"I tried, but he kept striding for his car, not bothering to toss a glance my way."

"Did he say anything?"

"Just that he was done playing a couple alone and was heading out for some 'me time.'"

"Any indication where?"

Veronica shook her head.

"You almost missed the shuttle," Kevin said, his deep voice echoing along the raised shuttle roof.

"Sorry." A lady with two blond ponytails and a pink snowsuit hurried for the open seats by Greyson and Riley. A tall man in gray attire followed her.

"Hey, Roni," she said as she passed her and settled onto the bench seat beside Riley.

"Allie, this is Jenny," Veronica said. "And Chad," she added as the man maneuvered around Jenny for the window seat. "And this"— her gaze fluttered over Greyson in his navy snowsuit—"is Noah."

"Nice to meet you," Jenny said. A shiver shot over the woman. "It's a cold one." She slid her hands into a fluffy white muffler. "How's it going, Roni?"

"Fine. Tate left today."

"I wondered how long that would take."

Riley shifted to face her better. "You know Tate?"

"Only from here. Chad and I happened to be here with them for our first visit and again for this one, so we've chatted, but I wouldn't really say we know each other. Neither are big talkers, but Kelly is definitely friendlier than him. He's like a wet sponge." Jenny leaned toward Roni. "Have you talked to Kelly since she left? I heard that fight she and Tate had. Wasn't pretty."

"You saw the fight?" Riley asked.

"No." Jenny blew a bubble with her gum. "I was walking by when I heard yelling, so I lingered a bit. Just to make sure Kelly was okay. Then the noise settled, and I returned to my room. In the morning she was gone." She twirled the pink bubblegum around her index finger, then popped it back into her mouth. "It's been an interesting trip with people leaving."

"People? As in more than Kelly and Tate?"

95

"Oh, just staff moving around." She waved off that topic with the flick of a hand. "Is Kelly doing okay?"

"Why would she not be okay?" Riley asked. "I mean, were you worried Tate might . . . hurt her?"

Jenny shrugged. "I don't know. I just wasn't a fan of the guy, and it was quite the heated argument."

Chad gave her a soft elbow in the side.

"What?"

"You're gossiping again."

Jenny rolled her eyes. "I'm just relaying information."

"Did you see her leave?" A second eyewitness would be great.

"Nah, but I heard. People around here talk, you know?"

Thankfully so.

Riley glanced up to find Kevin staring at them in the rearview mirror. They made eye contact, then he shifted his gaze back onto the road. Had he been listening to their conversation?

A half hour later, Kevin pulled to a bumpy stop along the ice-packed drop-off.

He shifted the shuttle into Park and opened the side-entrance door. "The trails start about five hundred yards in. They're marked, so you shouldn't have any trouble keeping to the paths." He looked at his watch. "We'll meet back here at four thirty sharp so we're all on board before it gets dark, but the sunset you'll see will be amazing."

One by one, he handed out equipment. Riley and Greyson went last.

Kevin held her skis for a moment's pause. "Be sure to stick to the trails. It's a big wilderness with wild animals. I'd hate for you to get lost."

Twenty minutes in, they'd lost the rest of the group—everyone heading off on their own trail, none in the mood to talk while in the midst of the activity.

"Shall we?" Grey pointed to a nearby slope with a glint in his eyes, a playful smile kissing his lips.

Might as well enjoy the time. "Race you," she said, taking off.

"Cheater," he hollered behind her, but it only took him a nanosecond to catch up with his long strides.

The two raced in tandem, the ice-laden snow crunching beneath their skis. The sun's warmth heated Riley's back, the sky a beautiful clear blue.

Silence surrounded them, save their laughter and the occasional flap of birds rustling in the evergreens. The slope took a sudden, steep decline, and Riley went flying down it, faster than anticipated. She wobbled but corrected, managing to stop by a massive tree trunk before heading over the drop-off.

Greyson shushed to a sideways stop, resting his hand on the tree. "You—" A flash of something zinged by faster than she could blink. Greyson grunted a millisecond before they heard a resounding thwack.

He grabbed her, flung her to the ground behind the tree, and covered her with his body.

Another thwack, bark splintering around them as a quivering buzzed through her ears.

Grey pulled to a crouching position, tugging her with him. Positioning her fully behind the thick trunk, he leaned around it, his gun at the ready.

Thankfulness that no one was around to see them blow their cover filled her.

Grey drew her attention to movement at the rock formation thirty feet to their three o'clock.

"Oh my goodness," Roni hollered, appearing around the bend. "What's happening?"

Brad reached Roni's side, and Grey slipped his gun back into his holster and zipped his jacket back up.

A snowmobile roared just beyond the tree line on the ridge above them.

"You're bleeding," Roni said, and Riley turned her attention to Greyson.

"You were hit?"

Riley studied the tear in his jacket. Not a bullet track. Her gaze shifted up the tree, fixing on two arrows sticking out of it, their vanes blue and yellow.

"Grazed." He shrugged his other shoulder.

"Enough to tear your coat and your skin."

"It's a flesh wound, luv."

"Let's at least get you back to the shuttle. I'm sure Kevin has a first aid kit."

Halfway back to the van, Kevin rushed up over the slope. "It was Tate," he said, out of breath. He bent, resting his hands on his knees and sucking in a shallow burst of air.

"Tate?" Riley narrowed her gaze. "What do you mean, Tate?"

"I saw the arrows fly and thought it was a hunter, so I went to let him know we were in the vicinity."

She took in the orange reflective vest he'd put on.

"And?" Roni pressed.

"I saw Tate running for a snowmobile with a quiver of arrows on his back."

"Whaaat?" Roni drew it out with a gasp.

"Tate shot at you."

EIGHTEEN

"IT'S HARD TO BELIEVE Tate shot at us," Riley said as she and Greyson disembarked the retreat shuttle.

"Are you okay?" Julie asked, rushing up to them. "You poor dears. I heard about Tate. I can hardly believe it."

"It is hard to believe," Grey said.

"We should get you to Peter," Julie said, striding to the far building.

Riley tilted her head. "Who's Peter?"

"He's our paramedic and also our Pilates instructor."

"Interesting combo," Greyson said.

"Well," Julie said, striding toward the far building. "We don't have much cause for a paramedic here, but we wanted one on staff should one of our guests get sick or injured." Her gaze raked over Greyson. "I never thought he'd be handling something like this. Anyway," she continued, "he's a fabulous Pilates instructor too. It's a great combination for us."

"Sounds like it."

Reaching the double glass doors, Julie opened one and held it for them to pass through.

"Third door on your right," she said, directing them down the hall past the yoga and Pilates room.

Greyson leaned in. "I can handle seeing to my injury myself."

He'd learned more than enough training in the military to butterfly a wound. They weren't talking major medical.

"Don't be ridiculous," Riley whispered back.

Of course, she'd fight him on it.

"I'll do it," she said in that determined voice of hers, hushed as it was.

"Everything all right?" Julie asked behind them.

"Fine," Greyson said. "I was just explaining that I appreciate that you have a medic on staff, but I'm quite capable of seeing to my own injury."

"Surely you're joking," she said, pausing on the threshold to the medic bay beside them.

"No, ma'am. I'm former military. I have the training."

"I'll take care of him," Riley said. "We'll be fine. We'll just need a few supplies."

"I really must insist," Julie protested as a tall, lean-yet-muscular man with dark hair approached in a black Under Armour T-shirt and matching exercise pants.

"This must be Noah," he said.

"How'd—" Riley began.

"Miss Julie radioed ahead," he said. He stepped inside the room and gestured to the exam table with white paper drawn over it. "Please have a seat."

"I appreciate the offer, but I have the necessary training, so we'll be seeing to it ourselves," Grey said.

"It's really no trouble," Peter said.

"I appreciate it, but if we could just have a few supplies, we'll be set."

"Okay." Peter shook his head. "If you insist."

"This is the oddest thing to happen here," Julie said.

"I would have thought him being struck by an arrow would have taken that spot," Riley said, and Greyson bit back his laughter.

"I . . ." Julie stuttered. "Well, of course. I simply meant—"

"There's no need to explain," Greyson said, then redirected his attention to Peter. "We'll need rubbing alcohol, gauze, Steri-Strips, and some antibiotic cream, and we should be set."

"Come here, Grey," Riley said, after they returned to their room. Taking his hand, she led him into the bathroom. "I thought Julie was going to have a conniption."

"You and me both." Greyson smiled.

"I know you take care of the team when one of us gets an injury on the job, but I didn't realize you had medic training in the military."

Because that part of his life was tied to pain. "Yep."

"Cool. Now take off your shirt."

He swallowed. Maybe this wasn't such a good idea. "I can do it myself."

"Don't be silly." She pulled out the first-aid items they'd collected from the medic's office and laid them on the vanity. "You sure you're okay with me tending to this? We can always go back to Peter."

What should he say? She was more than capable, and he preferred to involve the retreat staff as a little as possible. "I can always do it myself."

She tilted her head. "Don't be ridiculous. I can do this."

He didn't doubt she could. "All right," he said. "Thank you."

She nodded, and he grabbed the hem of his shirt and lifted, his injured arm smarting with pain. He winced despite trying not to.

"Let me help you," she said, stepping closer. Close enough her ocean-scented fragrance swirled around him in the enclosed space.

She raised his shirt up, her fingers brushing his chest in the process.

He took a sharp intake of breath.

She froze. "Am I hurting you?"

Not in the least. "No, I'm good."

"If you say so." She shimmied his shirt fully off his right arm

101

and bunched it by his neck. "Ready?" she said, empathy in her beautiful eyes.

He nodded.

"One, two, three." She pulled it over his head.

He ground his teeth.

"Sorry," she said.

He swallowed. "All good."

She inched his left sleeve down his arm and set his shirt to the side.

Her eyes widened as her gaze locked on him, and pink flushed her cheeks.

He angled his head. Was she checking him out? Nah. His mind was playing tricks on him.

She cleared her throat, reaching for the rubbing alcohol. "Ready?" she asked again before swabbing his wound.

He leaned against the sink, gripping the edge of the vanity.

"I think it's always better to put the alcohol on fast. It'll sting, but think of it as ripping off a bandage. Or," she paused, "do you want me to go slow?"

He wanted her to go slow just to have her close longer, but . . . "Fast," he said.

"Okay. Here we go." She did a quick swipe across the wound. Once. Twice.

He clenched his teeth, but it was over before it began, then she leaned in and blew on his wound.

Emotions and warmth rushed through him. Fearing his expressions would give him away—his feelings for her, the joy at her closeness—he schooled his features.

She studied him, a question in her eyes. "You okay?"

"Mm-hmm." He nodded.

"Okay. The worst part is over." She reached for the antiseptic cream.

"Ready?" she asked.

He nodded, trying to keep his thoughts off her and the fact she was touching him, even in the most innocent of ways—her hands soft on his skin as her fingers grazed his shoulder.

She slid the cream on the wound, then grabbed the bandages. She was so close. Her breath whispering across his bare skin. Her honeysuckle shampoo infusing the air mingling with the salt-air scent of her perfume.

He ached to pull her into his arms, yearned to kiss her, but he had to do the right thing. Had to stand by his boundaries. He cared too much about her to subject her to his secrets. Besides, kissing him was the last thing she'd want to do. He had to keep reminding himself she viewed him as a brother and a friend. Nothing more.

"There," she said, taking a step back.

The urge to pull her back seared through him, and he gripped the vanity harder. "Thanks," he managed.

"No problem." She dropped the first-aid items back in the bag Peter had provided and set it on the vanity. "We'll change it again in the morning."

He nodded. The thought warmed him. He cringed. He really was a mess.

"We can order room service for dinner and just stay in so you can rest."

"I'm good." He strode for the closet and grabbed a blue button-up shirt.

She followed him into the room. "You sure?"

"Definitely good." In regard to dinner—yes. In regard to his heart—it was shattering into pieces knowing she could never be his.

NINETEEN

"HEY, RI," Deck said, answering her FaceTime call. "How's it going?"

"Not so good." She glanced over her shoulder at Greyson as he gingerly slid his shirt sleeve over his wound.

"What's up?"

"Greyson got grazed by an arrow."

Deck dipped his chin and arched a brow. "I'm sorry. Did you say an arrow?"

"Yep."

"Well, that's a first. What happened?"

"We were cross-country skiing, and an arrow zinged by, taking a bit of skin off Grey's arm before hitting a tree barely a foot from him."

"Was it a hunter?"

"That's not what Kevin said. He's one of the trainers and handles the driving for the most part too."

"Who does he say it was?"

"Tate Matthews."

"He saw him do it?"

"He said he saw him driving away on a snowmobile."

Deck narrowed his eyes. "But you don't believe him?"

"I'm not certain of anything right now. Can you go by his place, see if you can find him and question him?"

"Sure. Did you guys file a report with the local sheriff?"

"Nah," Grey said in the background. "It was just a flesh wound."

"All right. We're on our way back from questioning Paige Wheeler, Tate's ex, in Rio Rancho. We'll head to Tate's next and keep you posted."

"He's up in Angel Fire. I'll text you his address from when we ran it."

"You got it. And, guys . . ."

"Yeah?" Riley raked a hand through her hair, mussed from her winter cap.

"Be careful. It if was Tate, he might try again—and not miss."

Two hours and a solid nap later, Riley strolled out of the bathroom in a burgundy dress that made Greyson's mouth go dry. Stunning didn't even come close.

She held two matching ribbons that hung down her neck. "Could you help me tie this?" She turned her back to him. "They just tie here."

He shook out the tingling in his hands or at least tried.

"Sure . . ." He cleared his throat. "Of course."

She glanced over her bare shoulder at him. "You okay? You sound parched."

"Yep. Just need some water."

"You can grab a glass first," she offered.

"No, I'm good." Better than good—always better when she was near. Her laughter, playfulness, reckless streak—even that he loved because it was what made her *her*.

He stepped closer, and the scent of salty sea spray wisping over him infused the air. How she smelled of the ocean in the middle of the desert amused and entranced him. Only Riley.

He took the satin ribbons from her hands and tied them, the excess ribbon ends trailing down her back. He ran his finger down along them, and she took a squeaked inhale.

"Sorry." He yanked his hand back. "Was just smoothing them."

Which was part of it—the soft touch of her skin the other, but he'd leave that out. No sense terrifying the woman with the notion he had any feelings for her.

"Thanks," she said, stepping forward then twirling around to face him, her dress hem fanning around her legs. "Look okay?" she asked, holding out the skirt of the dress.

Enchanting. "You look beautiful."

A soft smile curled on her lips. "You think I'm beautiful?"

"Of course I do. Have you looked in a mirror lately?"

"It's just . . ." She shrugged a bare shoulder.

He dipped his chin, looking her in the eye. "Just?"

"You've never called me that before."

Was that a good thing or a bad thing? "Is that okay? I mean, was it weird for you coming from me?"

"Coming from you? I don't understand."

"I know you view me as an older brother. Maybe not the person you want pointing out how enchanting you look."

Her eyes lit. "Enchanting?"

He took a stiff inhale. Of course he'd let that slip. But he couldn't take it back, and it was the truth. "Very."

The blush deepened on her cheeks. "Thank you. Now, are you sure you're up for this? Between dinner, dancing, and the casino, it's going to be a long night."

"I'm fine. It was just a flesh wound."

"All right. If you're sure." She opened the safe and reached for her SIG.

"Can't take the guns."

"Why?" She frowned.

"The casino is on the res according to the itinerary board. No concealed weapons allowed on the reservation."

She exhaled, returning her sidearm to the safe. "All right, I suppose. What could happen at the casino that would cause us to need our weapons, right?"

"Exactly." Though he didn't like the idea any better than she did. After the incident today, he couldn't help but fear things were just getting started.

He slid his black suit jacket on, easy over the wound.

Riley stood back and smiled, pink infusing her high cheekbones.

"What?" he asked, curious what had caused the flush.

"Nothing." She strode over and took the cobalt tie from his hand. Stepping close, she slid it around his neck and took hold of each side. "You clean up nice."

He furrowed his brows. Why did it feel like more was happening between them than there really was?

Tying it, she gave the tie a soft tug, then straightened the neck portion.

So close. All their years of friendship swooped up in this moment, this time together, but to another level—one he was rather inept at handling smoothly.

She smiled up at him. "There." She smoothed his jacket with a gentle slide of her hand.

He cleared his throat. Did she have any idea what she was doing to him with her innocent, tender touch?

She glanced at the clock on the nightstand. "Yikes! We're already late. We'll hear it from Julie. She drives a tight ship around here."

"She can wait a minute." He wanted to soak in the moment—the time alone with her. Just chatting, just being with her was all he needed.

Dinner was a blur, Riley still engrained in his brain.

"You've barely touched anything," she said as the wait staff removed their plates. "Are you sure you're okay?"

"Better than okay, luv," he said loud enough for their tablemates to hear. Then he took her hand and lifted it to his lips, brushing a whisper of a kiss across her knuckles.

She shivered.

"Are you cold? You can have my jacket."

"No." Her stare held his. "I'm good, but thanks."

The rest of the world faded away; their gazes locked. So much residing there . . .

"Aren't you going to dance?" Roni asked, breaking the spell.

The wood-plank dance floor was a large rectangular section at the other end of the dining area.

"Oh, I love dancing," Riley said, her eyes sparkling. "But you should rest with your arm."

"I'm happy to take Riley for a whirl," Brad offered, starting to stand.

"No." It came out far too blunt, and Brad halted half-seated, half-standing. "Sorry." Greyson cleared his throat. "I was just trying to say I'm more than fine for dancing, but thank you for offering."

He'd dance even if the arrow had shot him straight through. He wasn't giving up the opportunity to dance with Riley—just once. He stood and offered his arm. "Shall we?"

She smiled, stood, and linked her arm in the crook of his good one.

"Us" by James Bay came on—the melody slow, the words hitting closer to home than he'd like, but he shifted his focus off the words and onto the gorgeous, feisty woman next to him.

She stepped in front of him and raised her hand. He took it in his and raised it up to his left shoulder to rest on his neck.

Her gaze remained fixed on him as he tugged her close, wrapping his arm around her waist and positioning his hand just above the middle of her back, then he took her other hand in his. They began moving, slow and smooth, across their section of the dance floor.

Riley glanced over his shoulder. Leaning in, she whispered, "You're going to have to do better than that."

He frowned. "Better than what?"

"Julie and Alvin are watching us. You need to hold me closer." She was mere inches from him.

"You sure?" he whispered back.

She nodded, closing the space between them until she was flush with him—utter perfection. It was like she was made to be held in his arms. They moved to the music in perfect unity.

"Now lower your hand." Her whisper tickled the nape of his neck.

He swallowed. "Pardon me?"

"Julie's moved on, but Alvin's still watching. We have to make it look like we're in love."

Speak for yourself. I'm not pretending. But she couldn't ever know that.

"Lower your hand," she said under her breath.

He inched it down.

"Lower."

He inched it down more.

While Alvin's gaze was diverted, she took hold of Grey's hand and lowered it to the small of her back, settling it there. She looked up at him and blinked. "That okay? You just tensed."

More than okay. "All good."

They moved in sync with the music, shifting their gait as "I Cross My Heart" came on by George Strait.

He twirled Riley and swung them around, fixing his vantage point on Alvin standing against the back wall, his gaze fast upon them.

He returned the stare, and after a moment too long, the man shifted his gaze away.

"You tensed again."

"I don't like how Alvin's watching you."

"Trust me, I don't like it either."

He twirled her back around and drew her close.

She rested her head on his chest and shifted her hand from his shoulder to the base of his neck, her fingers brushing the edge of his hair. Any pain throbbing through his injured arm faded away until all he could feel was her. He pressed a kiss to the top of her head, and she leaned deeper into him. Closing his eyes, he sank into the moment. He could hold her like this forever.

After a time, he opened his eyes and found them moving with slow, soft steps to music that no longer played.

"All right." Julie clapped.

Riley lifted her head and scanned the room. "I didn't realize it stopped."

He studied her face. Had she enjoyed the dancing as much as he had?

"Hello?" Julie said far closer than she'd been. "Did you hear me?"

"Yes." Riley stepped back. "I . . . we were distracted."

"Clearly." Julie smiled. "But it's nice to see a couple as deeply in love as you two so clearly are."

They were? He'd say they were putting on a great show of it, but for him it was very, very real.

"The shuttle is leaving for the casino. You'd best hurry. You don't want to miss out on all the fun."

"Thank you." He reached for Ri's hand, wanting her close again. "Come on, darlin'. Let's scoot the boot."

"Don't worry. Alvin will hold it for you."

Great. More Alvin.

TWENTY

DECK KNOCKED on Tate Matthews's door after noting his car in the apartment complex's lot.

A tall, lanky guy with curly hair answered. "No solicitors. Didn't you see the sign?" He shut the door.

Deck slid his booted foot in before it fully shut. "We're not solicitors."

Tate raised two fair brows. "Oh? Then who are you?"

"I'm Deckard MacLeod. This is Christian O'Brady. We're private investigators."

"*Uh-huh,*" Tate scoffed.

They both held up their licenses.

Tate frowned and shifted his stance, his hand braced on the door. "What's going on here?"

"We're trying to find Kelly Frazier," Christian said.

"Isn't everyone?" He turned and stalked back into his apartment, leaving the door open.

Taking it as an invitation, Deck stepped inside, and Christian followed.

"I told them, and I'll tell you, she's just off on some adventure."

"You know that for a fact?"

"No, but it's what she does. It certainly wouldn't be the first time."

"Does she usually answer her phone on these adventures?"

"Sometimes. Look, I appreciate that you're trying to help Kelly, but you're looking for someone who doesn't even realize she's missing."

An odd way to put it.

"So if you'll excuse me," he said.

"Actually, there's one more thing," Deck said.

Tate exhaled in a whoosh. "Yeah?"

"Noah was shot by an arrow today."

Tate's eyes widened. "An arrow? Is he okay?"

"Thankfully, yes," Christian said. "It was only a flesh wound."

"But far too close," Deckard said.

"I'm sorry to hear that, but I don't understand what that has to do with me."

"Kevin from the retreat said he saw you do it."

"What?" His voice hitched an octave higher. "Is he insane?"

"You tell us. Where were you around three this afternoon?"

He shrugged. "I was here."

"Can anyone vouch for you?" Christian asked.

"Yeah, actually. I ordered DoorDash, and it got delivered to my neighbor Calvin by mistake, so he brought it down to me, and I asked if he wanted to join me. I got quite a bit, so I had more than enough."

"Okay. We'll confirm it with Calvin. Which apartment is he in?"

"3D."

"Thanks for your time." Deck stepped back.

"I hope you find who did it."

"Thanks," Christian said as Tate shut the door.

They turned and headed up the steps one flight to the third floor. Deck ran a hand through his hair. "It's weird. It's like there's two versions of Tate."

Paige Wheeler had been more than helpful, and her answers had been surprising—painting a completely different picture of Tate than the rumors running around about him. The only disturbance they had was one night he got into a barroom brawl with a guy who'd been flirting with her. According to her, it was

112

sweet and thoughtful, and the two only broke up because Tate was still carrying a flame for his ex. Someone named Claire, but that's all Paige knew about her—a first name. She said he had mentioned her once when he was drunk, and when she asked about her later, he refused to discuss it. Tate and Paige had split a year ago. Right before he started dating Kelly—based on what Kelly had told Roni.

"Maybe he's the moody sort," Christian suggested.

"Nah, it's something more. Like some of the rumors are just that—rumors. Maybe he's not so bad a guy after all."

"So if Tate isn't after Kelly . . ." Christian rounded the stairwell.

Deck leaned against the rail. "Then who is?"

The ride to the Jicarilla reservation took less time than Greyson anticipated. He glanced at their surroundings. As dark as it was outside, it was difficult to tell where exactly they were on the reservation that he knew all too well.

"I hope I have as much luck as Kelly," Roni said, strolling down the shuttle aisle past them.

"What do you mean?" Riley stood as Veronica paused to wait for other guests to disembark.

"Did I forget to mention she won ten grand at the casino her last night here?"

"Yeah. You did."

"Oh, sorry. I just didn't think anything of it." Roni shrugged and pulled out a cigarette.

"No smoking on the shuttle," Alvin called.

Greyson wondered how much of the conversation he'd heard and how it had come across to him. "We should head out," he said, resting his hand on the small of Riley's back.

Riley's phone vibrated as they stepped off the shuttle, leaving Alvin behind.

She halted two steps from the van, and Greyson nearly bowled her over.

He rested his hand on her shoulder and leaned in, keeping his register low. "What is it?"

She held her phone out for him to see.

Tate was home when Grey was shot at. He has
an alibi. Not thrilled with you two staying there.
I'd consider leaving.

"Everything okay out there?" Alvin asked.

Grey turned to find him staring at them once again, the shuttle door still open. "We're fine," he cut out. He wrapped his arm around Riley, and they moved for the casino door with gilded scrollwork and handles. No neon sign—in fact, no sign at all.

"If Tate didn't shoot the arrow . . ." she whispered.

"Then we have to find who did. I'm assuming it's whoever is after the key. They've found us here."

"You mean me. He's found me." She lifted her chin a notch to look up at him. "If that's the case, then that arrow wasn't meant for you. It was meant for me."

TWENTY-ONE

THE CASINO WAS different from what she'd imagined. More a high-stakes, high-elegance poker room with a couple other options, including two roulette tables and two blackjack tables. No flashy lights. No blingy sounds. Just black linen tablecloths and employees attired in white dress shirts and black dress pants with matching ties. Julie Chase stood near the entrance, greeting the guests as they arrived.

Riley narrowed her eyes. Why was Julie playing host at a reservation casino?

"Greetings," she said, interrupting Riley's thoughts. "Please enjoy yourselves and have some fun." Julie smiled. "Oh, and there's a five-hundred-dollar minimum to play."

"Very well," Greyson said, resting his hand on her shoulder, caressing her skin. "Shall we go have some fun, luv?"

She nodded, thankful the casino didn't resemble those in Vegas, but the tightness squeezed her chest all the same.

"What would you like to play first?" Grey leaned in and whispered, his breath tickling the nape of her neck. The very best kind of shiver shot along her spine.

She swallowed at his tenderness. "I think blackjack," she managed to utter.

"Blackjack it is."

He trailed his finger down her arm and clasped her hand.

She wasn't sure which was garnering more of her attention. The fact she was in a casino again for the first time since they'd fled Vegas, or the fact that Greyson was doing a very good job convincing people they were a couple. At this point, he was even convincing her.

"Good evening," the dealer greeted them as they stepped up to the blackjack table.

Grey nodded in reply. He pulled out a chair for her, then took the seat beside her.

"Thanks," she said.

"Always, luv." He winked, and her stomach did that weird thing. She didn't have butterflies fluttering about. She had squirrels, and they were at a rave.

"Ready for some blackjack?" the dealer said. He was clean-shaven and extremely bulky for a dealer. He looked more like a bodybuilder. Perhaps he was in his spare time.

"Yes, we are." Grey glanced at Riley, disarming her with a charming smile. He rested his hand on hers, caressing her fingers with his. "Aren't we, darlin'?"

She nodded. Okay, the man knew how to flirt. One wink with *that* smile, and she turned to putty. Not. A. Good. Sign. At least not for her heart.

The dealer dealt the cards, and the game began.

She blinked.

Please let the Vegas memories stay at bay.

———

A horrible, disconcerting floating sensation plagued Riley. She'd let the setting get to her, and a mix of rage and sorrow sifted through her.

"You did amazing tonight. You didn't lose a hand," Greyson said once they were back in their room. "Too bad we didn't learn anything new from the other guests we interviewed. But I think they really bought it."

"Bought it?" Riley asked.

"Us being in love."

She stiffened.

His gentle touch across her arm, his hand in hers—all of that, all of the deep emotions welling inside her, was fake. She had to remember that, though she'd already remembered far too many painful memories tonight. Her unrequited love didn't need to be among them.

"We have it"—he loosened his tie—"we just need to keep it up."

Have it? They didn't have anything. Not anything real. He'd just said it himself. Why did *all* of her have to care so deeply for a man who didn't feel the same way?

She dropped her clutch on the bed and pulled the rhinestone-lined combs from her hair, letting it fall across her shoulders. "You can't lose what you don't have."

"What?"

"You said 'have it.' And I'm saying you can't lose what you don't have. I learned that long ago." As much as she wanted everything happening between them to be real, it wasn't. Pretending was blurring the line between what was real and what was playing a part in her mind. She had to remember she wasn't his, as much as she longed to be, and he certainly wasn't hers. One more person in her life who was playing a role.

Emotions and a flood of memories crashed over her like a suffocating wave. Her feelings for Greyson, his lack of romantic feelings for her, her parents and everyone in her family—even her—playing roles to survive, the terror that had filled her over Pete's death. It all combined in a current that pulled her under and tossed her about.

Greyson stepped in front of her. A never-before-seen vulnerability radiated in his soulful eyes. "You have me. You know that, right?"

"Excuse me?"

"I'll always be here for you."

Just not in the way she longed for. Why was she getting so upset with Greyson? Yes, it hurt, especially after a night when it had seemed so real, but there was more there. Her past was coming back to haunt her. She'd let the casino get to her. Let her horrid childhood swarm back over her like a rush of locusts over crops, decimating them in one pass.

Unruly tears misted her eyes.

Greyson cupped her face. He swiped her tears away with the pad of his thumb. "I mean it. I'll always be here for you. I don't want you to think otherwise." The deep timbre of his voice resonated in her chest.

"I've heard that before." *Take a breath. You know what to do when you've been triggered. Stop this before you embarrass yourself.* She was being beyond rude, and Greyson was the last person she ever wanted to be so with, but here she was—all the hurt and anger that had roiled through her little body as a kid roiled through her anew. She slipped her slingback heels off and sunk her feet into the plush carpet, trying to ground herself.

Please, Lord. Don't let this happen in front of Greyson. Don't let this happen, period. I've left the panic attacks behind. Or she had until Pete . . . And now the casino tonight . . . the sounds of the roulette wheel spinning, the ice clinking in the crystal glasses.

"From who?" he asked, pulling her from her thoughts. He remained steadfast at her side. How could his presence be so comforting yet painful at the same time?

"We'll be right. Just play your part like a good girl." Hot tears spilled from her eyes. "My parents."

"Oh . . ." His face softened. "Come here." He tugged her into his arms, his hands splaying across her back. "I'm so sorry," he whispered against her ear. "I didn't stop to think about the casino bringing back old memories. I'm *so* sorry."

She sniffed, feeling foolish for crying on Greyson's shoulder, but his arms only held her tighter. "You don't have to be sorry. You didn't do anything." At least nothing real. It was all an act, and she needed to stop thinking otherwise.

He brushed her hair back from her face. "I hate to see you cry." Sincerity resonated in his eyes.

She nodded and stepped back with a sniff. She squared her

shoulders. She was stronger than her past. "I'm going to get ready for bed." She just prayed the nightmares that had haunted her for years after Vegas didn't return. She already had more than enough with Pete visiting her almost nightly in her dreams. Horrid dreams she prayed would stop.

Shifting his binoculars to see through the slit in the curtains, he watched Greyson Chadwick comfort Riley as she cried, and heat flared within him. He was coming to like the woman. Enough not to kill her? Of course not. He had a job to do, and in the end, she'd be the one to pay for Kelly's crime. But jealousy had rooted inside him, and the closer the pair got, the more he wanted to tear them apart. And he would.

Lowering his binoculars, he moved for the window, hoping to hear as well as see, and it worked. Greyson tried so valiantly to soothe her. What a pansy. When he had her, there'd be no comfort. Only pain until he got what he needed, and then she'd be of no more use to him.

TWENTY-TWO

RUNNING THROUGH pitch black, groping to feel with arms stretched out in front of her . . . Sweat drizzled down Riley's neck.

"Quicker," her mother hissed.

Her little legs burned. They'd been running forever. Would it never end?

Her mother looked back, but her stern face was marred in the moonless night.

"He's here," she clipped out. "Hide." She disappeared.

"Where?" Riley spun in the darkness. Where had her mother gone? Everyone else was still at the hotel. Hot tears pricked her eyes. She didn't know how to get back there. Sirens roared in the blackness.

Heavy footfalls crashed along the pavement.

Her chest heaved, her tiny throat closing.

"No!"

Riley bolted up. Sweat soaked her hair, drizzling down her neck and clinging like a beaded mist to her chest and arms.

Where was she? She blinked. What was happening? Terror clamped her chest, hard.

The bathroom door cracked, a beam of light sliding in the crack along with the muzzle of a gun.

She clamored for her weapon, her breath ragged.

"Ri?" Grey said. "Status?"

Her chest deflated as reality swarmed back into place. "It's clear. I'm okay." Far from it, but that's the story she was going with. Vegas was not going to demolish her like before. She was stronger than it. Stronger than before. Hot tears pricked her eyes. She had to be.

Greyson opened the door all the way and rushed to her side.

"Sorry to wake you . . . to startle you," she stammered. She raked a hand through her damp hair. "It was just a dream."

"Sounded more like a nightmare." He gestured to the bed. "May I?"

She nodded and scooched over.

He sat on the side and reached over, resting his hand on her calf, rubbing it in soothing strokes. "You okay, luv?"

She nodded. "The casino just . . ." She swallowed, the fear tracking through her.

"Ri?" He rubbed her calf again.

She bit her bottom lip, then admitted the shame. "It brought back memories best left dead."

Grey cringed at memories that were best left dead for him, too, but death already clung to those memories. He just feared for Riley. Flashbacks and nightmares that woke a person in the night and were worse still during the day—he'd seen it before. And he'd tried, but he couldn't stop the inevitable conclusion.

"Hey," she said, resting her hand on top of his on her leg. "You okay?"

She was asking if he was okay when she'd just been plagued by nightmares? "Why do you ask?"

"You just got this awful look on your face and you tensed way up."

"Sorry." He needed to be there *for* her, not the other way around.

"Don't be sorry. What is it?"

"Just an old memory." Apparently, memories haunted them both.

"Want to talk about it?" she asked, turning the nightstand lamp on.

"Nah." He shrugged a shoulder.

She shifted, pulling her knees to her chest. "Why do you do that?"

"Do what?" He frowned.

"Always pull back when it comes to something personal."

He didn't do that, did he? "I don't—"

"Oh, please, we spend hours upon hours together, and there's so much I don't know about you. You know everything about me, but you keep a guard in place, and I want to know why."

"Some things are best left behind."

"True, but clearly whatever it is isn't behind you. I've never seen fear on your face before tonight."

How bad had his expression been?

"Besides, it's only fair," she said, sliding closer to him.

"Fair?"

"Like I said, you know everything about me. Even the horrible parts. I want to know you like that."

He dipped his chin. "You want to know my horrible parts?"

"Yes. I want to know all of you."

Was she saying . . . ? No. She was just curious and being a friend.

"Please. Tell me where your thoughts went."

Did she think she could save him? He took a deep inhale. Funny thing was, she probably was the only one who could. And while being a couple was a farce, being friends was not, and she was asking as a friend. A dear friend. Dearer than she knew. "His name was David." He hadn't said his name out loud in nigh on a decade.

She sat there silent, waiting.

He shook his hands out. "We served in the military together. I was the supply guy getting what everyone in combat needed when they needed it and got some medic training along the way. But my friend David was on the front lines. He saw too much pain."

He took a steadying breath, or attempted to.

She looked up at him, tenderness in her eyes.

Swallowing, he continued. He'd started; he'd finish. For her. "After we got back, he had these horrid flashbacks."

"Did he see anyone about them?"

He nodded. "Yeah, he went to a counselor. Got diagnosed with PTSD and saw a doc and got some meds."

"And?" She leaned in.

"For a while it got better." He rubbed the back of his neck. Here came the excruciating part.

Sensing it somehow, she reached out and took hold of his hand, intertwining her fingers with his. He was coming to rely on the warmth and comfort of her hand in his. But soon it would stop. He'd still be part of her life but looking in from the outside again. Alone again. Why did the prospect knock the breath from his lungs?

"Grey? You all right?"

"Yes." He cleared his throat, dreading the words about to come out of his mouth. "He stopped taking his meds. His PTSD and depression worsened. I feared he might hurt himself. . . ."

She tightened her hold on his hand, caressing it with her thumb.

"I removed the guns from his house. I . . ." He swallowed again, his throat dry. "I tried to control the situation, but I failed." There. He'd said it. The words were out, and they sliced through him like a scythe on a festering wound—raw and tormenting.

Her eyes softened along with her voice. "What do you mean, 'failed'?"

He released a tremoring exhale. "David hung himself."

"Oh no." She pressed her free hand to her lips, compassion flooding her eyes, but he didn't deserve compassion. He'd failed a friend in the worst possible way. "I'm so sorry. I didn't mean . . . I mean, I shouldn't have made you share. I'm so sorry that brought back such bad memories for you."

Unfortunately, what happened to David was just one of the demons he wrestled with. But when Grey was with Riley, the memories—rather the waking nightmares—didn't nosedive his depression like usual. But hot tears burned his eyes for what was left to say. He exhaled and went for it before he retreated behind his wall. "I found him."

"Oh, honey." She cupped his face, caressing his cheek. "I'm so sorry."

He balled his free hand into a fist. "Me too." If he'd just stayed with him. Done more. Thought of every angle. David would still be here. Worse yet, Grey's judgment had faltered again when he was searching for the serial killer who murdered Cassie Williams. He'd failed them both, and he couldn't forgive himself. That was why it was better for everyone if he stayed out of the field.

Riley leaned close, engulfing him in her arms. She rested her head on his chest.

He swiped at an errant tear that escaped. "I learned that day control is a farce." He'd believed he had control of the situation, but the circumstances flipped, shattering his belief he could control his own depression. He'd seen the toll it took on his dearest loved one, then David with the added pain of PTSD. It'd been a decade of carrying sorrow inside . . . but somehow being with Riley brought a sliver of hope that one day *he'd* beat his demons.

"Hey," she said after a time of silence. "Why don't we raid the minibar and chat for a while."

He wasn't up for more intense talk.

"Just chat about whatever," she said, getting up and heading to the minibar. "The weather if you like. I'm just not ready to go back to sleep yet."

Of course. He'd been so focused on David, he'd nearly forgotten her nightmares had kicked this off. If she needed time and company before falling back asleep, he'd be honored to be there for her as she was for him—as a friend. His hand balled into a fist again, and he shook it out. Only a friend. That brought a different kind of sorrow.

After they'd each snagged a drink and snack from the shockingly expensive minibar—a can of Pringles, two cans of pop, and a bag of Skittles running them twenty dollars—Riley returned to the bed. Setting her Skittles and Sprite on the nightstand, she fluffed two pillows, wedging them between her back and the tufted fabric headboard. She shimmied about until she finally crossed her legs in front of her.

"Comfortable now?" He chuckled. How did she have the ability to bring laughter from his lips so soon after an intense talk? Because it was Riley. She was the light to his darkness. Always had been. And he prayed she always would be. The thought of her seriously dating someone, falling in love, getting married . . . He'd be happy for her, but it would wrench a knife in his gut.

"Come sit," she said, patting the space beside her on the bed.

"I can pull up a chair."

"Grey, we're friends. We sit right beside each other at work for hours on end."

Some of his best times.

"Come on and sit."

"Yes, ma'am." That brought a smile to those oh-too-kissable lips.

"So," he said, pulling the lid off the Pringles and setting it on the nightstand beside him. "What shall we talk about?"

"How about your dance moves or your ability to flirt? You proved me wrong there."

So she thought he danced well, and flirted well too. *Interesting.*

Riley jumped off the bed.

He frowned. "What's up? Spill your soda?" It wouldn't be the first time, or the hundredth for that matter. The woman was a klutz at times, but an adorable one.

She walked toward the window facing the grotto.

"What is it?"

"I saw movement."

He stood and retrieved his gun.

"I see it again by the grotto. Someone is out there."

"I'll go," Greyson said, sliding on his shoes.

She slid hers on beside him and grabbed a thin jacket.

He looked at her and realized an argument over her going would only waste time, and she'd end up going all the same.

Opening the door, they raced down the passageway for the

rear outer door, guns low at their sides. Thankfully, it was four in the morning, and no one was around—other than the shadow they were chasing.

Stepping out into the frigid night, he blinked, trying to adjust his eyes to the darkness. The lampposts were lit, but they lined the far side of the courtyard.

Grey rested a hand on Riley's arm. They held. Listened.

Footfalls.

They rushed for the grotto.

A shadow shifted through trees. They followed, entering through the hardy winter vegetation surrounding the hot tub.

They held up again, surveying the trees on the opposite side, searching for movement and finding none. No more shadow. No more footfalls.

They'd definitely lost him.

"Come on," Grey said. "Let's get you back inside. You're going to catch hypothermia with that thin jacket." He wrapped his arm around her waist, tugging her close to him and rubbing her arm.

The thought of sleep seemed even more difficult after another reminder someone was after them. It had to be the man after the key. He'd found them.

TWENTY-THREE

KNOCKING ECHOED in Riley's dreams. Sweet ones of her and Greyson chatting the night away, his hand in hers—the movement so comfortable and natural now. What was that ceaseless knocking? She opened her eyes and blinked, then it clicked. *The door.*

"Just a moment," she called, sitting up, sunlight streaming through the curtains.

"Room service for the happy couple."

"Just a minute." She chucked a pillow at Greyson's head on the sofa. She'd talked him into sleeping there rather than in that uncomfortable bathtub.

Befuddled, Grey grabbed the pillow and sat up.

"Room service is at the door," she whispered. "Quick, put your pillow and blanket on the bed."

He did so in a flash, and she mussed the cover on that side of the bed.

He strode to the door and looked back at her. *Ready?* he mouthed.

She nodded, pulling the blanket up to her shoulders.

Grey opened the door.

"Good morning. I have breakfast courtesy of the retreat," the service attendant said, rolling in a cart of covered trays.

"How nice and unexpected," Riley said.

"We aim to pamper our guests with a few surprises along the way. Miss Julie thought you might enjoy breakfast in bed."

"May I?" the man asked, indicating lifting the dish covers.

"Please," Greyson said.

The man removed one silver cover after another to reveal the delectable food underneath. "Brioche French toast, raspberry crepes, bacon, and seasonal fruit. May I pour you coffee?" he asked, reaching for the carafe.

"That's very kind of you. Thank you," Riley said.

"As I said, we want all our couples to be fully pampered. And, speaking of pampering, I hear you have a massage at nine."

Apparently, the staff knew everything, or so it seemed. "Yes, I'm looking forward to it."

"Oh, and fresh flowers for your room." He lifted a vase from a shelf underneath the cart. He set it on the dresser. "Unless you require anything else?"

Riley smiled. "No, but thank you."

Greyson held out a tip for the man, but the man shook his head. "Not necessary, sir. I'll leave you two alone. Oh, I almost forgot." He moved back to the cart and pulled up two leaves to make a round table. "Would you like me to move your chairs for you?"

"We're good, thank you," Greyson said.

"Enjoy, now." The man headed for the door and waved once before shutting it.

Riley hopped from the bed. "Everything looks delicious. It was nice of Julie to send this."

"Agreed."

She took a slice of bacon and ate a bite while Greyson moved two chairs over to the pop-up table. "I better hurry if I'm going to make my massage."

Twenty minutes later, she was headed for the door when Greyson exited the bathroom in a black Under Armor workout shirt that clung to his chiseled chest and a pair of matching black sweatpants.

"Going for a workout?" she asked, trying to keep her gaze off his handsome physique.

"Yeah. I figured it'd be a good way to try the lockers here without drawing too much attention. I'll ask for one to hold my stuff while I hit the gym."

"Sounds like a smart plan."

A sideways smile curled on his lips. "I'm full of them."

She shook her head. "Full of something else too."

He laughed. "Shall we?" He indicated the door.

"Thanks," she said, exiting as he held the door open for her.

They hurried across the snow-covered path to the gym and spa facilities building.

"Don't forget to mention your coconut oil allergy," Greyson said before they reached the building's glass double doors.

"How did you remember that?"

He shrugged. "Just have a memory for details." He opened the door and she hurried inside, stomping the snow from her shoes onto the rubber entrance rug.

They looked up to find Alvin at the check-in desk. "Here for your massage, Miss Bennet?"

"Yes."

"I'll be happy to get you checked in." He looked past her at Grey. "Gym is through that door." He gestured to it with a tilt of his head. "And down the hall to your left."

"Thanks." He nodded, then scooted close to Riley, pressing a kiss to her cheek. "Have fun."

She swallowed. He'd never kissed her before the retreat. First a kiss on the head and now on the cheek. Had it been for Alvin's benefit, or had he actually wanted to give her a kiss?

"You're all set. I'll show you to the lounge, and Annabelle will be right out for you."

"Thanks."

She hoped her masseuse or some of the ladies in the spa gossiped like the women at her Santa Fe spa. They needed a fresh lead before Kelly's trail went cold.

TWENTY-FOUR

"WE'LL BE RIGHT HERE." The masseuse gestured Riley to the first slotted massage space on the left. "I'll just pull the curtain while you get undressed. The table warmer is already on."

"Sounds wonderful."

"It is," the woman in the space across from her said.

Riley got on the table stomach-down and pulled the covers up.

"Are we ready?" Annabelle asked.

"Yes."

Annabelle pulled the curtain back. "I see we're starting on your back."

"Yes, it's been really tense of late. I think I pulled it at the gym." Before they'd come, and it was still tender.

"No problem. We'll get that taken care of." Annabelle moved for a dispenser and pumped oil on her hands, then rubbed them together before starting on Riley's shoulders.

"I was so mad." Riley recognized Jenny's voice coming from the next massage space.

"I'm so sorry," Jenny's masseuse responded.

"I always work out with Jared, and now he's gone, and I was stuck with Alvin."

"You don't like Alvin?"

"He's not nearly as good of a trainer, and there's just something weird about the guy."

After an hour of eavesdropping to all the chatter around her, Riley stepped inside the steam room and found Jenny sitting on the top bench.

"Hi," she greeted Riley.

"Hi." Riley smiled, taking a seat on the lower bench. "I'm glad I'm not the only one who Alvin creeps out." It seemed like a solid inroad to the previous conversation.

"Thank you!" Jenny said, lifting her arms up. "Everyone else says he's quiet or reserved, but he just feels off, if you know what I mean."

"Absolutely. Kevin makes me feel the same way."

"Yeah." She bumped down to share the bench.

"So you said you usually work out with who? I might have to sign up with him."

"Jared Henshaw. But apparently he's gone."

"Oh?"

"They said he's on vacation, but I had a training spot reserved with him the morning after he left. Guess he forgot to cancel it."

Interesting. "When did he leave?"

"He was gone yesterday morning when I woke. They said he left the night before, after his shift. That's the same night Kelly left. I was planning to see her here."

"Did Jared and Kelly know each other?" Riley asked. "I'm just curious since they left the same day."

"Oh. You think they maybe ran off together? How yummy of an idea."

"I'm not sure if that was the case. Just curious if it was possible. I mean, the timing is interesting at the very least."

"She definitely knew him. Worked out with him every morning at six."

"Wow. That's commitment."

"Yeah. I have the seven o'clock slot with Jared. Or I did. I can't say I blame her if she did leave with him. I heard she and Tate had quite the blowout the night before she left. He's another guy who rubs me the wrong way. But Kevin flat-out gives me the creeps. You know I saw him stalking around the grounds late last night."

"You did?"

"I got a call from my mom in the middle of the night. She's a very early riser and forgot about the time zone difference. She's on eastern. Anyway, I didn't want to wake Chad, my hubby, so I took it on the balcony, and there Kevin was, sneaking around."

"What time was this?"

"Four thirty."

"Are you sure?" What would Kevin have to do with Kelly or the key? It had to be Riley's stalker walking around, didn't it?

"Positive," Jenny continued. "Mom's always up at six thirty. Apparently, the news about her neighbor was too juicy to wait until our regular call."

"Any idea what Kevin was doing?"

"I have no idea. He was hedging around the building walls. I have a good angle of the gym building from my balcony and caught a glance of him in the lamppost light. Weirdest thing. I could have sworn I saw binoculars around his neck."

"Binoculars?"

"Yeah." Jenny shrugged. "Probably safety goggles or something. The moon just glinted off them weirdly."

Riley wrapped her arms around her chest. Had Kevin been spying on them, and, if so, why?

"Did he stay there long?"

"Not after I came out. He was heading around the back of the gym facility, probably for that building in the woods he always skulks off to."

"What building?"

"Well, I was curious why he kept going into the woods. So one day I followed him. I couldn't help myself. Chad always says I'm too curious for my own good."

"I get that too."

"Right?" She smiled. "So anyway. There's this building out in a clearing about . . . well, the length of a couple football fields away. It's nondescript. No name on the building. He goes inside and stays for quite a while. At least he did on the day I watched him. From the time I saw him go in and until he came back to the main center, it was probably a couple hours."

"That is weird."

"That's what I told Chad, but he just said I'm paranoid and have been watching too many *Spenser: For Hire* reruns."

"I love that show."

"Me too. Are you heading to the hot springs today?"

"Hot springs?"

"Yeah, I heard that's on the day's agenda. You'll love them. They're gorgeous and *very* romantic."

Great. Riley blew an errant strand of hair from her face. That'd make it easier not to fall any harder for Greyson.

TWENTY-FIVE

WHAT WAS WRONG with him? Greyson noted the clock, *again*, and grunted out an exhale. He'd finished his extended workout and figured Riley would be done not long after him, so he opted for some more push-ups but still no Riley. Five more laps around the track and still no Riley. A half hour went by slow as molasses and still no Riley. Just a half hour and he was missing the woman beyond measure. This was bad. Extremely bad. He was becoming dependent on her—as she was on him in some ways. The two of them were bound with an invisible connection he couldn't quite explain. But it was strong enough to crumble his guard and fill him with hope for a future that could never be.

Footsteps sounded on the hall's tile floor. There was a bounce in the person's gait. *Riley*.

She rounded the corner, and happiness swirled inside him. "How was your massage?"

"Great. How was your workout?"

"Good." Though his heart rate kicked far higher in her presence than when he ran on the treadmill. "Ready to head to the room?"

She nodded.

They crossed back over the snow-packed path to their building, and Greyson held the outer door open. "After you."

She smiled, stepping inside but waiting by the entrance. "Find anything exciting?" she whispered as she tugged his arm to lower his ear level with her mouth.

"Afraid not."

She nodded, but her smile waned.

They'd hit another dead end with the locker key. Where between the retreat and Riley's door had Kelly left it? And how could she put Riley in danger? It had come hard and fast, starting with the man outside her home. Frustration seared through him as a door shut down the passage. He shifted his gaze toward the sound.

Kevin strode forward, an odd expression on his face as if he'd just been caught stealing a cookie from the jar.

"Hi, Kevin," Riley greeted him as he strode toward them, fast and focused on the door behind them. She tilted her head. "You giving an in-room lesson?" she asked, stepping between him and the exit.

"What?" He frowned, his brow furrowed, his stance rigid.

"I just assumed you were in here because you were giving a lesson. What other reason would you have for being in a guest's room?" she asked with a smile—the one that emerged during a case when she was playing mental chess with a suspect.

"Right," he said, glancing at his watch. "I need to get to my next lesson." He wedged past Riley and exited the building.

Riley rested her hands on her hips, the yoga pants accentuating her curvy form.

He swallowed; his mouth dry.

"Shall we, honey?" she asked.

He blinked. "Wh—"

Another couple entered the building behind him.

"Of course, luv." He reached for her hand and she slipped hers in his. Her touch soft and warm. What did it matter—it was just for show. He swallowed again. But it did matter—more and more as their concentrated time together went on.

After Riley greeted the couple, they strolled to their room hand in hand.

Entering, she left her hand in his, not even hinting at moving away. Warmth spread through him.

"I think I'm going to take a shower."

"Sounds good."

"Why don't you join me?"

"Uh . . . what?" He'd misheard her. Surely, she didn't mean . . . "You . . . I . . ." *Great, Greyson, sputter like a fool.*

"Yep. Come on, honey." She pulled him with her.

What on earth was happening?

She tugged him into the bathroom and shut the door. Moving for the shower, she yanked back the curtain and turned the shower on. Water gushed then sprinkled out like heavy rain on pavement.

"What's going on?" he asked as steam wafted in the small space. No way Riley was truly suggesting what she'd said.

She leaned close and whispered, "If I was a betting woman, I'd wager the door we heard Kevin shut was to our room."

"Most likely."

"I say we go through the room top to bottom. See if anything is out of place . . ."

"Or missing." Their guns. He flung the bathroom door open and rushed for the safe. Punching in the numbers, he opened the heavy door. They certainly hadn't cheaped out on their safe choice.

He streamed out a long breath, the tautness easing from his shoulders—gun and badges still in place.

Riley stepped to the dresser, opening the drawers. He strode to her side. The intent concentration on her face as she studied the contents deepened.

He followed her gaze and heat rushed up his neck and into his cheeks. Silk PJ shorts and tops, ladies' garments . . .

She looked up at him, her eyes widening as she slammed the door shut. Her cheeks red as an apple, she sputtered. "I . . ."

He stepped away, indicating with outstretched hand that he'd search the clothes hanging in the closet.

An hour of meticulous searching later, they'd found nothing out of place or missing.

Grey dropped on the edge of the bed, wondering if Kevin was just that good at putting things back in place or if he'd been in the room for another reason. He surveyed the room, his gaze fixing on the vase and flower bouquet. Could it be . . .

Riley shot him a curious look as he stood and moved for the flower arrangement they'd received with breakfast. It was the only new thing in the room. Examining the crystal vase, he found nothing. Straightening, he eyed the flowers. Was it possible . . . ?

He dipped his head and examined the flowers one by one and bingo. A small white chip was nestled in one of the daffodils. He waved Riley over and noted the bug. She straightened; her beautiful blue eyes wide as she fixed her gaze on him.

Gesturing to the bathroom, he led the way. Once inside, the room full with steam from the still-running shower, he shut the door.

Riley leaned against the marble vanity.

He stepped close to her, standing so near they were practically touching. He inhaled the scent of lavender and was that eucalyptus? Must be from her massage because those scents hadn't been there earlier. But they smelled lovely just like her.

She waved her hand in front of his face.

He blinked. "Sorry. Was just running things through my mind." She needn't know what.

"Gotcha. Sooo," she said, drawing out the word. "I learned a few things at the spa."

"Oh?" He quirked a brow.

She shared everything—the fact that Jenny saw Kevin stalking around outside not long after the visitor to their window, and that a Jared Henshaw was gone the same morning Kelly left.

"That was a lot of information to get in thirty seconds," he teased. It was an inside joke from a sitcom they watched, but it held true. That *was* a lot of information to get in a short period.

She took out her phone and started typing. "I'm asking Deck if he and Christian can go check this Jared guy out ASAP." She stilled. "Do you think Jared could be the one Kelly is running from? I mean, they both were gone the same morning."

He crossed his arms. "I'd say it's fair to assume there's most likely a tie between the two, and that's one possible scenario. We need to dig deeper into the possibility."

"Agreed." Her phone vibrated. "Deck said they'll head to Jared's today. He lives in Red River." She shifted against the vanity. "I'm curious why they bugged our room," she whispered as the steam engulfed them.

"Maybe they know we're looking for Kelly," he said, the room warming by the second. "Maybe they're worried."

"Like they know what happened to her?"

"Maybe." He leaned against the counter beside Riley and planted his hands on the vanity behind him. "Or maybe they figured out we're PIs."

"Either way it's not good."

"Agreed."

She hopped up to sit on the vanity, her leg brushing his side as she got comfortable. He smiled.

Her lips quirked to the side, concern furrowing her brow. "I pray Kelly's okay. That she got where she was going after she dropped the key off with me."

"Oh!" she squeaked, her beautiful eyes widening.

"What?"

"It just hit me. What if the man I saw in the trees outside my house was Kevin? I mean, something isn't right with the guy. Maybe Kelly was running from him until she dropped the key at my house. Deck said the first car he heard left by the back way. And the second car came several minutes later and then left from the front of the ranch. Maybe he lost her trail and came back here."

Frustration with the danger Kelly had put Riley in reared again. "I pray he doesn't know you have the key."

"You and me both. But we can't rule out this Jared character either. It's extremely coincidental that they disappeared at the same time. And what if Julie lied about Kelly leaving of her own accord?" The questions kept coming and he couldn't help but smile.

When she paused to take a breath, he cut in. "Everyone here seems to cover multiple positions—Alvin, Kevin, et cetera. I thought it was simply because it's a smaller staff and they rotated, but what if Jared's job shifted to something far more sinister?"

Riley fanned herself, perspiration dotting her brow. "Interesting . . . We'll need Deck and Christian to dig deep on this guy."

He nodded, fighting the urge to pull his shirt off. It suctioned to his skin, the moisture-wicking fabric no longer doing its job against the onslaught of steam. He tried to ignore it, but to no use. It was no different from her seeing him in a bathing suit. Reaching his hand to the back collar of his shirt, he pulled it up over his head and slipped it off. "The heat was just too much," he said, flinging the shirt over his shoulder.

Red flushed Riley's cheeks. She stared at him, then cast her gaze to the side, clearing her throat.

He narrowed his eyes. Was she blushing because of him? *Nah.* She didn't look at him like that. Well, not normally, but she had been since they'd arrived at the retreat. But that was all for show, wasn't it? But no one was around to see it now.

"So . . ." Riley cleared the squeak from her voice. "What should we do next?"

Her close proximity warmed him more than the steaming shower, but he focused to keep his voice neutral despite the fast-paced feelings rumbling through him. "We pretend all is normal while we're in the room, or they'll know we found the bug and are on to them."

"And then what?"

"We dig deeper on the staff."

"Good idea, but that'll have to wait until we get back."

"Back from?"

"We're going to the hot springs."

Given the temperature of the shower steam and the unspoken heat radiating between him and Riley, he'd say they were already there.

A couple hours later, she and Greyson strolled down the empty passageway of the guest quarters. Not a soul around.

Riley studied him, hard.

"What?" he asked, one brow quirked.

"I'm curious," she began.

"Shocking." He grinned.

She smirked but continued. "I'm just wondering how it feels being back in the field after so many years away? You seem to really love it."

"I do, but . . ."

"But Cassie," she said with solemnness.

"And more."

"That's what you said." Her nose crinkled like it did when she was thinking hard. Her face blanched. "Oh . . ." She bit her bottom lip. "Never mind. Sorry I asked."

No doubt she'd just put the timing together.

"David wasn't the only reason I left the field," he said, holding the outer door open for her. Wind swirled the flying snow in wisps.

"Was it the combination of his death and Cassie's timing wise?"

"Yes." He nodded once. "But . . ."

"You don't have to share if you don't want to," she said as they caught sight of the shuttle waiting at the far end of the property, just outside the rear gate. "I'm sorry. I shouldn't have pushed."

"It's okay. To be fully honest, there's one more reason, but now's not the time." He gestured to Kevin waving them over from the far end of the retreat center. All the other guests appeared to be on board the shuttle. No wonder the place was empty.

"Okay. You tell me when you're ready. If you want to."

Shockingly, he *did* want to. It was the one secret he'd never shared with anyone, but something inside whispered for him to share with her.

But can I really do that, Lord?

It'll bring healing you so desperately long for.

I don't deserve healing. I let them down. I failed them. It's on me.

Stop carrying what isn't yours and watch your back. Evil is coming your way.

TWENTY-SIX

"I STILL DON'T THINK this is a smart idea, for the record," Greyson said as they hid behind the giant juniper at the edge of the woods separating the main retreat center from the secret building Julie and Kevin had entered. The sun was dipping toward the horizon, pulling the light with it.

Time hung heavy as the humidity still draped around Riley since they'd returned from a two-hour trip to the hot springs. While she should be freezing given the current temperature of thirty degrees and her still-damp hair, she was overheated. And she couldn't help but think the man beside her was part of the cause. If not the whole of it. Greyson in a swimsuit had been . . . *No. Focus. Don't ruin your shot.*

"They're coming," he whispered, a breath of a second before her feet were pulled out from under her.

She landed on top of him with a thump. He wrapped his arm around her and rolled them over, his body fully shielding hers as her back rested on the mushy, damp earth.

What was happening?

He held as still as one of the massive tree trunks surrounding them, and she followed suit.

Julie's voice echoed over the fallen log nestled beside them. Kevin's followed as the pat of footsteps against the earth reverberated across the narrow chasm between them.

A sprig of a fern twitched her nose, and she fought back a sneeze. If she didn't move her nose from it . . . Her chest heaved as she fought the burgeoning sneeze pressing at her rib cage, tickling her sinuses.

Greyson stiffened, his gaze flashing to hers.

Julie's and Kevin's voices trailed farther, but not far enough to let loose the sneeze.

Please, Lord. She held her breath. Like that would stop it. And when she sneezed, she went big or went home. She didn't have a dainty, feminine sneeze. Hers were headshaking, unfortunate as it was, especially at this moment in time. The sneeze would give their position away posthaste.

Greyson's eyes pleaded with her to remain silent.

I'm trying. She blinked back. Fearful to move her head an inch.

Greyson's heart raced against her rib cage. Now was not the time to note how perfectly his sandalwood aftershave mixed with their surroundings, but she couldn't help herself.

There. Distract yourself with him. It'd stolen the impending sneeze from her mind.

His chest rose and fell in bursts. Was his fear meter rising? Wait a minute. Grey doesn't fear. Worry, yes. Worry over her? Big yes. But fear?

The footfalls whispered away.

Greyson shifted, allowing her to move her head. The fern leaf slipped off her nose, and the stinging sensation to sneeze faded. Grey lifted his chin, his gaze peering over the log.

"There," he said, rolling to the side, his warmth leaving her. "That should do it. Are you okay?"

She nodded, and the burning returned in a fury. She covered her mouth and—"Auckshoo!"

His eyes widened, and she froze. He inched his head back over the peeling bark of the log.

Her heart raced—faster than his.

Please. Let them be too far away to hear.

Greyson's shoulders eased an inch. "We're clear," he whispered.

142

She released a long exhale.

Thank you, Lord.

He popped gracefully to his feet while she ungraciously scrambled to get up. He held out a hand. She took it and stood.

"Thanks." She swiped the bark and earth from her other hand and her pants. "Okay, let's do this."

"You still want to do this?"

"Of course." She rocked on the balls of her feet.

"I still think this is a bad idea."

"Duly noted," she said. "There's got to be something hidden in there for them to sneak in and out of a building that's concealed from the guests."

"It might just be where the building happened to be built. It's probably just administrative."

"I prefer to be an optimist."

"And I prefer to be a realist. And the reality is they could come back at any time and catch you."

She cocked her head.

"There it is." He shook his head.

She narrowed her eyes. "There what is?"

"That I'm-going-to-do-it-regardless look."

She stifled a grin.

"And there's that smirk."

She pulled her lips into her mouth.

"Too late. I saw it." He swiped his thumb across her pinched lips.

No brush of a finger should feel so good. "I'm going."

"Fine." He sighed. "But be careful. I'll keep watch."

"Deal," she said and shot off before he could argue.

She opened the storm door to find the main door cracked. Taking one last look around, she cracked it wide enough to slide in, then she pushed it shut behind her.

A desk sat to the right with an old-fashioned black leather desk pad, keyboard, single monitor, notepad, and pen cup. No pictures. No personal touch at all.

A pine bookcase flanked the otherwise bare wall in front of her, but no books stood on its knotty shelves. Two-inch black binders lined them instead.

Curiosity piqued.

She padded to the binders and pulled the top left one out. She flipped it open to an employee photo of the masseuse nestled inside a clear sheet protector. She flipped the page. A printout labeled with *Annabelle Anderson* across the top descended into the usual employment information. Date of employment and of birth. Social Security number. Home address . . . and the list continued. She flipped to the next page. Employee monthly performance evaluation. She leafed through. How many months did Julie hold on to? And why in old-fashioned binders instead of on her computer?

The computer purred in the distance. Ignoring it, Riley kept her focus on the binder, wondering if it held other information. White pages with black ink fluttered by until a heading caught her eye. *Personal Data.* Hadn't that all been on the first page? She scanned the page. It appeared to be a duplicate until phone records appeared. Narrowing her eyes, she trailed down the line of highlighted calls. Nearly all of them. Beside each sat one to two letters. *Bf.* Best friend? Boyfriend? *M.* Mom? *J.* The first letter of someone's name? She flipped to the next page and the numbers continued. She went one more page to find photographs in four-by-six clear plastic slots. One of Annabelle and a man labeled *Jason.* That solved that mystery of *J,* but what was Julie doing with what looked like surveillance photos of a staff member? Riley zeroed in on the date. Two weeks before Annabelle was even hired. What on earth . . . ? She counted the binders. *Twenty-four.* Did Julie have one on every employee?

A bird whistled. Check that. That was Greyson's attempt at a bird call. Was someone coming? Adrenaline surged through her limbs. Shoving the binder back into place, she scoured the room. A single door stood opposite the desk. Julie's and Kevin's voices sounded.

Oh, crud. She darted for the door, praying it was a side exit but found herself in a three-by-six box of a closet.

The storm door creaked, and the main door swung open.

"Thanks for actually remembering to shut the door all the way."

"Uh, sure."

"So the hundredth time was the trick to tell you that you have to slam it hard."

Please don't let Kevin say he didn't slam the door. Please. Jackets swept over her head as Riley backed toward the cubby space to her left. She inched, her pulse thumping in her neck, until she bumped into something solid. A suitcase. A pink one with a pineapple tag. That certainly didn't scream refined Julie.

"We need to find that thief and get that money she stole back in our safe before our high rollers come asking for it, or we're dead," Julie snapped. "Have you heard from him?"

"Yeah, at the hot springs."

"No one better have heard you."

"I took it in the shuttle while everyone was in the springs."

"And?" The tap of her heels sounded on the plastic mat Riley had seen under the desk.

"He's on the trail and gaining."

"Good. Tell him to find out where the witch stashed the money, then dispose of her."

"Oh, I told him. But the boss wants to be the one to get the location out of her."

"Is that right?"

Riley cringed at the pleasure in Julie's voice.

"Said this one is personal."

"Fine. Now, you need to find that key. Alvin checked their room while you all were at the springs, and nothing."

"She must still have it on her."

"Then you know what to do."

He chuckled. "Consider it done."

"Look. I told you," Julie snipped, shifting her attention, "I didn't leave that file on the desk."

"Check your drawers?" Kevin grunted.

Keys rattled, and a drawer opened.

Holding her breath, Riley braved a peek through the closet door slats.

Julie stood behind the desk rifling through drawers. Kevin oversaw from the front of the desk, his broad back to the closet.

"Got it," Julie said, lifting a blue file folder.

"Told you," Kevin clipped.

"Whatever. What's in the file on those two is far more important than where it was."

Riley swallowed and sank to her knees. They had a file on her and Greyson? A shiver snaked down her spine. How much did they know?

Finally, she heard the door close, and Riley's stiff carriage eased.

Climbing to her feet, she turned the door handle, then paused.

Something told her to check the suitcase out. Maybe it was the style that didn't suit Julie or maybe it was the Holy Spirit. Either way, she wouldn't ignore the feeling. She scooted back in the cubby and lifted the sparkly pineapple luggage tag.

Kelly Frazier.

Either she'd left her luggage behind by choice or necessity, or . . . she'd gone missing under duress. Given the key left at Riley's house plus Julie and Kevin's comments, it was definitely the latter. Deck needed to yank Joel onto the case pronto.

Snapping a photo on her phone of the suitcase and tag, she hustled out of the closest, sprinted across the office, and slipped out the door. Poor Greyson was probably having a cow.

"What took you so long?" he said when she reached his side in the tree cover.

"I found something."

He took her hand. "You can tell me when we're safely back at the retreat."

Heading down the winding dirt path, they hadn't fully cleared the forest when Julie's voice echoed their way.

Adrenaline seared her limbs.

Before she could blink, Greyson swung her against the nearest tree—the bark cold against her back.

His warm hand stroked her neck, his finger trailing down it.

"Wh-what are you doing?" In truth, she didn't care why he was doing it. She just hoped he didn't stop.

"Shh," he whispered, his lips mere inches from hers.

What was happening?

He braced his left hand on the tree beside her head and cupped her face in the other.

Julie's voice was just around the corner.

"Sorry in advance," he whispered.

"Sorry for—"

He dipped his head, and his lips melded to hers.

Sparks shot through her.

He shifted and trailed his fingers up her neck, then spread them through her hair.

She kissed him back, hoping she was doing it right.

A groan escaped his lips. He wrapped his arm around her back and tugged her against him, deepening the kiss.

Thank goodness the tree was holding her up.

His hand splayed across the small of her back. Was his hand shaking? Maybe she *was* doing it wrong.

Julie cleared her throat.

Greyson eased back, his forehead momentarily resting on hers, their rushed breaths mingling.

Julie cleared her throat again.

With a sigh and a drop in his shoulders, Greyson pulled back enough to turn his head toward the woman.

Riley dipped her gaze under his arm, his other hand still planted on the tree.

Julie and Kevin stood side by side.

"Can I help you?" Julie tapped her foot on the damp earth.

"No," Greyson said, his tone level, even. "We're good."

"What are you doing out here?"

"We just needed a little privacy." He smiled.

"I see." Julie crossed her arms over her chest. "Well, we'd prefer if you require privacy that you find it in your room."

"Of course." Greyson gave a nod.

Riley just stood there, letting the tree continue to hold her up as her knees knocked. Greyson had kissed her. She struggled to wrap her mind around it . . . around *them*.

"You should probably change," Julie said, directing her attention at Riley. "Before you catch a cold from damp hair."

She'd forgotten she was still in her suit under her winter coat and fleece-lined yoga pants. They'd barely made it off the shuttle when she'd taken her opportunity to dash for the building.

"We'll just be going, then," Greyson said, taking her hand in his as they made their way back to their room.

Head swirling, she hoped they picked up from where they left off, but certainly it was just a pretend kiss, just like the relationship she was coming to love. It wasn't real, and that stung more than she'd anticipated. She sighed. But it was for the best. It was time they got out of Dodge.

TWENTY-SEVEN

ENTERING THEIR ROOM, Greyson shut the door behind them and locked it. Riley had filled him in on her findings during their rushed walk back. They had stopped to warn Roni and Brad to leave, though he and Riley would wait until the shuttle left for a special wine-tasting supper, with Kevin likely driving as he had most other excursions.

They'd take the opportunity to disappear into the night. Hopefully no one would notice their absence until morning—putting hours between them and anyone who might try to follow them. He still couldn't believe Kevin's role. He had to be the one who'd ambushed Riley, broken into her house . . . Speaking of breaking in . . . He stopped and stared around the room, curious what Alvin had touched—what he'd learned.

"I think I'll take a shower," Riley said, gesturing him in once again.

"Good idea." He followed her into the bathroom, where she turned on the shower and shut the door.

"We need to catch Deckard up. He needs to loop Joel into this now. It's been forty-eight hours, and with Kelly's luggage still here, he can open a missing person's case now." Riley pulled her phone from her pocket.

Her cheeks were flushed, her lips still rosy from their kiss. He'd never experienced anything like that kiss. But he owed her an apology. He'd acted in the moment and taken a liberty that wasn't his from the one person he cared most about. If she only knew how much. And while the kiss had been out of this world for him, it'd probably been downright awkward for her.

He cleared his throat, the steam enveloping them. "About that kiss . . ." he began.

She lowered the phone as her bright blue eyes searched his. "Yes?"

He cleared his throat. "I'm truly—" he began, his voice husky.

"Don't say it," she cut him off.

"What I was . . ." He paused. Were those tears misting in her eyes, or was it the steam from the shower? He prayed the latter. If his kiss had caused her distress, he wouldn't be able to bear it. "I—"

"Don't say you're sorry," her voice broke. "Please."

He studied her. Was the kiss so upsetting to her?

She squared her shoulders. "Please don't negate my first kiss as something you regret."

His eyes widened, and he leaned back on the sink, needing something to hold him up. He'd taken her first kiss? On one hand, he reveled in the pleasure that he'd been the first to kiss the woman he loved, but on the other hand, he felt like a scoundrel for doing so.

She stepped from the room and shut the door.

After a staggering moment, he followed her out.

She sat on the sofa, texting. No doubt to her brother, who—if he found out about the kiss—would deck him. "I caught him up to speed," she said. "They said their latest visit was a bust. A neighbor said he was off on a two-week camping trip. Apparently, he likes outdoor activities too."

"That sounds familiar."

She nodded.

He ached to sit beside her, to tell her the kiss may have started as a diversion, but it meant infinitely more to him. But he let her be. Telling her his feelings for her would only make the situation more awkward and embarrassing.

He moved for the desk, searching for what Alvin had searched through. He scanned the room methodically—taking in one surface, one item, at a time. His gaze landed on the safe, and he froze.

Riley looked over at him and frowned. *What?* she mouthed.

He held up a finger and rushed for the safe. Bending over, he punched in the code. It opened, and he straightened, stiff as a rod. *Empty.* Their guns were gone.

Riley rushed to his side and looked into the empty safe then up at him.

"We need to go," he whispered in her ear. "Now."

She nodded.

He moved to the window and gazed outside. The courtyard was clear. The shuttle had to be loading.

Moving toward Riley, he lowered his mouth and whispered in her ear. "Get something warmer on as fast as you can. Grab your backpack and shove only essentials in. As soon as that shuttle takes off, so do we."

TWENTY-EIGHT

RILEY OPENED the bathroom door after changing to find Greyson holding up her boots in one hand, her coat in the other. Taking the boots, she sank onto the end of the bed and pulled them on, then stood.

Ready? he mouthed, holding out her winter coat.

She nodded, and he helped her into it. She grabbed her backpack. He did the same.

He cracked the door and peeked into the passageway, then stilled. He eased the door shut and locked it. "We need another way out."

Agreeing with another nod, she moved for the oversized window on their back wall.

He helped her through, then followed.

Their front door opened as his boots hit the ground. He eased the window shut, and they bolted for the wrought-iron doors of the outer gate.

Reaching the Rover on the other side of the wrought-iron fence, Greyson opened her door, and she climbed inside. He raced around and hopped in the driver's side. He turned the ignition. *Click. Click. Click.*

He took a deep breath and turned again. *Click. Click. Click.* "It's rolling over but no catch. Hang on." He climbed out and lifted the hood, then hurried around to her side. "Come on. We've got to go. Someone took our spark plugs."

She jumped out, now noting the flat tires.

Greyson popped the trunk and lifted the cover to the spare tire and tools. He reached into the cubby to the side, and relief swelled in her chest when he pulled out an auxiliary handgun and gave it to her. Then he reached over into the space above the wheel well and pulled out his dismantled rifle, put the pieces together, and loaded it. He looked over his shoulder, and she followed his gaze. *Clear.* He opened the toolbox and pulled out two flashlights and his compass.

"Where are we heading?"

"Into the mesa."

His gaze shifted to the building next to the parking lot. "We need to move."

Kevin and a man she didn't recognize stalked down the building's well-lit hallway, headed straight for the glass exit door and them.

"Move," Greyson hollered. His hand firm on her lower back, he shoved her forward, and they ran.

Snow crunched beneath her boots as they hit the mesa, and she prayed the sound didn't give their position away. Thankfully, new falling snow rained down, hopefully fast enough to cover their tracks.

"We need to get a hundred yards out. Past that cleft for some cover." His words clipped out in sync with his stride.

Adrenaline singed her limbs, heat swarming down her thighs with each elongated stride. She faced forward, fighting the urge to look back. To see if the men had spotted them fleeing in the darkness, the moon shadowed by snow-filled clouds.

"Down!" The word rushed out of Greyson's mouth on a heavy breath.

She dropped and slid on her right side behind the rock formation in the ravine.

Greyson dropped beside her, then rolled on the ground, wincing at the movement across his wound. He anchored his rifle on one of the rocks and set up the shot.

"What kind of range do you have on that?" she asked as he sighted in.

"Up to three hundred yards with the long-range scope."

More than enough.

They lay flat, waiting. . . .

The men headed to the Rover. Kevin spewed out something, but they were too far away to hear. Both men strode the length of the parking lot, checking other cars.

"We remain still until they're gone," Greyson whispered.

The chill of the ground seeped up through her clothes, spreading through her bones.

Keeping her breath even, she lay as still as Greyson.

Kevin gestured the other guy over to the mesa.

"Here we go," Greyson said, his eye fastened to the scope.

Kevin and the man spread out with flashlights, the beams dancing over the snow and ice.

"Very still," Grey said so low under his breath, she nearly didn't hear him.

She pressed deeper into the frigid ground, hoping her teeth didn't chatter.

The light swept over the ground fifty feet in front of them.

She clutched the SIG Greyson had given her, ready to fire if the men attacked.

Crunch. Crunch. Snap.

The snow and twigs sounded under Kevin's feet. He walked closer. *Twenty-five feet.*

She prayed the brush, rocks, and ravine covered them. She fixed her aim on Kevin's center of mass.

"Anything?" the other man hollered.

Kevin stopped fifteen feet from them. "Nah. This is a goose chase. Let's head to the office and track them the right way."

"Roger that," the other man said.

The two turned and strode back for the center.

Relief whooshed out of Riley, her taut frame easing.

Greyson held until the two men disappeared through the gate.

"Let's go." He got to his feet, slid his rifle over his arm, and pulled out his compass. "Four clicks ahead is a rock formation. Hard to see it on a night so dark, but it's there. Once we reach it, we cross over the dry riverbed and head northwest, straight for the res."

She held her phone out. Zero signal.

"We're in no-man's-land," he said.

"It worked at the retreat."

"They must have a cell booster. But not out here."

"What do you think Kevin meant by tracking the right way?" she asked as they headed out into the wilderness.

"I'm guessing they mean checking the monitors to see if they missed finding us somewhere on the property. Hopefully they won't think to play back the recording to watch us head this way."

"I hope not, but I doubt it." She cringed. "Where are we headed?"

"To my friend Phillip's on the reservation."

"How far is that?"

"Depending on our pace, I'd say roughly ten hours. We should hit it about sunup."

"You think the men will try and track us on foot?"

"I think they'll be tracking the roads, but we need to keep moving at a good clip just in case. They seem determined to find us."

TWENTY-NINE

RILEY BLEW ON HER FINGERS, then shoved them back into her coat pockets, her gloves too thin to fight off the chill of a December night.

They hiked at a good clip, side by side, but had remained quiet for the last two hours, focused only on moving and occasionally looking over their shoulders. So far, all remained still and dark behind them.

"Take my gloves," Greyson said, pulling them off with his teeth, not relinquishing his hold on the rifle.

She'd slid the SIG into the back of her pants but could draw the weapon in a flash. Hours upon hours of practice with Deck had trained her well. It was nearly rote muscle memory at this point.

"I'm not taking your gloves."

"I'm not asking."

"I'm not taking them," she reiterated.

He shook his head. "You're so stubborn."

"Pot. Kettle."

"I'm trying to keep you warm."

"And I'm trying to keep you warm." Though she'd rather be held in his arms than hiking through the cold mesa en route to a reservation she'd never been on to meet a friend of Greyson's that she never knew he had. So much she didn't know, but so much she was learning. Really intimate stuff on a different level from casual friendship. And that kiss held far more passion than friendship—at least for her. But she must have misread his body language, how he'd deepened the kiss after she'd kissed him back, the racing of his heart against her chest . . . How had she misread all of that?

She studied his profile in the falling snow. What if she hadn't misread it? What if . . . ? A smile graced her lips.

He looked over. "What's up?"

"Nothing."

"You smiled that smile."

"What smile is that?"

"Your curious one."

"Ah."

"What is it you're curious about?"

"It can wait." She wanted to hold on to the possibility a little while longer before he crushed her hope.

He gestured to the endless mesa ahead. "We have time. As long as we keep moving."

"You think they're still coming?"

"I'm afraid so."

"Then it can definitely wait." Before he could answer, she continued. "I should try my phone again. I'm sure Deck's worried. We always check in at night." She pulled out her phone but no signal. She slid it into the back pocket of her ski pants.

"I think we can definitely rule Tate out now."

"Unless it's something wild and he's in cahoots with the retreat, I'd wager you're right."

Rumbling sounded in the distance.

Greyson scanned the area. "Move for the cave dwellings. Up!"

"What is it?" she asked, already in motion.

"Four-wheelers." He raced beside her.

"I'd ask if you thought it was them," she said in spurts as she scaled the rock face for the dwellings above. "But we both know the answer."

The headlights of two four-wheelers came into view. Ridden by two bulky, shadowed figures. Kevin and the unknown man.

Greyson halted and scanned the rock face.

She waited, reading his mind. The dwellings were too high to make it in time.

"That crevice," he said, pointing to a narrow opening in the rock.

"*That* crevice? It's too narrow."

"It's wider than it looks."

Miraculously, Greyson was right. She managed to slide inside and scooted back until she was flush with the cold rock. He slid inside, shielding her with his body. "If they see you, we're trapped, and you're dead."

"Not happening." He held his rifle against his chest.

She took a breath, but it was shallow in the confined space. Dark with no wiggle room, the top of the rock mere inches from her face.

"Here they come."

THIRTY

SOMETHING CRAWLED along Riley's leg in the tight confines, and she bit back a scream—her skin crawling as much as whatever was moving up her leg.

The men's boot steps grew near in tandem with their flashlights.

Greyson sat dead still as the boots stopped at the edge of the rock face.

"What does the tracker say?" the other man asked.

"It don't say anything, Steve. That's the problem. Zero flipping reception out here."

"Well, this was the last area it blipped before it went out. I bet they're up in one of those cave dwellings."

"You expect us to search them all?"

"There's only a half dozen, and it's what the boss would want us to do," Steve said. "I don't know about you, but I'm not calling him and telling him we failed."

"Fine. Let's go up the back side," Kevin said. "It's an easier climb. We'll start from the top and work our way down systematically."

Once the boot steps and flashlights faded away, Greyson spoke low. "We need to move to the tree cover before they crest that ridge. You ready?"

She nodded.

Greyson slid out, helped her up, and they bolted for the tree cover, just making it before flashlights crested the ridge.

"Keep moving," he said. "Stay behind the tree line."

If only it wasn't so sparse.

"We need to figure out how they're tracking us," Riley said.

"There are more caves up ahead at the edge of the tree line. We'll stop there and figure it out."

Branches slapped her face as she ran, but she kept going, her thighs burning, her lungs heaving.

Soon the copse of trees thinned, and another, denser, tree line lay ahead.

"To the right. Ten yards," he said.

She followed his directions and reached the cave.

"Okay," he said, once they were deep inside—far enough he could turn on the pencil flashlight and it wouldn't be seen from the mouth of the cave. "Strip everything off."

She blinked. "I'm sorry, *what*?"

"They've got some kind of tracker on us. I'll go in the tunnel on the right. You take the one on the left."

She nodded. The tunnel was dark save for the thin beam of her flashlight that she positioned on the floor. She hated to think what was crawling outside the beam of light.

She stripped down, thinking of Greyson doing the same not far from her, then chastised herself. They were running for their lives. She should not be thinking about . . . him.

Once she finished taking everything off, she shook out all her clothing and turned everything inside out. Nothing.

Lifting her boot, she felt under the sole lining and, sure enough, found an AirTag.

"You dressed?" Grey asked.

"No, give me a minute, but I found the tracker."

"AirTag in your shoe?"

"Yeah."

"There's a river nearby we can dump them. They'll be tracking them the opposite way we're going. That is, once they can pick them up."

Reaching the river, they placed the AirTags on floating pieces of ice heading downstream, while they'd be trekking up. Night encompassed them. Its dark fingers wrapped tightly around them.

Some time later, a charley horse attacked her right calf and she limped through the pain.

Greyson halted and, turning his back to her, hunched over. "Hop on."

"What?"

"Hop on. I'll give you a piggyback ride."

"You're joking."

"I never joke."

"Your arm still isn't healed. The last thing you need to be doing is carrying me."

"You're a slip of a lass."

"Lass?"

"Sorry. Family heritage kicking in. My grandpa used to say it to my grandma."

"That's sweet, but I'm still not doing it."

"We can move faster if I carry you."

She sighed. He probably had her there—at least for a little while until it stopped smarting. "Fine, but for the record I think it's a bad idea for your arm."

"Noted. Now come on."

"Okay." She climbed up. "You're sure I'm not too heavy for your injured arm?"

"We did dead-body drills in the military all the time. You're a feather compared to some I've carried, and I've done it injured before. This flesh wound is nothing."

"All right."

"Now settle in. You feel like a robot, sitting back all stiff."

She bit her bottom lip and went for it, resting her head against the back of his neck and cuddling into him. He was so strong and solid, and if they weren't being hunted, she'd be in bliss.

She just prayed they reached Greyson's friend before the men reached them.

THIRTY-ONE

DAWN LIFTED from the darkness, and relief swept over Greyson. Light always made things better—unless you were trying to evade discovery. He glanced over his shoulder again. Still clear. No sign of Kevin and Steve since the cave dwellings. He prayed they were still following the AirTags' path. But that would only last so long. At some point they'd reappear—it wasn't a question of *if*, it was a question of *when*.

"Hang on. I'm going to see if I have signal yet."

"Good idea." Riley tightened her hold on his neck.

He choked. "Maybe not that tight."

"Sorry." She eased up.

He slid his phone from his pocket. "Yes! Two bars. I'll call Phillip."

"I best do the same with Deckard. I'm sure he's worried sick."

A few minutes later, they both returned their phones to their pockets.

"Phillip's on the way."

"I think Deck's still worried. I told him I'd update him more once we're at your friend's."

"We should be there soon."

She took a deep inhale and sighed it out.

He arched a brow. "What's on your mind?"

"Why do you think I have something on my mind?"

"I know *you*. So let's have it, lass. Out with it."

"Again with the lass?" A spark of joy filled her voice.

"It seemed to tickle you, so expect it more. Now, speaking of tickling . . . are you going to make me tickle it out of you?" There was a thought. A smile tugged at his lips. Being a couple with her filled him with joy. His smiled waned. *Playing* a couple with her, but now even that was over.

She fidgeted with the collar of his coat. "I have a question for you . . ."

"All right." Her nervousness shifted to him. What was coming?

"Did I do it . . . right?"

He frowned. "Do what right?"

She stiffened against his back. "Kiss?"

"Darlin', you have no idea how right it was." The words bypassed his brain and slipped out of his mouth before he could stop them. He squeezed his eyes shut. *Course correct. Course correct.*

"Really?" she asked. Her innocence was so endearing, he couldn't lie to her.

"Yes." It was the best kiss of his life. "But," he continued, "I know it must have been awkward for you, and I'm sorry."

"Awkward for me?"

"I mean, I'm your big brother's friend, and you're . . ."

"And I'm the baby sister you had to kiss for a diversion." She shifted, and he did in return to keep her balanced. "I'd like to get down now."

"Are you sure? We still have a little ways to go until the pickup point."

"Positive." An edge bit her voice. "My leg is fine. It was just a charley horse."

He frowned. Was she upset with him?

She hopped down, and he studied the tight line of her jaw. She *was* mad. Did she think the kiss meant nothing to him?

"Hey, Ri," he said, taking advantage of the last bit of time they had alone before Phillip arrived.

"Yeah?" She looked up at him, walking beside him at a good clip.

Don't do it, man. Don't say it. He reached for her hands, cupping his around her cold ones. He rubbed them.

She blinked, her big blue eyes staring up at him.

"I . . ." He swallowed. "I don't want you thinking that the kiss was without . . ."

"Without?" she pressed, the sun inching above the horizon and casting its rays across her beautiful face.

"Uh . . ." He scuffed the ground with the toe of his shoe. "Was . . . without feeling."

She tilted her head. "What are you saying?"

"I don't want you to think that it didn't mean anything to me."

Her eyes widened. "It did mean something to you?"

He nodded as a reservation police SUV came over the ridge, saving him from sharing too much.

Phillip stepped from the SUV and strode toward him. "Grey?" He clapped him in a man hug, then turned to Riley. "And who is this?"

"I'm Riley."

"A pleasure to meet you." Phillip's gaze shifted between Grey and her. A far too intuitive gaze. "Your Mali, huh?" He chuckled.

Riley narrowed her eyes. "What's a mali?"

Grey rubbed the back of his neck. How was he going to explain this one away?

"The trackers have signal," Kevin said. He and Steve had just arrived back at the retreat center after spending most of the night on a blasted goose chase. "We've got them pegged."

"Well, don't just sit here," Julie said. "Go get them. We need that key and them out of the picture."

"Not to talk out of turn," Steve said, "but won't two dead PIs draw more attention?"

"Not if we spin it that our thieves took them out when they got too close."

"Smart," Kevin said, reclining in his chair.

"We need that key and where it goes to—get it out of her."

"She's always with Chadwick."

"Then kill him first, get what you need from the girl, and dispose of her too." Julie rested her hands on her hips. "It's not like it's the first time one of you has hidden a body. I can pull Alvin in on this instead of you if you'd rather."

"No way." This was personal now. "I've got this."

"Good. Now, get up and get back on their trail. I want them taken care of today."

"And Kelly?"

"I'm shifting Steve over to aid Brent. He's taking too long, and the boss isn't happy. He wants her yesterday. You understand?"

"Yeah," Kevin said, standing. He'd do his job, not because Miss High-and-Mighty was bossing him around, but because he had a job to finish, and it wouldn't be done until both PIs were his.

THIRTY-TWO

KELLY TRUDGED ON, the cold burning her lungs. She could do this. They had to do this.

The rumble of two motors sounded in the distance.

"The trees," he said. "We'll take cover."

A few minutes later, a couple stopped their snowmobiles a few feet from them and cut the engine.

Had he sent a couple after them?

"Did you see someone, Hector?" the woman asked her companion.

"Yes. I wonder where they went?" Hector scanned the area, his gaze following their footprints in the thick snow right to them. He cocked his head. "Good morning."

Kelly turned to Jared, and he shrugged.

"Morning," he said.

Hector rested his hands on his hips. "Did you see a deer back there or something?"

Both people's hands were visible, and she saw no weapons.

"Yep," she lied. "We were trying to be still to see more."

"Sorry if we disturbed them with the mobiles."

"We're just out for a morning ride," the lady said. "It's usually so quiet this time of day, but you're the second hikers we've seen."

Kelly stiffened. "Oh?"

"Yes, we met the nicest gentleman maybe a mile back. He asked where we got the snowmobiles, so we pointed him in the direction of the rental shop."

"I told him they weren't open yet," Hector explained. "We rented ours yesterday, but he seemed determined to get one. Probably waiting there now until they open. Anyhoo, sorry if we disturbed your nature watching. We'll be on our way now."

Kelly's shoulders relaxed as the couple drove away. She turned to Jared "We've got to move."

Tracking through the underbrush of the trees to avoid leaving any more prints in the snow, Kelly rushed forward, Jared a handspan behind her. The slope beside them edged a fifty-foot drop to the ice-floating river below.

"We're not far from my car," he said. "We've only got a mile to go, and we're at our exit point. If we can just reach it before he reaches us."

The same rumbling echoed up the mountain pass. She prayed it was the couple just circling around, but she knew better. It was him. She could feel it.

The snowmobile reared over the slope, and the man driving scanned the area, then turned his gaze on them, and a smile spread over his lips.

Brent stopped the snowmobile, climbed off, and headed for them, gun in hand. Stuck between him and the drop-off, they had no choice.

"Kel, no," Jared said in the rush of the wind.

"It's the only way." Squeezing her eyes shut a moment, she leapt over the edge as bullets flew overhead.

Jared hit the ground.

She looked up between free falls, smacking into trees, then rolling past them. He tumbled down the steep incline, but she couldn't tell if he'd been shot or was just following her lead.

Ramming into something hard, her hand split open. Warm blood oozed into her tattered glove as her slide continued. Jagged rocks lay ahead. Trying to avert them, she held out her hand to grab on to something—anything to stop her free fall—but the ground cover and brush only tore at her hand more.

Her ski pants ripped as pain shot through her thigh, and she collided with the frigid water.

A second splash sounded.

She prayed there wouldn't be a third.

Bullets splayed the rough water, hitting an ice floe mere inches away. She ducked under—the cold stealing her breath. The water stabbed like icicles lancing her skin.

She hoped the river would carry them the rest of the way to the exit point—and fast. If they didn't get out of the water and into their car soon, they'd die of hypothermia, and all would be lost.

THIRTY-THREE

THE RIDE TO PHILLIP'S HOME was short, and soon they were in a cozy adobe home, a toasty fire in the kiva fireplace.

"These are beautiful," Riley said, striding to one of the black-and-white landscape photographs covering the wall.

"Yes, they are," Phillip said, slipping his fingers through his belt loops. "Mali took them."

"Who's Mali?" Riley asked, wondering again at the name.

"Yes, dear?" A woman in a long rust-colored skirt and black button-down shirt rounded the corner. Her long black hair was pulled into a braid, and she had high cheekbones and cinnamon eyes. She was lovely. "Oh, Greyson." She embraced him in a hug. "So good to see you." She fixed her attention on Riley. "Hi, I'm Mali." She smiled.

Riley's jaw loosened. Mali was Phillip's *wife*? He was saying Grey had found his wife? Her gaze darted to Grey, and a wealth of emotion resided in his eyes. Had he . . . did he . . . did the kiss mean more than he was letting on, and if so, why was he downplaying it? "I'm sorry," she said, shaking the thoughts from her head, at least for the moment, and extending her hand. "I'm Riley."

"Riley." The woman gave a nod with a warm smile and wrapped her arms around her. "Welcome to our home."

"Thank you so much."

Mali straightened and studied Grey, then Riley, until a full grin graced her lips. "Let's get you seen to."

Deck's cell rang. He lifted it from the table at Betty's Diner. "It's Ri," he said to Joel, who sat across from him. They'd had an early morning hockey practice, and his thighs were still aching from the drills. "You okay, kid? You had me worried." All night with nothing then only a brief call this morning letting him know she'd call back.

"I'm fine," she said. "We're at friends of Greyson's—Phillip and Mali Longshaw."

Deck winced at the memories he knew flooded Greyson whenever he was back on the res. He uttered a quick, silent prayer for his friend. "You know you had me worried sick. Still do."

"I know, but I couldn't help not having a signal all night."

"It's good you didn't, with them tracking you with AirTags."

Joel's brows arched.

"I'm going to put you on speaker, Ri. Joel's with me."

"Hey, Riley. I'm worried about you on this case too." He leaned in, resting his forearms on the Formica tabletop.

"I appreciate it, but—"

"You've never backed down from a case," Deck finished for her.

"Yeah, and I'm not starting now."

"Okay." Joel rubbed his chin. "Be careful out there. I've filed an official missing person's report for Kelly and talked with Roni. She and Brad arrived safely back in Jeopardy Falls late last night."

"Oh good. I was terrified to leave them there. I'm glad they're home safe."

"You come home safe too," Deck said.

"Will do."

"Look, I know you're fully competent on your own, and a fierce force to be reckoned with, but I'm glad Grey's with you."

"Me too."

"I've given Kelly's picture to the news stations and police departments throughout New Mexico," Joel said. "And I put a BOLO on Kelly's car."

"Jared Henshaw has been gone more than forty-eight hours as well," Riley said.

"But no one has reported him missing yet," Deck said. "Mom's deceased. I tracked his dad down in Georgia. He said Jared called and told him he was heading off on a camping trip with no reception for a couple weeks. Not that they talked much, apparently, but the dad said Jared went off on camping trips often. He doesn't believe he's missing at all."

"Great." She exhaled on the other end.

"If we feel there's a tie there," Joel said, "I can put a BOLO on Jared's vehicle. We may find it at a camping trailhead."

"Or we might find Kelly being chased by it."

THIRTY-FOUR

AFTER A SHOWER and fresh change of clothes, thanks to Mali's sister who'd left clothes in the guest room and was about the same size, Riley felt like a new, clean, and warmed-up person when she joined the other three at the dining table.

Grey was in a black brushpopper shirt, dark-wash Wrangler jeans, and a pair of cognac Lucchese cowboy boots with matching belt. His hair was mussed from the shower, and the five-o'clock shadow he'd left in place made for one stunning man.

"Please join us," Mali said, waving her over.

"Thank you." She sat.

"Coffee?" Phillip asked.

"Please."

He took the cup from her place setting and poured the coffee from a clay pitcher with a black wolf howling at the moon painted on it.

"Thank you."

"So dare I ask what happened?" Phillip said, setting the pitcher down.

Grey caught his friend up to speed.

"Why am I not surprised?" Phillip said. "Trouble seems to follow you."

"Not so much follows me as some of us chase it down," Greyson said, casting his gaze on Riley, a soft smile on his lips.

She shrugged with a smirk.

"You said the retreat is claiming their casino is on our land?" Mali asked.

Grey nodded.

Phillip sat back and crossed his arms. "I'll have to pay them a visit. Sounds like an illegal one to me if they're trying to pass it off as one of ours."

"It definitely felt underground to me," Riley said. The setup, the people working it, the dark room, high-stakes poker tables. Far different from the flashy casinos in Vegas, at least.

"I concur," Greyson said.

"All right. If it's not on our reservation, I don't have legal jurisdiction. I'll call the county sheriff, Mack Gaines. He's a good guy."

"I think that's who Roni called when this started."

"Good, then he'll already be familiar with the basics of the initial case. I'll explain the situation as of now with the retreat and that you found her luggage. Knowing Mack, he'll call the gaming commission in to determine if it's an illegal casino or not and head out there to poke around and see what can be found."

Greyson leaned forward. "It's definitely far worse than an illegal casino."

"Based on the missing woman and the men chasing you, I'd say so." Phillip set his coffee cup down. "Have you reported her missing to anyone else?"

"My brother Deck reported it to our local sheriff, Joel Brunswick, since Kelly is a Jeopardy Falls resident and she was in Jeopardy Falls the morning she left the retreat—leaving something on my doorstep." She rubbed her hand along the outline of the key in her Levi's pocket. "Given what we've found and the amount of time passed, Joel filed a missing person's report on Kelly."

Her cell rang, and she pulled it from her pocket. "Speaking of Deck . . ." She stood. "Excuse me a moment." She took the call in the other room. "Hey, bro. What's up?"

"We got a lead. They just found Kelly's car in Las Cruces."

"You're kidding? That was fast."

"Yeah, I told you Joel was on it. The police found it less than fifteen minutes ago."

"You think they're trying to run for the border?"

"Looks that way."

"Guess we're heading south as soon as we get a car."

"There's more," Deck said.

"All right?"

Deck hesitated, and he *never* hesitated.

Nervous tingles shot through her. "What's up?"

Grey joined her, and she switched the phone to speaker.

"I found something that ties Jared and Kelly together—or is an enormous coincidence."

"You know I don't believe in coincidences," she said, leaning against the wall by the roaring fire.

"I know you don't."

She twirled a strand of hair around her finger. "What did you discover?"

"Kelly and Jared both lived in Vegas until a year ago."

Vegas—twice in as many days. Please keep Vegas out of this. Don't lead the investigation there.

She hadn't been back since *that* night, and she'd sworn she never would.

Grey glanced over at her, compassion welling in his stormy eyes.

"You okay, kid?" Deck asked.

"Yep." She'd make herself be.

THIRTY-FIVE

"IT WAS EXTREMELY NICE of Phillip to let us use his extra truck," Riley said fifteen minutes later as she climbed into the driver's side of the 1970 burnt-orange Chevy so Grey could work, running everything he could find on Expressive Wellness and its employees.

"He's a good guy," Grey said, shimmying his laptop out of his backpack.

"Anything?" Riley asked, a half hour into their drive for Cruces. The snow was easing, the sun's rays poking through the cloud cover. It streamed through the windshield, warming her face despite the frigid temps outside.

She checked the rearview again, but no sign of a tail—*yet*. But they would be coming, of that she had no doubt.

"A money trail," he said, "but one that holds more questions than answers." He shook his head. "The retreat center is owned by Lansing Global. It's a shell company if ever I've seen one. No board of directors, a PO box for an address, and the banking is done through an institution known for shady customers in the Bahamas."

"Bahamas?" She smiled.

"That's what you picked up from that?" He chuckled.

"It's freezing here. Investigating in the Bahamas sounds really nice right now."

"True."

"Anything on the staff?"

"I pulled up the retreat employee page and scrolled through the faces and bios. In addition to Jared, I recognized them all from our stay, save two, a Brent Walters and a Steven Marandi."

"The latter being the man with Kevin in the mesa."

Grey nodded. "I dug deeper into both. Brent has a record for assault and possession of an illegal firearm. A military-grade assault rifle not approved for individual citizens to own. Steve is former Army."

"So both have training with or own firearms. *Great.*"

"And Kevin, he's former Marines. Dishonorably discharged."

"Brown Eyed Girl" chimed on her phone. "It's Deck." She put it on speaker and answered. "Hey, Deck—"

"You're going to want to turn around."

"Why?"

"Joel just got a call from a witness who spotted a woman matching Kelly's description and a man matching Jared's at a clinic in Kayenta."

"Kayenta? Rerouting."

Grey pulled it up on the GPS.

"It's a four-hour drive away." Thankfully, they hadn't made it too far south. "Let's pray they're still there."

"According to Joel, he talked to a helpful nurse at the clinic. She said the pair came in, and the woman had an injury, but the nurse wasn't allowed to say what. Although she did share that they paid cash and left quick."

"Any idea how bad an injury?"

"She said the woman would need some recovery time."

Riley glanced at Grey. "You think they holed up somewhere so she could rest?"

"That's my line of thinking, but this is your area," he said. "What do you think?"

"I think sitting still is dangerous . . . but moving injured and risking more injury will just slow them down. I bet they found a motel in a neighboring town and are shacked up for at least a day, maybe two."

"Joel's talking with the county sheriff there now. Bringing him into the loop," Deck said.

"Hopefully, he'll keep Joel in it."

She tapped the wheel as the December wind rattled the windows. "I guess our question about whether Jared is after Kelly or with her just got answered. No way he'd take her to a clinic if he was there to harm her."

She glanced over, and Grey met her gaze. "They're in it together," he said.

"So if Jared's not chasing Kelly, then it's got to be Brent who's after *them*," she said, looking back at the road.

"How do you figure?" Deck asked.

"With Kevin and Steve after us, it only leaves Brent missing from the retreat. My money is on him." She exhaled. "Let's just pray we find them before Brent does."

THIRTY-SIX

REACHING KAYENTA, they drove through the Navajo Nation town, checking the parking lots as they passed.

"I'm betting they drove out a ways," Riley said. "It's what I would do."

"There's not much outside of Kayenta. Let me look at a map." Grey pulled it up on the laptop, continuing to use his phone as a hot spot.

"If I were on the run, I'd go around the Four Corners area," she said.

"Because?"

"It's less than an hour's drive from Kayenta, and the towns there get such a flux of tourist traffic from Monument Valley that it'd be easy to disappear in the throng of tourists."

"To the Four Corners, then?" he asked.

"Yep." She headed north at the next juncture, hoping they'd lost Kevin and Steve for good, though men like that were relentless. The question was, Who were they being relentless for? Who was the man Kevin had referred to as the boss?

■ ■

Jared opened the motel room door and helped Kelly inside. She winced every few steps, so he aimed her straight for the bed.

"What if someone recognizes your 4Runner in front of the motel?"

"One step ahead of you. I'm going to ditch it and get us a new pair of wheels. I'll be back soon."

"I thought a stolen car would put too much heat on us? That's why you had us hitch a ride with that hiker back to the 4Runner in the first place."

"I think it's necessary now."

"Why?"

"Just trust me."

"Fine." She sighed, something far more important on her mind. "Before you go . . ." She attempted to sit up but winced hard and lay back down.

"Yeah?" Jared asked, his hand on the knob.

"I figured out why the locket looks familiar."

"Oh?" He came and sat on the bed.

"Do you remember that heiress, Kathryn Buford, who went missing in Vegas, not long after Claire joined the cult?"

"Oh yeah, her picture was all over the news." His eyes widened. "Her parents said she had a star-shaped locket she never took off. She was wearing it when she went missing, according to friends who were with her on vacation there."

"The locket in the safe had the initials K. B." She swallowed. "What if she was part of the cult?"

"Because Lance had her locket in his safe?"

"Yes, plus Claire said there was a woman who left the cult not long after she arrived. She only learned later that Lance didn't *allow* anyone to leave, so she knew the lady must have broken free, and it gave Claire the courage to do the same."

"You think that could've been Kathryn?"

"I don't think we can rule it out."

"I don't remember the news mentioning anything about a cult."

"They probably had nothing to tie the two together then."

"Then?"

"While you were stashing the car, I did some digging. Kathryn's body was found here last year while they were doing new construction," she said, pulling out her phone and showing him the general region by the cult house.

"It's a solid mile away."

"Who knows how far Lance's property extended."

"Good point."

"She could have been recruited just as Claire was. I looked back at the news reports, and Kathryn's friends said she met a guy she really liked. The next day they saw her leaving with a man who didn't fit Lance's description."

"Maybe Lance used a courier."

"You know . . . the man they described who was seen with her . . ."

"Yeah?"

"I think Alvin fits the description her friends gave. Tall, muscular, dark curly hair, and brown eyes."

"The very opposite of Lance with his blond hair, lanky build, and one-love kind of style. At least back then."

"Alvin was from Vegas, and he has the creep factor. What if he was Lance's courier all those years ago?"

"You think Lance killed Kathryn because she tried to escape?"

"I believe Lance would do whatever he had to do to protect his enterprise. Swindling money out of rich women like Kathryn while sucking the life from them. Denying Claire the kidney medicine she needed under the guise of healing her. If Kathryn left and told authorities what was happening there, it would ruin it all, and he'd go to jail for swindling."

"And for running the cult."

"Unfortunately, cults aren't illegal."

"Are you kidding?"

"No, but the point is if anyone told the police about scamming money away from these women and practically or actually holding them captive, he'd go away for a long time. It's why, when Claire made it free and called the police, by the time they got to the cult house to question Lance, he was already in the wind. The two other cult members they did find after the fact were still so brainwashed they only protected him."

"That's messed up."

"Yes, but now we have proof to tie Lance to Kathryn. And whoever else the other items belonged to." Her eyes widened. "You don't think they belong to other women he killed?"

"Knowing him and how evil he is, it wouldn't surprise me."

"And now he's doing it again. Trying to kill us off to protect his assets and hide the evidence that could put him away for life. We need to tell the cops," she said, straightening on the bed.

"That's a discussion for later. Right now, you need rest, and I'm going to lose my SUV and get us a new set of wheels." He handed her the Glock before standing. "Don't open this door for anyone. Someone comes through it without me announcing it's me, you shoot first, ask questions later."

She nodded.

"And try to get some sleep. It's been days." He kissed her on the forehead. "Put the chain on behind me."

Like a chain would stop Brent, but crossing the room, she put the chain across the door and double-checked the lock, then sat on the bed with the Glock aimed at the door. She wouldn't be sleeping a wink until Jared returned.

THIRTY-SEVEN

"I'M JUST CURIOUS . . ." Riley said as they closed in on the Four Corners area.

"Uh-oh." Greyson smirked.

"Very funny," she said as two more cars passed them on the road. She kept expecting to see Kevin and Steve in one, but thankfully, not yet. They'd really given them the slip for now, but her gut said it wouldn't last long.

"Ri?" Grey said, shifting to face her, the shafts of sunlight silhouetting him on the frosted window.

"Sorry. Mind drifted. I was just thinking about Julie's comment about needing the high rollers' stolen money back."

"And?"

"And I wonder who actually broke into the safe—Jared or Kelly. I mean, I just can't believe Kelly would do something like that, though I didn't know her that well, obviously." Still, she would never have pegged her for a thief. Part of her hoped Jared was the one running it all, and Kelly had fallen for the guy and just gotten in over her head, but the clues weren't pointing that way. If anything, it looked like they were very much in it together.

"Does it matter who broke into the safe? They both took the money and ran."

"No." She sighed. "I suppose it doesn't, and depending on who the high rollers are and how much money they lost, they could come after Kelly too. I saw it happen in Vegas more than once."

He reached over and clutched her hand. "I can't imagine what all you saw growing up there."

She sighed. "I try not to think about it, but it lives in the back of my mind."

"I'm sorry, luv."

"You just called me luv again."

He swallowed. "Would you prefer I not?"

"No. I just didn't expect it after we left the retreat and stopped playing a couple."

"Right." His voice dipped. "Just playing." He nodded and leaned back, slipping his hand from hers. "I better get back to searching," he said, opening his laptop.

"Right. Work." She took a steadying breath, but it didn't help. She was far from steady.

He tapped on the laptop keys as she drove, the silence loud between them.

Hours of searching motel parking lots in the nearby towns and showing Kelly's and Jared's pictures to the people working the front desks resulted in no leads.

"It's time we find a hotel and get some rest," Grey said.

"All right."

He hadn't expected her to agree so readily, but the string of yawns from her said she needed her rest.

Before long, they were settled in two connecting rooms on the back side of the Lucky Eight Motel. The snow that'd subsided for the past few hours fell again in a fury, and he was thankful to have Riley inside a warm hotel room.

"I guess I should get ready for bed." She grabbed her backpack and headed for the bathroom.

The water ran, and a few minutes later, she returned, face shiny.

He stood and stretched, and she strode to him. Standing right in front of him. So beautiful and right there. The ache to pull her into his arms was unrelenting.

He leaned against the dresser.

She stepped forward, halting mere inches in front of him.

He cocked his head. "What are you doing?"

"I want to try something." She rested her palm on his chest.

"What?" He swallowed.

"This." She leaned in and brushed her lips across his.

"Ri . . ." He breathed, his entire being lit with feelings he'd locked down so long ago. "We can't." He gripped the edge of the dresser.

"You said the kiss wasn't without feeling."

He nodded. What was he doing? *Get it together, man.*

"Then what is it?" she asked, not moving back. She tipped her head up to look him in the eye. So much emotion welled inside. "Please tell me you don't still view me as a kid sister?"

Warmth powered through him, and dizziness swarmed his head. "Believe me, brotherly is the last thing I feel for you."

With that, she raised up on her tiptoes and pressed a soft kiss to his lips.

His heart thudded in his ears. "Ri . . ." he whispered against her neck, her sweet ocean scent enveloping him, her skin so soft against his. "We shouldn't."

"Is that what you really want?" she murmured as she ran her fingers through his hair at the nape of his neck—her forehead pressed to his.

His breath came in short spurts.

"Hmm?" she whispered, her lips right there. "Don't you want to kiss me?"

"More than you know." His willpower crumbled, and he engulfed her in his arms, kissing her with all he had—all the feelings he'd carried for her for so long.

She kissed him back, and he deepened the kiss, his hands splayed across her back. Time stood still.

When he finally managed to pull back, he rested his forehead against hers again, his touch tender, his breath still ragged. He trailed his finger along her throat, feeling her pulse quicken beneath his finger. "You're breathtaking, you know that?"

She leaned deeper into him. "You think I'm breathtaking?"

"You steal mine." He kissed her again, and a happiness he hadn't felt in years overcame him.

This was bad. Very, very bad. He had to tell her. She had to understand why they could never be, and why he never should have let this happen—as amazing as it was.

THIRTY-EIGHT

TIME EVAPORATED until Greyson finally managed to pull back and avert his gaze. If he looked into her eyes, he'd be lost. He'd acted on feelings, not logic. He knew where feelings could take things, and he'd vowed to always want the best and always do the best for Riley. And the best wasn't him. He had to stop. They had to stop.

Her lashes fluttered as her beautiful blue eyes opened, her lips rosy pink. She smiled, then studying his face, she stilled. "What's wrong?"

"We shouldn't—"

"It's a little late for that," she said, stepping back and resting her hands on her hips.

He nearly laughed. Leave it to Riley to be as blunt as a butter knife. "I'm sorry," he said, regaining composure and a brain. "I—"

"You can't tell me you didn't feel something. Not with kisses like that."

"Of course I felt something." She had no idea how much. "But I let my feelings take control, and that's dangerous."

She narrowed her eyes. "*Dangerous* is a bit extreme."

Feelings could be extreme. That was the crux of the problem. "You deserve someone . . ."

"Someone?"

"Other than me." She deserved the world.

She swallowed and wrapped her arms about her, taking a pronounced step back.

His stomach bottomed out. He hated hurting her, but if they continued, he'd likely only hurt her far worse. He knew the shadows that lurked deep within him and feared with his entire being that one day they'd overtake him as they had David and his sweet mom. He couldn't risk burdening Riley with that. He was doing the right thing, as excruciating as it was. "I need to explain."

"That would be nice."

He had moved to sit on the bed when boot steps echoed outside.

Reaching for his gun, he stepped to the window. Easing back the curtain the smallest bit, he spotted Kevin in the exterior lights, headed straight for their door.

"It's Kevin. We need to go." He raced to the dresser and grabbed his backpack.

"He's here?"

Grey nodded. "Get in the other room, quick."

Riley didn't argue, just went through the connecting doors, grabbing her backpack as she ran by the bed. He followed. The main door handle jiggled as he slipped through the opening and pulled the connecting doors shut, locking the one on their side.

"Out the window," he said. "Hurry."

She did as instructed. They were halfway to the truck when Kevin jumped down from the adjacent room's bathroom window.

Near-silent shots whizzed by their heads, their windshield shattering into a spiderweb of cracks.

"Get in." Greyson held the driver's door open while he covered her. She jumped in and slid across the bench seat as another shot pinged off the hood. "Stay down," he hollered, firing back at Kevin, who bobbed and moved in a zigzag pattern.

Grey shot again, and this time, Kevin dove behind his car.

"Stay down," he said to Riley, climbing in, but she didn't listen. Instead, she took the SIG from him and rolled down her window as he reversed. She fired. Once. Twice. She hit Kevin's front right tire, dodging his bullets in doing so. She fired again and hit the rear tire. He wasn't going anywhere for a while unless he had two spares. She'd bought them time.

"Nice shots," he said, swinging the wheel around and turning onto a curvy back road. The tires screeched, and the burning odor of rubber wafted up.

He clutched the wheel around the sharp turn, the angle of the road switching incline directions fast.

He slowed around another turn as the guardrail became the only barrier between them and the steep drop-off. His headlights bounced off an icy patch, and he pumped the brakes, then stiffened. Something was very wrong. Brakes shouldn't feel that way.

"Is everything okay?" Riley asked, studying him in the dim dash light.

He took a deep breath. "The brakes don't feel right." In fact, they felt incredibly wrong. He tested them one more time, and all warmth drained from his face. He pumped a third time and nothing. He took his foot off the gas on the steep decline, but the truck only flew faster.

"Hold on," he said.

Eyes wide, Riley grabbed hold of the bar over the door. "What's happening?" Fear clung to her voice.

"No brakes."

THIRTY-NINE

THEIR SPEED INCREASED as they flung around the switch-back, entering a zigzag section of road, but another decline lay ahead.

Please, Father, give us safety in this moment. Please don't let any harm come to Riley.

"Grey."

His name on her sweet lips burrowed deep in his heart. He reached over and clutched her hand. "It's going to be okay."

They barreled down the hill.

"Grey . . ."

I love you, he wanted to scream, but he bit his tongue and grasped her hand tighter. "We're going into that snow embankment," he said, indicating the wall of snow the plows had left along the side of the hill.

"Are you crazy?"

"It's our only chance not to go over the edge. Brace yourself."

Please, Lord, let no harm come to her. Not Riley.

She gripped his hand harder.

They plowed forward and slammed into the snow embankment. His head lashed forward, nailing the steering wheel with a thwack—the truck too old to have air bags. Stars lit his eyes. He looked over at Riley. She held her head.

Fear tracked through him. "You okay?"

"Fine. I just hit my head on the dash."

He squinted in the darkness engulfing them. He turned on the overhead light. The ruptured snow wall collapsed down, enclosing the truck in a white cocoon. One focus at a time, and right now, Riley was it.

"You're bleeding."

She reached her fingers to her forehead and pulled them away. Blood clung to them.

"Here," he said, pulling his handkerchief from his pocket.

"Thanks." She held it to her wound.

"Apply a little pressure to get it to clot."

She nodded, wincing as she did so.

"How's your neck?"

"Tender. What about yours?"

"I'm fine."

"No, you aren't. You've got a bloody nose."

He'd been so preoccupied with her that he hadn't noticed the warm liquid drizzling down his face.

"Here," she said, handing him the handkerchief back.

"No, you keep it." He gently moved her hand back to the cut on her temple.

"What are we going to do?"

He tried the doors, but they were too packed in by snow. "I'm going to call for help." He lifted his cell, and his heart sank. *Dead.*

"I've got no signal," she said, shifting her phone around to try to get one.

They'd have to wait for help. Pray someone other than Kevin found them. "I'm going to try and see if I can get something up on the antenna to alert anyone driving by."

"Smart idea."

He rolled down the window, and snow fell in. He managed to get a rag he found in the glove box up on the antenna, then he rolled the window back up, leaving an inch for air to keep the exhaust from building up in the truck if the tail pipe was blocked, and given the snow that tumbled down behind the truck, he had a feeling it was.

"I found a flashlight under the seat," she said. "And a knife, but don't suppose that'll do us much good."

"No, but the flashlight will." He propped it facing out the back window.

Riley sat, her arms wrapped about her, the flush of cold coloring her cheeks and nose.

"You're freezing," he said as wind whistled through the window's opening.

"It's better than dying from exhaust fumes," she said.

"No arguments here."

A voice echoed in the distance. It was muffled like it was working its way through water.

"Here," he hollered, straightening.

The voice grew a little louder, and snow began to shift.

"Here," he called again.

"Someone found us," Riley said, closing her eyes, her lips moving in silent prayer.

Scraping and slushing sounded at the rear of the truck. A shovel rasping in the snow.

Soon the rear windshield was clear, and a semi's lights permeated the vehicle.

A man waved. "I'm going to get you out," he said.

Riley smiled, and Greyson offered a wave of gratitude. More than the man would ever know. Eventually Kevin would be back on their trail, and if they had been still stuck in the snow embankment when he found them, they'd have been sitting ducks.

FORTY

"WHERE YOU HEADED?" the trucker asked after they'd climbed into his rig.

No towing companies were open until morning, so they'd have to stay the night somewhere nearby and pray Kevin and Steve didn't find them.

"We need to find a hotel," Grey said.

"I'm headed for Tonalea, which is less than a half hour down the road," he said. "They've got a couple motels there, or there's sleep bunks at the truck stop and hot showers."

Grey looked at Riley, and she nodded. "The truck stop would be great." Way less chance of Kevin looking there than at motels.

The man dropped them at the T&T Trucker Stop. They thanked him, and they got one room. Grey opened the door to reveal one bunk and a small side table.

"You really should get a bunk," Ri said. "I know you. You'll have me sleep while you sit on the hard floor."

"No way I'm leaving you alone, even next door."

"Fine, but then we're sharing the bunk."

"I'm fine on the floor."

"You're being ridiculous. We're both just going to sleep."

"I've got an idea. I'll be right back."

He returned fifteen minutes later with a rolled mattress in hand.

"I'm not even going to ask," she said from the bed.

He unrolled the mattress he'd gotten from the room he'd paid for next door and settled it on the ground, spreading out the blanket he'd garnered too.

Riley shifted onto her side, propping her weight on her elbow. "I'm glad you're getting some rest."

"You too. I never sleep in this late, but I'm setting my alarm for eight just in case. I want to call the local tow company as soon as they open and be ready to go."

"How's your hand and leg?" Jared asked, bringing Kelly a soda and selection of snacks from the vending machine.

"Fine. I'm fine. We need to keep moving."

"Eat, drink, and rest a little longer, then we'll get on the road." He sat on the edge of the bed.

She nibbled her lip. "I really think—"

"We've been over this," he cut her off, popping his soda open. "We can't go to the cops."

She sat forward. "I think he murdered Kathryn Buford."

"But we don't know that for sure."

"I bet if I do a search on the high school ring we found, with the parameters we know, we can track down another missing woman. There may be more bodies buried in the desert that just haven't been found yet. Besides, Kathryn's family deserves to see her murderer behind bars."

"If we call the cops, they might discover what we did and take away the money before we can make things right. And we'll go to jail."

"Lance is the one behind this. He *owes* Claire's family the money. They're still paying off her medical and funeral bills. They deserve it."

"Right, and if we call the cops, the Greaveses might lose everything we've worked to give them. It took five years just to find him, plus the last year of putting everything in motion. Besides, Lance's got to have his high-rolling investors on his back with the money we took from the safe. Maybe they'll kill him, and the problem will be solved. Now, have something to eat and rest. We'll head out tomorrow evening."

She frowned. "Why wait until evening?"

"Better to go under cover of night. Besides, it'll give you longer to rest."

"What about Brent? Aren't we sitting ducks here?"

"The risk of being seen is much higher in the daylight. We wait and hope he doesn't find us."

FORTY-ONE

GREYSON OPENED HIS EYES and stared at the yellow-painted concrete block.

"Morning, sleepyhead," Riley said. "Come see what I found." She gestured him toward her bunk, the laptop balanced across her legs.

He stood and stretched. He wasn't sure which was less comfortable, the retreat's bathtub or the truck stop's floor. He hopped up on the bed. She sat with the lone pillow stuffed between her and the unforgiving wall.

He stifled a yawn and glanced at his watch. *5:55 a.m.* How long had she been up? He glanced over at her, remembering their kiss. She'd kissed *him*, and a knockout kiss it was. He hadn't thought any kiss could beat their first, but it had—the intensity of emotion heightening it.

He raked a hand through his hair. He'd told her how he felt—well, far more than he'd ever planned to. What had he been thinking? He'd been thinking that the woman he loved was kissing him. But he had to stop. Had to explain. Once she understood, she'd pull back, and while it would be agony, it was the right thing for her to do.

"Hello?" Riley waved a hand in front of his face, pulling him from his thoughts. "Where'd you go on me?"

"Sorry." He shook himself out of it. "What did you find?"

"I ran some property searches around the retreat center. I got to thinking the owner might want to live close to his enterprise."

"Smart. And by the smile on your way-too-perky face for this early in the morning, I'm guessing you found something?"

"Yes." She handed him the computer.

It was warm against his jeans—the bunk room a tad on the chilly side.

She pointed at the screen. "A man named Ralph Masters bought five acres of land only a half hour from the retreat the same day the retreat land was purchased by Lansing Global."

"You have an address for Masters?"

She smiled up at him. "Sure do. I'm going to call Joel now."

Fifteen minutes later, she hung up.

"Well?"

"Joel's calling Sheriff Gaines to check it out."

"Good. I'm anxious to see what comes of it."

"I'll keep digging on Masters in the meantime."

Grey nodded. "So what was the great part?"

"Huh?"

"You said 'great news' to Joel."

"Oh, right. The Navajo Nation police in Kayenta shared with Joel that a black '90s Honda Accord was stolen from a restaurant parking lot there. It's one of those twenty-four-hour diners, and the short-order cook who worked the night shift came out at five this morning to head home and his car was gone. There's a BOLO out on it."

"If they stole it sometime between when the cook went on shift at nine p.m. and came out at five a.m. that means they can't be more than eight hours away at maximum. The real question is, where are they headed? So far their wild directions make no sense."

"Not necessarily true." She sat with her legs crisscrossed.

"No?" He furrowed his brows.

"May I?" She reached for the laptop, and he passed it over.

He grabbed his pillow from the floor and squished it behind him as Riley had done with hers.

She pulled up a map of the Four Corners states. "They abandoned Kelly's car in Las Cruces, I'm guessing so we'd assume they were headed for the border, but then they came somewhere up in this region. Given the camping gear Jared's neighbor saw him loading in his vehicle and the outdoor survival books in Kelly's apartment, along with her penchant for snowy adventures in particular, I'm guessing they were in one of these mountain ranges." She pointed to several possibilities.

"Then why Kayenta?"

"I don't know. Maybe they had a tie there or were comfortable there. Or maybe it's a point along the route to where they're headed."

"Which is?"

Her shoulders deflated. "I don't know. We need another blip on the map."

"I'll grab Phillip's car when it's ready, but until that blip comes, what's the plan in the meantime?"

"We work."

"Here?"

"They sell food in the truck stop, and we have plenty of privacy."

"True. It's off-grid enough that I doubt Kevin and Steve will come looking for us here."

"Speaking of Steve, I wonder why it was just Kevin at the hotel?"

"I don't know. They could have split up to cover more ground."

"Or they moved Steve onto Kelly and Jared with Brent."

"Either way, I doubt he's out of the picture."

Jared dropped Kelly at the bus depot after dark. "Grab us two tickets while I stash the car back at that restaurant parking lot."

"Roger that," she said, heading toward the small ticket office at the Kayenta bus depot. Walking by the row of lockers stacked four high with similar keys, she hoped Riley had kept the key safe. It was their only bargaining chip should something go wrong, and their only physical proof tying Lance to Kathryn Buford.

With her hair dyed black and cut short and a baseball hat on, she purchased two tickets to Flagstaff, which would only be a misdirection stopover. They'd find a car there and head up to Vegas to see their vow fulfilled. Clutching her backpack full of cash, she approached the service window.

Keeping her face down, she slid a few bills across the counter. "Two tickets for Flagstaff, please."

"Yes, ma'am." The clerk checked the clock. "It leaves in fifteen minutes. Far bus around back."

"Thank you." She slid the tickets into her pocket, anxiously awaiting Jared.

FORTY-TWO

A TEXT DINGED on Greyson's phone at the Waffle House adjacent to the truck stop. "Do you mind seeing what it says?" he asked, deep in research mode.

"Sure." Riley reached over, careful not to get her sleeve in the syrup on her plate. She scanned the screen. "Oh my word."

"What?"

"George called from the garage."

"And?"

"There was a hole drilled in the brake line."

He set his mug down with a shake of his head. "Kevin's smart. He must have used it as a backup measure in case we got away. It takes time for a brake line to lose fluid. Driving out in a blizzard, the roads treacherous. He could have killed us if we'd pushed fully through the snow wall to the drop off below."

"Thankfully we didn't."

"God saved us on that one," he said.

"Yeah, He did, but I'm curious what else Kevin has in store. No way we've lost him for good."

"No. But I think we've thrown him off our trail for now. Speaking of which, I'm going to let Phillip know I'll cover the truck, but I think we should get a different set of wheels. Kevin, no doubt, will be looking for the truck, and it stands out. We need to get a more nondescript vehicle."

"Agreed."

He glanced at the dark sky. The sun had slipped away while he'd had his nose in the computer. "We better take an Uber to the closest rental car place before they close."

"Good idea."

An hour later, they pulled out of the rental lot in a white Chevy Traverse.

Riley's cell rang. "Hey, Christian," she answered on speaker.

"Hey, Cool Whip. How's it going?"

"Still no sign of Kevin, so I can't complain."

Though he could always be waiting in the wings for them to lead him to Kelly and Jared. Maybe he and Steve had taken that tack, which was all the more dangerous. Riley was the tracker, and it seemed now as if the roles had been reversed.

"I've got some good news for you," her brother said.

"Great. What's up?"

"Joel called. Police found the stolen Honda stashed in another restaurant parking lot in Kayenta."

"Interesting. Do you know which restaurant?"

"Uh, hang on . . . Okay, The Three Pigs."

"Seriously?" She chuckled.

"Yep." Christian chuckled as well. "Apparently, it's a highly rated barbecue place."

"Okay." She ran her hand up Greyson's neck, slipping her fingers through his hair.

He shot a quick look over at her with warm eyes, then fixed them back on the road.

"I'll run a search for the restaurant on Google Maps," she said, still rubbing his neck. They both were sore head-to-toe from their adventures so far.

She punched in the name on the laptop keys. "Got 'em, I think. It appears The Three Pigs is within walking distance of the bus depot."

"The bus depot." Grey smiled, pride for her in his voice. "Guess we got our next ping. Good work, guys."

Greyson held the bus depot office door open for Riley. They approached the first window.

A bored-looking twenty-year-old glanced up at them. "Ticket?" he asked.

"No." Grey pulled out Kelly's and Jared's pictures. "Have you seen either of them?"

"What are you, cops?" the young woman asked.

"Private investigators," Grey said.

"Cool." She bobbed her head.

"Have you seen them?" Riley asked.

"No, but I just came on duty. You should ask Adam."

"Okay. Where's Adam?"

"He just headed for the locker room. I'll grab him." The kid jumped up and returned with a short blond man—probably midthirties.

"Casey said you're looking for someone?" the man asked.

"Yes." Greyson handed Adam the pictures.

He stared at them for a long while. "I recognize the face, but . . ."

"But?" Grey leaned in.

"She's got short black hair, not blond."

"She might have changed her physical appearance."

"She on the run from something?"

"Yeah."

"Well, I sold her a couple tickets to Flagstaff."

"Flagstaff? Are you sure?" Riley said.

"Positive."

"Thank you so much," Grey said.

"Why Flagstaff?" Riley asked as they exited the depot and headed back for the Traverse they'd rented.

"I doubt they'd take the bus to their final destination, in case someone discovered where they were headed. Flagstaff is on the way to Phoenix and Vegas."

"Vegas again?" Riley's face paled.

"I hate to say it, but I'm leaning there."

"Why?"

"It's a great place to launder money, get fake passports . . . that type of thing. Plus, they're from there. They must have connections. They can probably blend in and have coverage during their time there."

"Not a great place to stay hidden."

"No. But it might be a stopover," he said as they settled in the car and pulled out of the lot. "I've been thinking about all the books on Kelly's shelf Deck mentioned. He said there were books on outdoor survival, solar panels, and composting. What if they weren't just to prepare Kelly and Jared to go on the run in the wilderness?"

"What do you think?"

"What if they're heading for an off-grid location? Some place out in the wilderness where they plan to lay low and not be found."

"Okay, so they launder money in Vegas and then head for an off-grid location. Any idea where?"

"There's a lot of open land in Nevada."

"True. It would be like finding a needle in a haystack."

"Agreed. So let's hope we catch them in Flagstaff."

"And if we don't?"

"Then I think we should head to Vegas."

She swallowed, her throat closing in, her pulse kicking into high gear.

"I can call Deck and Christian to go," he said, reaching for her hand.

"No. I'm in this for the long haul."

"You sure?"

"I'm not going to let my past stop me from doing my job."

He clutched her hand, and she didn't let go.

FORTY-THREE

THEY SPENT HOURS searching Flagstaff motels and twenty-four restaurants and even the local bus depot, but no one recognized Kelly or Jared. But getting off a bus made it a lot easier to stay hidden than buying a ticket did.

"It's late, and we need some rest," Grey said. "I say we hit Walmart, get some fresh clothes and toiletries, then find a motel as long as our tail continues to look clear."

"I hate stopping," she said.

"I know, but we can't go without sleep, and for all we know, they're settled in a motel and heading somewhere tomorrow."

"Or they're on the road, and we're losing time."

"If they are on the road, we don't know which direction yet. Phoenix or Vegas. If we choose wrong, we could lose them for good."

"Fair enough."

After their pit stop, they pulled up to the Park Hyatt hotel.

"You sure they won't find us here?" It was a big change from their out-of-the-way motels.

"I think they'll be looking for something more low profile like the last motel, and I doubt the adjoining room trick will work again. I'd rather go someplace with staff covering the door and the front desk."

"Suits me," she said.

The bellhop greeted them, but with only their backpacks and shopping bags to their names, they saw themselves to the check-in desk and up to the two-bedroom suite Greyson had reserved on the key card–access-only floor.

"It's beautiful," she said, opening the double doors. A large living room greeted her with a damask-covered sofa with large red velvet pillows and rich, cocoa-hued satin bolsters.

Grey followed her in, and she didn't need to turn around to feel his presence mere steps behind her.

A vase of fresh flowers with bright yellows against startling red sat on the cherry drop-leaf coffee table with the sides down.

"Your room," Greyson said, his breath tickling the back of her exposed neck. He stepped to her side and gestured to the left.

Her gaze followed to find two open white-frame doors. She strolled toward them to find a gorgeous canopy bed with a yellow damask duvet and neatly stacked piles of fluffy white pillows spread across the headboard.

"It's gorgeous." She turned back and felt moisture pooling in her eyes, despite the smile she attempted. Grey enveloped her in his arms, and she rested her head on his shoulder.

"Do you feel confident they're going to launder the money?"

Greyson hesitated before answering. "I do. Given everything we've learned about the retreat and those who run it, I wouldn't be surprised if it was marked in some way."

"That's sort of how my parents got caught."

"Really?"

She nodded. "They conned the wrong man."

"Deck said his name was Big Max."

"Yeah." Her voice sounded strangled.

He rubbed her back, and after some time had passed, he asked, "You okay?"

She nodded and stepped from his hold, wrapping her arms about her. "It was a long time ago."

"But it was traumatic, I'm sure."

"That's one way to put it."

"So I take it they stole money from him?"

"Yep, and they didn't know there was a tracker chip in one of the bundles. That's how he found us. Killed my dad, and to avoid dying too, my mom turned herself in and is serving time in a Nevada state prison."

"She turned herself in? I didn't know that. That was a bold move."

"Or cowardly. She just didn't want to risk death. And didn't care about the kids she abandoned in the process."

The muscle in his jaw twitched, but he pushed that wound aside as more tears sprang into her eyes.

"Hey," he said, taking her hand and leading her to the sofa. He angled to face her, his knees rubbing hers. "We've got this."

"*We*? Are you saying we are a 'we' now?" Hope filled her eyes.

He swallowed. He couldn't let things move forward until . . . check that, couldn't let things move forward *period*. He should have never started. It was selfish on his part. Riley was the last person he wanted to hurt, and he was about to, but it was for her own good. She'd understand and even agree once he told her the truth. And if he was wrong and she didn't understand, if for some foolish reason she didn't want to accept it, he'd give her no choice. He cared too much about her to let her do otherwise. He couldn't saddle her with his family history.

Taking a deep breath, he tried to bolster his courage. She deserved the truth.

"What's wrong?" she asked, cupping his cheek.

He leaned into her touch, wishing it wasn't the last time he felt it, but it had to be.

He took her hands in his. "I'm so sorry. But we can't . . . I can't . . . continue like this."

She arched a brow, hurt reflecting in her eyes. "*This?*"

"Going down this path . . . I can't give in to my feelings for you."

She cocked her head. "Are you saying you can just shut off how you feel about me?"

He let the question hang.

"I see." She leaned back, wrapping her arms about her waist. "Then I suppose we don't feel the same about each other after all, because I could never just shut off my feelings for you."

The free expression of her feelings echoed how his mom had lived . . . wild and free . . . until . . .

"What's wrong?" Riley said, shifting to face him better.

"What?"

"Your expression just rapidly changed."

He cleared his throat as he still grappled to gather his courage to spill something so painful and delicate, but if he could trust anybody, it was Riley.

"What is it?" she asked again. "You're scaring me."

"I'm sorry. I didn't mean to. I just need to tell you."

She scooted closer. "Tell me what?"

He rubbed the back of his neck. Now or never. "The reason I shouldn't be in a relationship isn't because I don't care about you. It's because I do."

She tilted her head. "I don't understand."

He longed to take her hands back in his, but he let her have her space, as painful as it was. "My father was a . . . cruel, cold man who didn't deserve my warm, loving mother."

She bit her bottom lip, shifting to face him better.

"My dad was all logic and perfection. I can't tell you how many times I got the belt for missing the mark by a hair or for playing with my mom."

"He punished you for playing with your mom?"

He sighed. "My mom and I used to play in the woods, making fairy houses and toad houses. I often thought my mom was half fairy." A sad chuckle slipped from his lips. "My father said such play was nonsense and not for real men."

"But you were a child, right?"

"It didn't matter. Not to him." His arms trembled, and Riley rubbed them. "My mom, on the other hand, was sweet and loving— you remind me of her."

"I do?"

"She was free-spirited, compassionate, and followed her gut."
He reached over and caressed her cheek. "Like my wild girl."

Riley smiled, but his heart sank with the words to come, at the memories flooding back.

"But . . ." He slipped his hand to his side, balling it into a fist. "All that changed. Not overnight. It was gradual at first. My mom stayed in her room more. She grew quieter. We'd still go out in the woods and build fairy houses, but her heart wasn't in it, no doubt because of him."

Riley remained quiet, and he continued, his heart breaking both for his mom and for hurting Riley. He wanted to be with her more than anything, but he couldn't.

Continuing to ball his hands into tight fists, he forced himself to continue. "She got diagnosed with depression when I was ten. It took the light out of her eyes at times."

"I'm so sorry. That must have been hard."

"It was brutal to watch." He shook out his hands. "I graduated high school, and I hated leaving her, but she told me to go and live my life. I went into the service and was deployed. When I came back stateside, she'd worsened. I begged her to come live with me. I didn't want her staying with that cruel man, but she wouldn't leave. To this day, I don't know for sure, but I think she did it because she wanted the best for me and didn't view herself as it."

"That sounds familiar," Riley said tenderly.

She had him there.

"I'm sorry." She reached for his hand, and he slipped it into hers—one last touch. "That had to be awful."

He looked down. "It was."

She caressed his shaking hand.

"But it gets worse . . ." He shifted his gaze to her, and concern filled her big blue eyes. "She . . ." How did he say this? He stalled. "For a time, she seemed better again, until one day . . ."

Riley tightened her grip on his hand at the shudder that echoed in his voice. How embarrassing. He would not break down and cry.

"Grey?" She said it with such compassion, he nearly broke.

"I got a call one day . . . she died by suicide."

Riley cupped his face, tears welling in her eyes. "Oh, honey, I'm so sorry."

He got to his feet and pinched the bridge of his nose. If he remained close to her, he feared he'd give in to his feelings rather than stay strong. "So you see why I can't be with you."

Her brows pinched. "What am I missing?"

He tapped his foot and rested his hands on his waist. Why wouldn't they stop trembling? "Ri . . . I have depression too. I could end up in the pit one day like her."

She popped to her feet and to his side, rubbing his arm. "Just because you have depression doesn't mean it'll be the same."

"I did the statistical research. My chances are higher than someone who doesn't have suicide in their family."

"But I know you. You wouldn't do that. You'd get help."

"I have. I take medicine. I see a counselor. But I won't saddle you with my family history."

"Family?"

"My mom and her sister both died by suicide. That legacy. It's why I can't have a relationship, especially not with you."

"Especially not with me? I don't—"

He exhaled. "I can't burden you with that . . . *with me*. Depression is hard. And in some people, like my mom's case, it can be crippling. I can't risk laying that on you."

"I know *you*, and you're a fighter. You'll fight your way through it and never give up." She reached up and caressed his cheek. "And I want to be right there at your side, depression or no depression. I want you, *period*."

He clutched her hand, bringing her fingers to his lips, and breezed a kiss across her knuckles. "I can't tell you how wonderful that is to hear, but—"

"Nope." She shook her head. "We're done with the *but*s. We care deeply about each other. The rest will sort itself out."

"You can't assume for the better."

"And you can't assume for the worst."

"Don't you understand? You can have a much better life with a normal guy."

"Please. Normal is relative." She tugged on his sweater. "You are so much more."

"I'm trying to do the right thing. I want the best for you, and I'm not it."

Her hands landed on her hips. "You're wrong."

"You don't know how severe depression can get," he said, stepping back and shaking out his hands. "I haven't experienced it to a severe level yet, but I've seen it affect my family terribly."

"Did you love them?"

"What?" He frowned.

"Did you love your family members with depression?"

"Of course."

"Depression and all?" she pressed.

Understanding dawned. Of course she'd outplayed him. "You don't understand."

"Would you have wanted them, or expected them, to walk through it alone? To never love anyone or be loved?"

"Of course not. But I'm trying to protect you."

"It's not your choice to protect me, and this is hardly something you have to protect me from." She returned to his side. "You are an amazing, intelligent, sufferable man. Besides, you're not the only person with depression I know."

He quirked a brow. "No?"

"No. My friend Mandy from barrel racing struggles with depression, but she's awesome, hilarious, and uber-loving with her family. Depression isn't a red mark to be avoided. It's just one facet many wonderful people deal with. It doesn't define a person. You are *you*. You need to stop anticipating the worst. You can't live in fear of something that may never come to pass."

"My father said I'm just like her and I'll end up like her," he confessed. He knew better than to listen to the man's poison, but try as he might, he couldn't shake it. Couldn't lose the fear tied to it deep inside.

"Your father is wrong and sounds dreadful."

"He is. You know, on the day of her funeral, he sat talking with his golfing buddies and coworkers or whoever the men I didn't know were. The minute the pastor was done with the service, he walked away without a second glance."

"I'm so sorry. I bet you stayed."

He nodded. "For a while. My mom loved poetry and always collected wildflowers on our walks, so I put her favorite poem and a bunch of flowers inside her casket before they shut it. I bring both with me when I visit her grave."

"Oh, honey . . ." Tears spilled from her eyes as they misted in his. "I'm so sorry," she whispered. "I can't imagine how painful that must have been."

"I wish she could have met you. She would have loved you."

"Really?" She smiled.

"Absolutely."

Her smiled faded. "Please tell me this"—she pointed between them— "isn't over."

"I just don't see how it can work," he said, the moisture welling in his eyes.

"Will you do one thing for me? Will you pray about it? See what God says about it and what's holding you back?"

"I can do that, but I still don't see a way. . . ."

FORTY-FOUR

"I TOLD YOU THEY WERE ONTO US," Kelly said as she and Jared raced down the sidewalk. A mere hundred yards separated them from Brent.

"I thought we lost them," Jared said. "Just keep going."

The cold night air lit up her lungs, her thighs burning.

They bobbed and wove around the string of people populating the downtown Flagstaff sidewalks.

She glanced back, eyeing the man rounding the corner. *Eighty yards.*

Brent was gaining on them.

Slam. Kelly bounced back, holding her head.

"Hey, lady!" The man she'd bolted into grunted and rubbed his head. "What's wrong with you?"

"Sorry." The word rushed out as she fumbled forward, her feet feeling like they were running independently of her body.

"Building . . . ahead." Jared's words came out between puffs of air.

"Building?" Was he kidding? "Won't he trap us?"

"Have . . . an . . . idea," Jared puffed. "Just do it."

Lights shone out the building's windows and door, flooding the concrete sidewalk, slipping across the passing cars. People milled in and out. An event?

Rounding the edge of the circular parking lot, her hair damp along the side of her face, Kelly bolted past the beautifully dressed people and into the building.

Heat washed over her in a rush at the entrance but evaporated as she flew into the expansive hotel lobby filled with even more people.

"Now what?" she said over her shoulder to Jared as she slowed into a power walk in an effort not to terrify the guests and to blend in better, but given the beautiful dresses and the giggling bridesmaids shuffling by, that wasn't in the cards.

She moved through the bodies. "We're about to the end," she said. Only elevators stood in front of them. "Jared?" She shot a glance back to see Brent enter the building, his gaze searching. He pinged her.

"He's here."

"The elevators," Jared hollered. "Fast."

Like she didn't know that.

She broke into a run, practically slamming into the gold doors. She pressed the Up button. Harder and harder. "Come on. . . ." Her leg bounced.

Jared put his body between her and Brent. "He won't open fire with all these people."

"You sure about that?" Her heart thumped. "He's mid-lobby," she said, leaning past Jared's broad shoulder.

Ding.

Thank you, Lord. The doors slid open, and Jared shoved her in, nearly barreling her into the exiting couple.

She backed straight into the rear of the elevator. "We're trapped."

Jared pressed the Close button in a frenzy. "Come on. . . . Come on."

Brent bumped a woman, who released an offended cry.

Eighty feet. Seventy feet.

His hand slipped into his jacket. His gun.

The doors started sliding. "Come on!" she yelled, and heads turned.

Brent's face, twisted in anger, showed between the final slit before the doors sealed shut.

Relief swarmed through her belly, and she collapsed against the side of the elevator.

Jared rested his hand on the gold rail running the length of the back wall. Mirrors blanketed the space above, the illuminating floor numbers reflecting in them.

She looked for the depressed button. "Why the third floor?"

"Totally random." He ran a shaky hand through his hair.

"What now?" she asked as the floors dinged by, the lights dancing across the line over the door. Two. *Ding.* Three. *Ding.*

Jared held the door open but didn't step off the elevator.

"What are you doing?"

"You get off here, and I'll hit four."

Her belly dropped. "Split up?"

"It's the only way I see us getting out of here." He swallowed, his Adam's apple bobbing. "Or one of us."

"Jared . . ." She reached out and clasped his clammy palm.

He stepped closer. "We knew this was a possibility." He squeezed her hand. "We'll be fine. We'll meet at Gus and Amy's. Just like we planned for this contingency."

She bit her lip.

He cupped her face in his clammy, trembling hands. "It'll be okay."

He seemed even less convinced than her, but she did her part. She nodded like she believed him.

Placing a quick peck on his lips, she whispered, "I love you."

"Love you. It's going to be all right. Take the stairwell. One at the end of the hall if you can. I'll see you at Gus's."

"Can't we pick a place to meet up outside of here?"

"We need to split up. He's getting too close. Now, go."

She did so, forcing herself not to look back. She raced for what she hoped was the far stairwell, her boots thumping along the plush, mosaic-style carpeting.

Doors flew by in a blur. She shoved the stairwell door open as the second elevator dinged. She glanced back, and everything in her wished she hadn't as she made eye contact with Brent.

Her pulse raced in her neck. She sprinted forward, nearly tumbling down the first set of concrete steps. She rounded the landing, her moist grip on the rail tentative at best. She swung around another landing when the door above slammed open.

"I've got you," Brent said, his voice deep and harsh.

Her legs, feeling like wet noodles, somehow managed to carry her down.

A bullet pinged off the rail inches in front of her hand, ricocheting into the concrete block wall.

A suppressed retort sounded.

Panic sifted through her. She prayed someone had heard that and would come, but with the buzzing noise of the lobby crowd emanating up the stairwell, she doubted it.

Lobby. It would have the most people. If she could make it.

Another shot, this time into the wall inches from her head.

She ducked and ran in a crouch. *One more floor.* She just had to make it one more floor.

Her heart in her throat, she burst out the door, stumbling into the hotel lobby. Halfway across, she turned. Brent exited the steps.

"Gun!" she hollered at the top of her lungs. "Gun!"

The entire lobby filled with people erupted in screams. People ran in a swarming mass for the front glass doors, Kelly among them.

Please, please, please. She fled out into the night as two security guards rushed forward.

"I saw him. He's tall, dressed in a black sweater and black trousers."

"Thank you, miss." The first radioed in the description, and whoever was on the other end replied the police were rolling.

She bolted down the street in the opposite direction from the one they'd come, having passed not much else. She hoped there would be more this way.

Screams still filled the night as footsteps trampled out of the building.

She rounded the first corner she hit. An alley. Had she just trapped herself again?

She eyed every building she ran past until her gaze fixed on a side door. With no clue where it led, she burst inside to find herself in a commercial kitchen. Everyone turned to look at her.

"Sorry," she said. "Lost."

"The party is out that way," one of the men said.

"Thank you. My abusive ex is chasing me. If he comes in— dressed in black and angry—could you please not tell him you saw me?"

"Sure, honey," a female chef said.

She followed the direction the man had pointed and shimmied sideways down a narrow corridor, then out a subsequent door into a . . . *Museum?*

A long black banner had *Walter's Art Gallery Gala* printed in gold script.

She'd walked into a gala? She cringed at her jeans and long-sleeve tee, but there was no time to care what all the people staring her up and down thought.

She pressed through the crowd, heading for a service elevator. She took it to the top floor.

"Always keep moving. You stay still, you die." Jared's adage raced through her head.

Exiting on the fifth floor, she scanned the space, her heart pounding. How much fear could it take before it burst from her chest?

Stop. You've got this.

Finding a stairwell, she entered, the memory of the last one clutching her chest in a vise. She worked her way down it, slowly. Exiting this time on the far side of the gallery, she eyed the glass exit doors and the space around her. No sign of Brent.

Taking a steadying breath, or as steady as she could manage with shallow heaves, she strode outside. The cold night air swept over her, instantly cooling her skin with a chill. Gooseflesh rippled down her arms.

She approached the first taxi in a long line.

The driver rolled down his window.

"Ride?" she asked.

"Yes." The man nodded.

"Great." She climbed in back and slouched low. "Could you take me to . . ."

"To?"

"Just drive. I'll figure it out."

"Suit yourself." He shrugged and pulled out onto the street.

She stretched up barely an inch to look out the rearview mirror and swallowed at the sight of Brent still searching for her. She slouched back below the window.

"Where's it going to be, lady?" the driver asked.

"A car rental agency."

"You care which one?"

"Nope. Whichever one is still open."

"Most are open all night at the airport." He punched the airport name into his GPS, and a twenty-minute estimated route appeared on the screen.

"Are there any rental places outside of the airport?" she asked. Airports had more cameras.

He tapped the clock. *10:00 p.m.* "Not open this late."

"Okay." She swallowed. "The airport it is." If only she could get on a plane and fly away. *Anywhere.* Escape all of this. But she and Jared had a duty to fulfill, and she wasn't going to let Lance steal it from them like he'd stolen from Claire. Finally, after six years, they were going to make this as right as they could.

A half hour later, Kelly pulled out of the rental car lot, having used her fake ID. After using it at the clinic, where they'd been tracked, it was probably useless, but she had no choice.

She escaped into the night, leaving Flagstaff behind and fleeing for the safety of Gus and Amy's. At least, she hoped she was headed for safety. It'd been in short supply.

FORTY-FIVE

GREYSON hit his knees.

Father, I have always been so certain of my path in life. In how to protect loved ones—by not having them. But that hasn't seemed to work. I've fallen even harder than I thought for Riley. What I didn't anticipate was her returning my feelings.

He took a deep inhale and released it.

She's asked me to pray, so I'm here. Show me the way, Lord. An unknown future is difficult to grapple with—especially in my case. That's why I'm doing this. Protecting her.

Protecting yourself.

Swallowing, he opened his eyes. Was that true?

Riley's footsteps padded in the other room. He got to his feet as she opened her bedroom door to the main living space of their hotel room. Her eyes, red and puffy, gave away her tears.

"Do you want to talk about it?" he asked, knowing he was the cause. The thought of hurting her, even if it was for her best, gutted him.

She shook her head. "Just something from the past, and I like to keep it there."

Vegas.

He hated the idea of taking her someplace where she'd endured so much trauma. All of the siblings had been traumatized by horrific, criminal parents who used them rather than raised them. But

217

Riley, being the youngest, took the brunt of it. She was the sweet little girl, so no one saw the scams coming while she was in tow.

He moved to sit beside her on the couch as she took a seat. "I could just go if it leads to Vegas."

"No way, mister. I will see this case through, wherever it leads."

He got it. At some point, you had to face your demons, and Vegas was hers. He reached over and tipped her chin up a notch. "You are the bravest woman I know."

Her gaze darted to the floor. "That's hardly true."

"Look at me," he said, his voice gentle.

She met his gaze, moisture brimming in her eyes.

"It's very true. I promise, and you know I never make a promise I don't mean."

A tentative smile slipped across her lips, then something caught her eye over his right shoulder.

He followed her gaze to his open laptop.

"Were you working?" she asked, her voice soft. "It's four thirty in the morning."

"Yeah." He ran a hand through his hair. "I couldn't sleep." Not after the pain radiating in Riley's eyes when he'd told her there wasn't a way. He'd prayed hard, but unless God was going to answer in a completely different way than he anticipated, he had to stand by what he thought was best for her. "I was doing some searching while you slept."

"You need rest too," she said, rubbing his shoulder.

"I'll get some." When this was over, or when it felt safe enough to sleep. For now, it didn't.

She cocked her head.

"I will." He gave a sideways smile. "At some point."

She sighed and shook her head, then looked back to his laptop. "Did you find anything?"

"Actually, yes. I just got a hit on the fake identity Kelly used at the Kayenta clinic. I've been keeping an eye on transportation options, and Joel followed up on it for me. Kelly just rented a car from the Flagstaff airport under her assumed name last night."

Her cell rang.

"I better get that. If Deck is calling this late, it's for a reason," she said, seeing her brother's name on the screen. She grabbed it and answered. "Hang on, putting you on speaker."

"It's late. Why are you still up?" Deck asked.

"How do you know you didn't wake me?" she countered.

"Because I know what you sound like when you first wake up."

Her eyes narrowed. "I don't think that was a compliment."

"I'm just saying . . ."

"Any news?" Grey asked, anxious to hear. Ri was right. Deck wouldn't call this late just to chat. In fact, Deck never called just to chat.

"Yeah, Joel just called. A kid working the counter at a Circle K called in a tip. He spotted a woman who looked like Kelly."

Riley shifted forward. "That's awesome."

"What'd the kid say?"

"That she came in, bought some snacks and a pair of sunglasses, and left."

"He recognized her from her photo on the news, I'm guessing?"

"Yes. I think it helped they added a rendering of her with short dark hair."

"Did he see Jared too?"

"No, that's the interesting part," Deck said. "He said she was alone and there was no one else in the car."

"That is interesting." Ri's brow furrowed. "I wonder why they split up now?"

"My guess is Brent may have gotten too close, and they split for a better chance to escape. Or Jared let the man trail him so Kelly could get away."

"Where was this?" Grey asked.

"That's the other interesting part," Deck said, his voice extra gravelly with slumber.

"Oh?" Riley shifted again, planting her feet on the floor.

Grey smiled. The woman could not sit still when she got hold of a clue.

"Kachina Village."

"Kachina Village?" Grey repeated Deck's words. "It's the opposite direction of Vegas."

"I know. Maybe they're headed for Phoenix after all."

Maybe. But it didn't sit right with him. Vegas made sense. Phoenix did not. Not compared to a place where they had lived, where they had connections, and that was a known hot spot for money laundering.

"I guess so." Greyson shrugged. "But it doesn't—"

"Feel right." Ri finished the sentence for him.

"Well, let me know what you guys decide," Deck said. "I'm going to catch some winks. We can catch up more in the morning."

"Sounds like a plan. Night, bro."

"Night, kid."

Riley ended the call, then stood and moved to the laptop.

"Whatcha doing?" Greyson moved to stand behind her, longing to rub her shoulders, but he kept his hands by his sides. He'd made the hard choice, and now he had to stick by it.

"As much as I'd love for it to be Phoenix, it just doesn't feel right," Riley said, typing away.

"Agreed, and I also agree with Deck about why they split. I bet Brent got too close, and Jared tried to lead him away from Kelly."

"I hope Jared's okay." Ri glanced over her shoulder at him. "I mean, I know what he and Kelly did was wrong, but I don't want any harm to come to them."

"Of course not."

"It's weird." She sighed, her shoulders dipping. "I just can't get over Kelly being a thief. I can't wrap my head around it."

"Maybe there's a reason behind it we're not seeing."

"Yeah, could be, but to break into a safe, you have to have some experience."

"Everyone has a first time," he said as she turned her attention back to the computer.

"Very true." She pulled up a map of the state and zoomed in on the area in question. "Huh. I wonder . . ."

He waited, but she just kept moving ahead, pulling up Facebook and clicking on Kelly's profile. She scrolled down through pictures of Kelly and a couple—skiing, hiking, kayaking. Then she settled on a house by a river.

"Whose place is that?"

"Kelly's friends Gus and Amy."

"The ones who are in Europe?"

"Uh-huh."

"You think she's headed there?" He furrowed his brow. "Where is *there*?"

"Just outside of Cottonwood on the Verde River. There's a lot of pics of Kelly on Facebook kayaking there."

"And Deck said Jared had a kayak with him when he left his place."

"Which makes me curious. Did they bring the kayak for part of their exit strategy, or was it just to make it look like Jared was heading on an adventure like he said?"

"Could go either way. Losing someone by river is a solid strategy, especially if the river has lots of exit points."

"Which the Verde River does." She pulled it up on Google Earth and scrolled through them.

"Or is heading away from Vegas just a diversion?"

"I'm sure they had a meet-up point just in case anything went awry."

"True."

"And what better place than your friends' house where you've spent a lot of time—and with the house now empty."

"So we're heading to Cottonwood?" he asked.

"Yep. I better get changed."

FORTY-SIX

FINDING THE SPARE KEY inside the hanging plant where Amy always left it, Kelly pulled it out, looked around one last time, and opened the door.

The alarm beeped, and she shut it off, closed the door behind her, then turned the alarm back on. Jared knew the code. Anyone else coming in the house would not, and the alarm would signal help before Brent could kill her. Or so she hoped. She'd lost him in the Uber, but she doubted it was for long. Lance Winslow's reach was illegal and extensive. But she was seeing this to the end. Claire deserved it. Claire's family deserved it. And Lance deserved to go down. Not only for Claire but for Kathryn Buford, who he'd no doubt killed and buried in that shallow grave. Why else would he have her locket?

Money was not enough for him to lose. His life was due, whether it was in the death penalty or life behind bars. He deserved no mercy and no freedom. Jared disagreed, but she had to do what was right.

They'd left the safe's contents in a locker. It would be leverage if Brent caught up with them. She just prayed Jared made it away safely. *Prayed.* She exhaled. She still prayed. She'd done something unlawful, but to right an awful wrong. Surely God would understand that, so then why did *"It is mine to avenge; I will repay"* keep whispering through her soul? She didn't doubt He could avenge, but He hadn't, so she and Jared had taken matters into their own hands.

Moving through the silent house—save for a creaky floorboard here and there—she left the lights off. It needed to appear empty since Gus and Amy were still in Sicily.

Stepping into the kitchen, she chugged a glass of water, anxious for Jared to arrive. He *would* arrive, right?

She took a deep breath—the kind Jared made her take when she freaked out—then counting to seven, she released it nice and slow.

Shaking off the fear that would eat her alive if she let it, she continued moving through the house, a small flashlight in hand. She needed some light. She kept it directed at the ground and away from the windows. The closest neighbors were acres away, but she took the precautions all the same.

An hour passed and still no Jared. Acid burned up her throat. What if something happened to him? What if . . . ? *No.* She squeezed her eyes shut. She couldn't allow her thoughts to go there.

She returned to the kitchen—the farthest room from the front of the house—and closed the blinds. Enough of the moon slipped through the narrow slots between each blind that she didn't need the flashlight any longer. Not once her eyes adjusted, and thanks to the small night-light near the pantry.

Glancing at the butcher-block holder and the silver knives arranged evenly in it, she pulled the biggest one out and clung to it. She curled her fingers around the handle.

She'd ditched her phone as Jared instructed, both fearing Lance was somehow pinging them. Come their stop in Vegas, she needed to grab a burner cell. There hadn't been time before fleeing Flagstaff.

The door opened, and the alarm went off. She tightened her grip on the knife handle, the silver cold against her moist palm. The alarm beeped. *Please shut off. Please be Jared.* Her heart thudding in her chest, she strode as silently as possible for the kitchen door, flattening her back against the wall beside it. The alarm shut off. *Thank you, Lord.*

"Jared?" she called, not budging.

"Kelly." He raced through the door, nearly running into the point of the knife as she stepped forward.

"Whoa!" He fumbled back. "It's me." He tripped over his feet and fell backward onto the ground, bracing himself on his bent-back hands. He looked rather like a crab playing Twister.

She dropped the knife on the counter and helped him up, wrapping her arms around him. "I was so scared something happened to you."

"I had to lose the tail."

"You mean he followed you here?"

"No. He picked me up about forty miles out, but I lost him about twenty miles back."

"It won't take him, or more likely Lance, long to figure out where we are, with all the illegal resources he has."

"Which is why we need to keep our contingency plan in place."

———————————◼ ◼———————————

No lights shone from the house as Greyson and Riley pulled into the already crowded driveway. Three other cars sat parked in it—Kelly's rental car, a dark sedan, and a black SUV.

Kelly, Jared, and Brent, Riley was betting.

"I hope we're not too late," she said, leaping from the door the second he shifted into Park.

Greyson jumped out, and they headed for the dark house. Dawn was just breaking, but shadows still covered the land.

It took them a solid five to clear the large house, but it was empty. A small waterproof duffel sat halfway zipped on the table.

"They must have left in a hurry. The rapids are dangerous enough in the day. I doubt they'd have taken to them before sunrise without Brent chasing them. We better hurry."

They passed the three cars out front and hurried down the hill. "There's a kayak rack," Riley said. Five slots, two kayaks. One tandem. One single.

"We're going to need dry suits, or we'll catch hypothermia," Grey said, looking to the open doors of the shed. "Maybe in there?"

"That would be my guess."

Ten minutes later, in dry suits that mostly fit, they had started climbing into the tandem kayak when a small black bag caught Riley's eye by the back corner of the shed. "Hey." She pointed.

"Grab it," Grey said, hanging on to the kayak.

She tossed it inside and helped him push off, climbing into the rear seat.

The sun inched above the horizon as a class IV rapid swirled them sideways. They paddled with it and broke free as it crashed down with white water splashing over the sides. Thank goodness for the dry suits. It was cold enough with them. They'd have frozen without them.

Wind gusts rifled Riley's hair as they rode the rapids. A quarter of a mile downriver and still no sign of them. She tightened her grip on the paddle. How far behind were they?

FORTY-SEVEN

"WE'VE GOT TO MOVE FASTER," Riley said as frigid water sloshed over the side. The dry suit kept her body warm, but her hands were freezing. There'd been no gloves in the shed.

The sun rose higher in the sky, streaking through the clouds, glinting off the class IV rapids.

"Heads up," Greyson hollered over the roar of the rapids. They swirled up and curved around a series of treacherous boulders.

"That was close," she said as they managed to traverse their way around. She caught a glimpse of movement ahead, but it vanished as quick as it'd come.

Water sloshed about, twisting the front of the kayak as they steered against the swift current. Nearly too swift to counter. Sunlight reflected off a swirling pattern in the water. Was that a . . . ? "Whirlpool!" She paddled, praying they could avoid it.

"Too late," Greyson yelled. "Hold tight."

It sucked them in, spinning them. She clutched her paddle, trying to push them out of the whirlpool, while Greyson tried steering them with his. They pulled free.

She took a deep breath.

Thwack! A rock splintered before them.

"Down!" Grey yelled as the kickback from a gun echoed through the hollow.

She ducked a breath of a second before another thwack. Then kickback.

Keeping his head low, Greyson steered them through the swirling rapids, bouncing them along the roaring river, likely trying to make them a harder target.

But how had someone gotten behind them on the river? The house had been empty.

Peeking over the edge, she stiffened at the sight of Kevin, riding a rapid nearly on top of them. He'd caught up. But how? Her chest squeezed. *Brent.* He must have alerted the rest of the crew to Kelly and Jared's trail.

Kevin steered across the rapids at them. He bumped their kayak, shoving them up against the line of jagged rocks to their left, pinning them. Then he let the rapids slam them.

Greyson pushed him back with his paddle, and Kevin did the same. On the highest peak of the rapid, Kevin rolled them. She grasped the duffel strap before everything went pitch-black as water threatened to burn up Riley's nose. She fought the desperate instinct to breathe—her chest caving in with pressure.

Greyson's hand grabbed hold of her arm. At least she prayed it was Greyson. He hauled her up.

Greyson. Thank you, Lord.

Greyson swam to the kayak, paddle in hand, thankfully. They'd both managed to grab theirs before going underwater. And she'd maintained hold of the duffel.

"Ready?" he roared above the rapids.

She nodded and took her paddle straight out on the left side, and then at a 90-degree angle, knowing Greyson was doing the same.

It took three tries, but they righted the kayak just in time to hit another whirlpool. It yanked Riley under just as Greyson's voice cried out.

"Riley!" he hollered, his voice muffled by the raging rapids.

She pushed above the raging rapids, foam slapping at her mouth. She moved into a swim position, letting the rapids carry her, swinging her body to avoid rocks.

A hand clasped her hair from behind and yanked her up by it.

Kevin.

She kicked and flailed, but he kept pulling until she was over the side and into his kayak. She slammed her elbow back, and it collided, the crack of a breaking bone following.

Kevin swore and released his hold on her. She lunged back into the water, but not fast enough. He grabbed her foot, pulling her back. This time leaving her in the water and shoving her head under it.

He was saying something, but the words were lost in the water.

She fought for the surface, struggling, but half her body was under the kayak, the other half shoved under water.

A shot reverberated through the water, and the hold on her vanished.

A hand reached around her arm, pulling her up.

She gasped and spit out water.

Greyson pulled her up against him, her back to his chest.

They disappeared around a bend, and Kevin didn't follow—at least not while the bend remained in their view.

"Did you get him?" Her chest heaved in a frigid breath, her lungs crackling.

"He was bobbing too fast. I only got him in the shoulder—not the chest."

"He's going to have a hard time controlling the kayak with a wounded arm."

"You think he'll bail? Hit an exit to get treatment?"

"He can't keep going without getting the bullet out and at least wrapping it. I bet we've bought several hours."

"Good," Grey said, using his paddle as they soared up on a rapid, then crashed down into a bubble bath of white-water foam. "Let's see if we can catch up with Kelly and Jared."

She sat back in her seat, wedging the duffel between her feet—wondering what, if any, clues it held. But now was not the time to look. Now was for catching up.

FORTY-EIGHT

TIME FLEW, the rapids keeping them on their toes, Riley's arms burning, her lungs seared with the cold morning air. She couldn't let Greyson see her shivering, or he'd likely stop the pursuit to get her warmed up, and they didn't have the time.

"How far do you think they're going?" he asked over the roar of the rapids.

"First stop is at a town named Camp Verde," she shouted. "But what if they didn't stop at a town?"

"My concern exactly," he hollered back. "I haven't seen a kayak up on shore yet."

"Neither have I. Though I suppose, if they went ashore, they'd pull it into the trees at the very least."

"Agreed. It's what I would do."

"So we follow the river to its end?" They couldn't push that long. Nine hours was the maximum kayaking trip. Not a rule, but a fact among expert kayakers. Gratefulness for all her hours white-water kayaking settled inside her.

"No, I say we stop at the first town and assess the situation. See if we can find if they got off or where they might be going. Even without my laptop, I can do a lot on my phone," Greyson said. "They must have a plan." He lifted his chin and pointed with his paddle. "Camp Verde."

She nodded, and they maneuvered the kayak over to a flat

229

landing, where stacks of rental kayaks stood against silver racks layered with more.

"Hey, guys." A kid in his late teens greeted them, helping them pull the kayak ashore.

"This is the fourth kayak I've seen land this morning. Not that common this time of year. Usually, it's just me staring at the river for most of the day."

"Really?" Greyson said. "Must have been our friends. Blond-haired dude with a lady with short dark hair."

"Yeah."

"And a single guy?" Ri said.

"Yeah. The couple landed about a half hour ago. The other guy maybe fifteen minutes after them. Both asked me to hold on to their kayaks for them."

"Any chance they said where they were going?" Greyson asked. "We were supposed to meet them here."

"Nope. Sorry." The kid ran a hand through his tousled hair.

"Okay." Riley smiled. "Thanks."

"Could we trouble you to watch our kayak too?" Greyson said. He pulled a bill from his wallet and handed it to the kid.

The guy smiled. "Thanks, man." He jutted his chin toward the kayak. "I'll take good care of her."

Riley stripped off her dry suit and stashed it with the kayak. Grey did the same.

"So what now?" she asked, stepping out of earshot of the teen.

"Let's look through the bag they left behind at the house now that we can breathe. Maybe there's a clue to where they're headed."

They wandered over to a picnic table, set the waterproof bag on it, and opened it.

Greyson pulled out the contents one item at a time. "Sunglasses. Two walkie-talkies. Interesting . . . if they were staying together."

"Maybe they were planning to split up at some point."

"Maybe, but not at a far distance with these things. While these are good, they aren't the best, so we're probably talking about a twenty-mile range."

"I wonder what for."

"I don't know." Greyson pulled out a pocketknife and a flashlight.

"That it?" she asked when he paused.

"Just checking the side pockets." He held the bag up and reached around. "Hang on. . . ."

"What is it?"

"A pocket within a pocket."

She leaned forward. "Anything in it?"

He pulled out a strip of paper and unfolded it to reveal an address. "Let's see where it leads." Greyson lifted his phone and punched in the address. "Got it."

"What is it?"

"A private airline."

"What?" Her brow furrowed.

"Yeah, it's got a pilot's name. He's got a Cessna, based on the picture, and it's based at . . . Montezuma here in Camp Verde."

"I didn't know they had an airport here."

"Neither did I, but doesn't look like much of one. More like a private airstrip."

"I guess we better see if we can find an Uber to the airport, or we've got a walk ahead of us."

Greyson used his app. "I'm so thankful Uber's available in this remote area."

"Me too." She took a deep inhale and released it nice and slow, trying to ease the racing of her heart.

He looked at his watch. "The driver should be here in fifteen."

"Great. But they've got a solid start on us."

"If we don't catch them before they take off, we can talk to the pilot when he returns and find out where he took them."

"If he's willing to talk."

A few minutes later, a white economy car approached. It pulled up beside them. "Uber for Greyson?" the driver said.

"That's us."

As they climbed into the back seat, Riley prayed they'd be able to intercept Kelly and Jared before Brent did. This whole time she'd been so focused on saving them from Brent that she hadn't stopped to wrap her mind around the fact that the woman she thought she knew was a criminal.

FORTY-NINE

"THE AIRPARK is straight ahead," their Uber driver said. "Remember, ask for Randy. He's the best pilot there."

"Thank you so much," Riley said. "But I don't see the airfield?" Only a mesa.

"It's on a plateau, so you can't see it from the highway, but we'll be there in two minutes. Fast, like you said."

Greyson handed the man a cash tip when they stopped.

"Thank you. Randy with Free Air is in the last hangar." He pointed down the narrow row—too narrow for cars to maneuver down. The only cars on site were in a small lot at the beginning of the row.

"Thanks again," Riley said, climbing out.

Grey lifted his eyes. "Ready for a run?"

She bounced back and forth from foot to foot. "I've got so much adrenaline coursing through me that a run will do me good."

A plane engine thundered.

They looked at each other and bolted into a run. Just over the rise, a Cessna Skyhawk roared down the airstrip.

"No!" Riley said, heat searing her limbs as they raced forward.

The Cessna gained speed and soared into the air.

She slowed her run, Grey beside her. Her chest rose and fell with the heightened breaths. "I hope that wasn't them, but . . ."

"With an airfield this small and the same kind of plane as the one shown online . . ." Grey said.

233

A man, *their* man according to the Uber driver, strode out of the last hangar and took a long sip from a mug. He wore a Red Sox baseball hat, a white T-shirt, and jeans. His gaze followed the bird in the sky until it vanished into the clouds.

"Our guy," Ri said, pointing at the man.

Grey nodded, falling in step beside her as they hurried across the tarmac. "On a full tank of gas, a Cessna Skyhawk has a distance of around six hundred miles. So we're talking max flying time of four hours, maybe less."

"How many hours is Vegas from here?" She slipped her hair over her shoulder, grabbed the hair binder off her wrist, and whipped it up into a ponytail.

Grey blew out a breath. "I'd wager a little over an hour."

They came to a stop in front of Randy.

"Can I help you folks?"

"We're looking for a flight. Our Uber driver said to ask for you."

"Where are you two headed?" he asked before taking another sip.

"We aren't positive," Grey said, explaining situation.

"Huh." A curious expression blanketed Randy's face. "I've never met PIs before. Kind of cool."

"Any chance you know where their pilot took them?" Grey asked.

"Yeah." Randy took another sip of the steaming liquid, then met Grey's gaze. "Vegas."

"I knew it," Riley said, fear tracking through her at the very name.

Heated frustration stiffened her body. Why did she still allow it to affect her so?

"We'd like a ride there," Greyson said, giving her shoulder a reassuring squeeze. Silently letting her know he had her.

"I'll get the plane ready," Randy said. "Be ready to roll in ten."

"Thanks." Grey shook the man's hand and then paid him.

"Y'all can take a seat if you like." He gestured to two metal folding chairs Riley hadn't even noticed. Adrenaline burned her limbs, anxiety rattling her. She couldn't sit still if her life depended on it.

"I'm going to make a quick call," Grey said, pulling out his phone. "I think your brothers should join us."

"I can face this on my own." Well, *with* him. After the Lord, who was her ultimate rock, Greyson had become a rock for her too. Even if he didn't believe they could be together, he'd go to any lengths to protect her, regardless of their relationship status. She trusted in that and in him.

He rested a hand on her shoulder. "I know you can do it alone, but the fact is you don't have to."

"Neither do you," she said.

He held her gaze, a deep expression passing across his features, and then a soft smile curled on his lips.

A smile? Interesting.

"Besides," he continued, "we've got a big city to comb. Having two more feet on the ground will help. We need to catch up to them before Brent does. He won't stop hunting them."

Taking a steadying breath, she nodded. Having her brothers there would be a blessing.

As Greyson guessed, the flight to Vegas took just over an hour, and as they cruised above the strip, a flood of horrid memories pummeled over her, threatening to drown her.

"I've got you," Greyson whispered in her ear as he clutched her hand.

She held on tight, her stomach quaking. The old hollow feeling in her gut that she'd carried as a child came rushing back, and they hadn't even landed yet.

Focus on the case, God whispered to her soul. *I've got you. Even when your mother and father forsake you, I will take care of you.*

A sliver of peace penetrated her tortured heart.

Focus on the case.

Grey was right. They had to track Kelly and Jared down in Vegas or they'd be looking for a needle in a massive wilderness. Time was not on their side.

FIFTY

"WHERE TO FIRST?" Greyson asked, exiting the airport terminal. "Oh, hang on. I have a text from Deck." He tugged her back from the line of taxis.

"What's it say?" She rose on her tiptoes and gazed over his shoulder at his phone.

Flight leaves at five. Take care of our girl.

She bit her bottom lip.

"I promise it'll be okay," Grey said, shimmying them to the side of the hustle and bustle and to the far end of the pickup line. He needed to reassure her. He wrapped his arms around her.

"I'll always be here for you. You know that, right?"

She looked up at him with such hope.

He brushed a loose strand of hair from her face and stared into her eyes.

How could she have so much hope in him? He swallowed. The world disappeared around them. He tipped her chin up. "I've been praying."

"And?"

How did he put it? "I feel God tugging on my soul, but I can't see through it all yet."

She scrunched her nose. "*Through* it all?"

"Yes, unless . . ." He tugged her farther into the concrete cubby he'd found at the edge of all the terminal chaos. "Unless God gives me peace that my depression won't hit that low, unless I can see a normal future for you with me . . ."

This time her whole face scrunched as she studied him. "None of us can see the future or be guaranteed of a certain kind. That's where trust and daily dependence on God comes in."

And there was the problem. Daily dependence. Surrendering control when that was the only thing stabilizing him. Though his illusion of control in relation to saving David was just that—an illusion.

I'm sorry, Lord, but that's just too frightening. To just let go . . . and trust.

"I could die tomorrow," she said, nudging him. "I could be hit by a car or die on this case. I almost did die in the water."

"Frighteningly true."

"We don't get to know the future, but God does."

"That doesn't mean it's going to be good." Not knowing how bad it could get was brutal. He'd seen the worst happen twice, and it had nearly broken him.

"No, we aren't promised no pain or hurt, but we are promised God is with us through it all. And the fact that I don't know when God will call me home, I, for one, want to live each day gifted to me as boldly as I can."

He chuckled despite the serious nature of the conversation. "You've got the bold part down."

"And," she said, tugging on his shirt, bringing him mere inches from her. "I want to spend it with those I love." Her eyes searched his.

Wait. Was she saying . . . ?

"I love you, Grey."

He staggered back, nearly tripping over his own feet. She loved him? The woman he loved desperately loved *him*?

"You love me now, but not as I could be."

"You're borrowing trouble."

"What?" he asked, his thoughts still zooming around the fact that she loved him.

"You live each day for *that* day. You're worried about something that may never come to be. And," she continued before he could argue, "you're super proactive about it. You take medication, you see a counselor. You take good care of yourself health-wise." Her gaze raked over him. "You can't fear a life that may never come to pass. Otherwise, you're living it out in your mind all the time instead of enjoying the blessing of the moment."

"But—"

"*If*"—she cut him off—"your depression hit a terrible low, we'd get through it together. It's like saying to someone with a heart-attack risk or a cancer risk that they shouldn't be with anyone."

"That's different."

"How?"

"That's a medical situation."

"And depression isn't? It's a chemical imbalance in the brain. I'd say that's medical. There's such a stigma around depression, and it sounds like you're buying into it." She cupped his face. "Your depression isn't you. You are intelligent—sometimes annoyingly so." She winked. "And you're witty."

"Witty, huh?"

"At times. Now, don't go getting a big head on me."

A horn blared, setting off a series of horn blares.

She looked behind them. "We better go. We can continue this conversation later."

Given how his head continued to spin as her blissful words swirled in his mind, later was probably better, but all he wanted to do was pull her into his arms and tell her he loved her too. But he couldn't take that leap unless God changed something in his heart.

Please, Father. For the first time, he wanted how he viewed things to change, but he didn't know how to start.

"Taxi!" Riley whistled and waved one over.

She glanced back at him, love shining in her eyes. Love for him. How had he missed it all this time?

FIFTY-ONE

"WHERE TO FIRST?" she asked. Joy at telling Greyson she loved him was liberating. No matter his response.

"We should get a hotel room. We need a base and some fresh clothes and such. Who knows how long we're going to be stuck here."

She bit her bottom lip. *Stuck in the mire and muck of my nightmares.* Seeing the first of the hotels on the strip radically shifted her thoughts of loving Greyson to shadows of her past back to haunt her.

He reached over and clutched her hand. "I'm so sorry we have to be here," he whispered, caressing her hand. "I can always stay and wait for your brothers and put you on a plane home."

"Not on your life." She wasn't running scared. She'd left Vegas that way once as a child. She refused to do it as an adult despite the echoes of fear riddling through her.

"I figured." He held up her hand and pressed a kiss to her knuckles. "My brave lady." He exhaled. "But I had to offer. I'd do anything to spare you pain."

"I know." She squeezed his hand. "And I love you for it."

"You guys picked a hotel yet?" the driver asked.

"Any place other than the MGM," she said, her muscles coiling just at the name. "Why don't we stay at the Argo?" she suggested.

"Where Kelly worked before she moved to New Mexico. Smart," Grey said.

"I have my moments." She smiled. Something she never thought she'd do in Vegas, but she had Greyson, and he wouldn't let anything happen to her. *She* wouldn't let anything happen to her. She wasn't that scared little girl anymore, despite how the feelings and heightened sensations roller-coastered through her.

"You okay?" he asked under his breath as they traveled down the strip.

She nodded. "The Argo is just another block that way. Let's get checked in, grab a meal"—her stomach growled as if on cue—"and grab some stuff from the stores downstairs, then we can start hunting."

"It's a plan," he said.

"Do you think Brent is still on their trail? I mean, we only saw one plane take off."

"True. But even if they eluded him for a while, I doubt it will be for long. I'd bet Brent is already on the ground."

"I wonder how he's tracking them. Maybe AirTags like they did with us?" she suggested.

"Maybe, but if they're smart, they'd have figured that out by now. Could be malware on their phones."

"Or maybe Julie or this Ralph Masters guy has the funds to buy the passenger lists from an airline. It's the easiest way to get the information needed to start tracking someone." It was downright scary the information she could garner from the passengers' flight and booking information she bought from airlines when stuck on a case.

"For that matter"—Grey shifted, the pleather seat squeaking beneath him—"they could be using it to track us."

She exhaled. "True." That was a horrible thought.

"The Argo," their Uber driver said, wedging his way through traffic into the hotel drop-off lane.

"Thanks," Grey said, tipping the driver as a man from the hotel opened Riley's door.

She took his gloved hand, and he helped her out.

"Welcome to the Argo," he said with a smile.

Welcome wasn't the word she'd use, but she thanked the man all the same.

Her cell rang. She stepped to the side of the long line of doors to the casino hotel.

"Hey, kid," Deckard said when she answered. "I've got an update."

"Okay." She moved farther from the entryway to the single exit door and beyond, covering her other ear with her hand. "What's up?"

"I hear Vegas in the background."

"Yeah. Its sounds are pretty memorable." Just the wrong kind.

"Are you sure you don't want Grey to—"

"No. I'm staying."

"Okay. Can't blame me for trying to look out for you."

"I know, and I appreciate it."

He chuckled. "No, you don't."

She'd been hearing that a lot lately. "So what's up?"

"Sheriff Gaines and his deputy went to talk to Masters. His housekeeper said he'd left and let them look around. Apparently, it looked like Masters left in a hurry, and so far, there's no sign of him."

"Great, we've got the guy who is probably behind all this on the loose."

"Yeah. And there's something else I found. Ralph Masters didn't exist before six years ago."

The house sat quiet except for a lone crow perched on the barbwire fence pole.

"It's clear," Jared said, hunched on the dirt beside the old shed, the weather vane rattling in the burgeoning wind.

"I don't know," Kelly said, crouching beside him, the metal siding cool against her skin, anxiety rushing heat through her limbs.

"I just have this bad feeling." Though if she were honest with herself, she knew what it was, and it had nothing to do with whether Claire's parents' house was clear for the money drop.

"Where are we dropping it?" Jared asked, his head pivoting as she scanned the desolate ranch at the far edge of the county.

It'd been six years since she'd stood on Claire's family land, and it'd grown barren and still. Just like they all had when they stood at Claire's graveside. Silent and torn asunder.

Heat surged through her afresh, her resolve fortified. Lance couldn't get away with it. Not again. He'd murdered Claire, even if he hadn't pulled the trigger. He'd murdered her all the same. By the time she'd fled the cult and gotten away from the horrid, scheming con, it'd been too late. The kidney disease he'd promised he'd healed, most likely so he could have the exorbitant amount of money she'd spent on the medicine—the same medicine that her mom took and the cost of which was clearly breaking them—had ravaged her body. She'd died within days, her ex-boyfriend Tate at her side. She'd left him for the cult, breaking his heart, but he never stopped loving her or she him. They were reconciled before she faded away. That day, Tate vowed with them to do whatever it took to make things right, and he'd played his role as a diversion for the case to perfection. He'd kept Riley and Greyson looking into him long enough for them to get a solid head start. It'd all worked so well.

"You okay?" Jared nudged her arm.

"Sorry." She shook off the painful memories, even more convinced of what she had to do. Money alone wasn't enough. Not anymore. She swiped her nose. "I'm good." She scanned the arid land, wind lashing the storm door and spinning the weather vane. "I say we leave it on the passenger seat of her dad's truck. I'm worried if we leave it on the front stoop, it could get seriously tossed about in this wind." It whipped her hair about her face as if to say she was right.

"Okay, but how can we make sure they see it?"

"I'll turn the wipers on."

"Smart."

"And I'll hit the bell and run. I can be behind the shed and in the car before they make it to the door." With the older couple's bad health, it wouldn't be hard to outpace them.

"You ready?" he asked as she gripped the thick canvas bag full of cash. Cash that had been laundered just to be safe. They couldn't risk anyone coming after Mr. and Mrs. Greaves.

She rocked back and forth on her haunches, preparing for flight. "Ready." She didn't wait for any kind of response or well wishes. She dashed across the small patch of land separating the house from the shed.

The old red Dodge pickup sat parked at an angle to the door, the windshield fully visible. A creak reverberated through her ears as she opened the driver's door. She shoved the bag onto the seat, did a quick hot-wire, then hit the wipers. They screeched across the bone-dry glass.

Holding her breath, she looked toward the door, praying no one had heard a thing, but she was being foolish—the sounds louder in her mind than they must really be. She bumped the truck door shut with her hip.

She crept up the front steps leading to the house, a piece of loose siding flapping in the wind. Her finger shaking, she hit the bell, then jumped down the steps in one fell swoop. She bolted back behind the shed and hopped into their friend Carl's car.

The engine purred.

"Wait," she said. "Inch the car forward. I want to be certain they got it."

"We're risking being seen," Jared said, grasping the wheel.

She laid her hand atop his, stilling him. "I want to see."

With a sigh, he did as instructed, inching the car forward in time to see Mr. Greaves hitching down the front steps. He hollered something over his shoulder, moving for the truck. He opened the door and reared back, then he lowered his head to his hands and started weeping.

Kelly's chest warmed. "We can go now," she said. "Take the back road."

Jared eased the car back and then pulled slowly down the road, not really hitting the gas hard until they were past the copse of lonesome trees. "We did it!" He banged the wheel with a smile. "We did it."

She looked over and smiled. *Only part of it.*

FIFTY-TWO

AFTER LUNCH, a quick shower, and a change into fresh clothes, Grey and Riley entered the Argo casino. Blazing lights ran along the ceiling of the never-ending room, slot machines buzzed and flashed. The entire room was one big neon sign.

People cheered, cussed, and cried—the room a maker and breaker of dreams. Riley loathed this place. Loathed everything about it. Her skin crawled with each step they took. Each employee they interviewed was stiff and unrelenting. Even when they'd showed the photographs they'd brought of Kelly and Jared.

They stood in the bar, waiting to speak with the bartender next.

An employee in an Argo uniform—white blouse, short gold skirt, and cobalt blue vest with *Argo* stitched in gold thread on one side of it—approached the bar, took a seat on a stool, and slipped off her vest, setting it on the empty stool next to her.

She ignored the staring men and kept her gaze fixed on the bartender. He strode to her side of the bar. "What can I get ya?"

"Hey, Simon," she greeted the bartender. "I'll take a martini, dirty, two olives."

"You got it, honey."

She unbuttoned the sleeves of her crisp white blouse and rolled them up. Always pristine white shirts, always looking so professional when they dealt lies, even if they didn't know it. The entire

245

place was one big illusion, one big lie. Riley's life had been saturated in them.

"Rough day?" Simon asked.

"You could say that. My feet are killing me, and I had a player who insisted I cheated."

Called out for cheating. Flashes of Riley's childhood came roaring back. The entire building enveloping her in its claws.

"Hey." Greyson leaned over and whispered, "You've got this. *We've* got this. Yeah?"

She nodded, but the words wouldn't come. *I'm stronger than this place. I'm stronger.*

"Hi." Riley found her voice and shifted into work mode. She could do this. God was with her. She would not fall. "How's it going?" she asked the lady.

"Could be better." The woman pulled out a vape, took a stiff inhale, then blew it out. "You a player?"

"No. I'm Riley and this is Greyson," she said, gesturing to him, and he lifted a hand in greeting.

She lifted her chin, greeting him back as she eyed them warily.

"We're looking for two friends." She handed the woman Kelly's and Jared's pictures.

"Friends, huh?" the lady said, not buying a word of it.

Time to take a different tack. "We're private investigators. We're looking into the disappearance of these two," she continued, holding the photos up higher.

"Can't help you," she said, as another employee took a seat at the bar, pulling off his vest in turn.

Riley went for broke. "Kelly *really* is my friend, and she's in great danger."

"Oh yeah?" The lady actually made eye contact this time. "From who?"

"A man who has gone by the name of Ralph Masters for six years."

"Six years, huh?" the lady said. "That's an interesting amount of time."

"Please, could you help us?" Riley said. "I don't want anything bad to happen to Kelly."

"And why do you think this Ralph Masters guy would harm her?"

"They stole a lot of money from him."

"Kelly stole money?" The woman laughed.

"She and Jared. They're on the run and being chased."

"Maybe they shouldn't have stolen the money." She took another vape, then blew the misty white cloud out.

"True. I have a hard time believing Kelly did it myself, but regardless, I don't want her to die because of it. He already sent a man after us who tried to take us out numerous times."

The lady's eyes widened. "And why would they also want to kill you?"

"Two reasons," Grey said. "One, because Kelly sent Riley something that's apparently of great interest to the people at the Expressive Wellness Retreat and Spa that Ralph Masters owns. And second, because they don't want us reaching Kelly and Jared first."

"Why not?"

"Because we'd protect them."

She arched a brow. "Even though they stole?" She twirled the tiny swizzle stick in her empty glass and motioned Simon back over.

"I have to believe they stole the money for a reason," Riley said. That didn't make it right, but she truly believed in her heart it wasn't just a theft for theft's sake.

Riley glanced at the woman's nametag she'd been too sidetracked to notice until now. "Kimmy," she said, "I know this is a lot to take in, but I'm really worried about her."

"Because some spa owner is after her?" she chuckled.

"It's far from a regular spa. They run a racket through their illegal casino."

"They bugged our room," Greyson added, taking a sip of the Coke the bartender set in front of him.

"Seriously?" Kimmy asked, her jaw slackening.

Riley nodded.

"Hmm." Kimmy frowned. "And how long ago did you say that owner appeared?"

"Six years ago."

Kimmy looked at Simon as he set a new drink in front of her.

"You don't know it's him," Simon said.

"Him, who?" Riley asked, leaning forward.

"There was a man out here named Lance Winslow," Kimmy said. "He disappeared six years ago."

"Is that right?" Grey rested his forearms on the bar.

"Yeah," Kimmy said. "He ran a cult outside of town. The house is vacant now. Has been since he left, but he did terrible things there."

"Such as?"

"Well, Kelly and Jared's closest friend, Claire, was one of his . . . I don't know, what's the word for someone who joins a cult?"

"A convert, maybe?" Grey offered.

"Sure," Kimmy said. "Let's go with that."

"Kim," Simon said, trying to hush her. "It's none of their business."

"If it could help Kelly and Jared, I'm going to help."

Simon shook his head but moved to the next customer.

"What can you tell us about Claire and the cult?" Riley asked.

Kimmy lifted her vest off the stool next to her and gestured for Riley to take the seat.

Grey remained in place.

Simon watched out of the corner of his eye while helping the other customer. But Kimmy continued, "Lance took in girls with a solid amount of money. He took the money for himself—claiming he was freeing the girls of the burden of worldly possessions like money."

"And Claire?" Riley asked.

"She used to be a regular here before the cult."

"A player?"

"Mm-hmm. Came in daily to play the slots. She and Kelly were good friends. And Jared too. And one day she stopped coming in.

Kelly said she'd gone with some man to his place out in the desert, but she didn't know where. They searched for her but couldn't find her until she returned to town a waif."

"A waif?"

"She had this kidney disease. Said Lance promised he'd healed her. By the time she came back, she was on death's door, literally. Died a few days later. Her ex-boyfriend, Tate, never recovered, and neither did Kelly or Jared. They were—"

"Wait." Riley narrowed her eyes. "Did you say Tate? As in Tate Matthews?"

"Yeah, Tate Matthews." She blew out a vape puff. "You know Tate too?"

Riley turned to Greyson.

"Yeah, we do," he said. "That explains the conflicting stories about Tate."

Riley nodded.

"What conflicting stories?" Kimmy frowned.

"Long story. You were saying they were set on finding Lance. Did they find him?"

"They found the cult house, but he was long gone. This was six years ago. Police went out, too, but by the time they got there, everyone had vanished, and it looked like they left in a hurry—clothes on the floor, drawers open, that sort of thing."

"You think Ralph Masters could be Lance Winslow?"

"That retreat crap sounds like a scam he'd pull."

"Can you tell us where to find the cult house?"

"Sure, but why would you want to go there?" She took a sip of her drink, then set it down. "It's just an empty property the townie kids use to party in."

"I've learned to chase down leads wherever they head," Riley said.

"Little Riley MacLeod," a baritone voice said with a hint of sadistic pleasure.

The familiar voice sent shivers down her spine. *Please, please, no.*

"It's gotta be you. You look just like Carla. You must be her daughter."

"*MacLeod*?" Kimmy said, disgust forming on her face. "You're a MacLeod kid?"

"Was. *Was*," Riley repeated, then stood and turned to face the man who'd killed her father.

FIFTY-THREE

"BIG MAX," Riley said, and the name suited him even better now. Still tall and looming, the man had added another sixty-plus pounds to his already robust form.

"Little Riley MacLeod." He smiled, but there was zero warmth in it. He was the only man who could send shivers down her spine with a smile. "The sweetheart scammer."

Her stomach flipped at the nickname.

"What are you doing back in Vegas?"

She took a stiffening breath.

"She's looking into Ralph Masters, a.k.a. Lance Winslow," Kimmy said.

"Is that right?" Max chuckled. "A scammer looking for a scammer. How apropos."

She grit her teeth. "I'm a private investigator, and I'm looking to bust him."

Max burst out laughing, his belly jiggling as she'd always pictured Santa's doing when she was a kid, though Santa had never visited her.

She held firm.

"Oh, you're serious." He laughed even harder.

"Thanks," she said, angling her head at Kimmy.

"Hey. You're a MacLeod. You're no better than Lance Winslow."

Riley shifted her balance from one foot to both—she needed all the grounding she could get. "That was a lifetime ago." And she was just a kid.

"Sure, honey. Keep telling yourself that." Kimmy hopped down from the barstool. "I'm outta here."

"Wait. Please tell me where the house is."

"House. What house?" Max asked.

"The old cult house," Kimmy said before walking away.

"What do you want with that place?" Max asked.

"It pertains to our investigation."

"*Our?*" His brows furrowed.

"My partner Greyson and me," she said, gesturing to Greyson, whose carriage was taut, his hands balled in fists at his sides.

"You really turned PI?" Max rubbed his chin. "Interesting."

"I don't suppose you'd help us by telling us where the old cult house is?"

"All right," Max said after a moment's reflection. "I'll help you, if you help me."

Of course he'd go there. A solid for a solid. What was she getting herself into? "What do you want?"

"You to tell me where your dad is."

"My dad is dead. You killed him."

"Oh, I planted the car bomb, but he wasn't in the car."

Her brow furrowed. Why lie about that? But he *had* to be lying, right?

"Now that you know what I want, I'll tell you what you want."

He rattled off the location. Had Big Max really just helped them?

"Oh, and the pair you're looking for"—he jutted his chin at Kelly's and Jared's photos on the bar in front of Greyson—"try the underground."

"The tunnels?" she said.

"The network," he said. "Now, remember your part." He pinned his gaze on Riley.

"Riiight," she drew the word out. "I'm supposed to tell you where my dead dad is. He doesn't even have a grave, thanks to you."

"That part is true, sweetheart." He studied her a moment. "I believe you don't know now. But when you discover the truth, PI, say hi to your dad for me."

FIFTY-FOUR

"WHAT WAS THAT ALL ABOUT?" Greyson asked, wrapping his arm about her waist as they stepped from the bar.

Riley shook her head. "I have no clue. I think he was just trying to mess with me." But he'd seemed so sincere, and she saw right through crud, always able to read lies. She'd been well-versed in them. She'd swear Big Max had been telling the truth, but there was no way.

"What are the tunnels he referred to?" Grey asked, resting his hand on her lower back—his stance protective, his gaze firm.

"There's a tunnel system that stretches the entire underground of the city. Kelly and Jared could be anywhere in the labyrinth, or we could have just been sent on a wild goose chase."

"You think the lead's no good?"

"No, I think it's real, but like I said, we could search for days and never find them."

"So you don't want to go there?" he asked as they strolled toward the lobby.

Everything in Riley's being wanted to be out of this world. Ached for the fresh air she always longed for as a child but never got. Always smoke. Always lights. Always sounds whirling in her ears.

"Oh, we'll go there, but I want to visit the cult house first." It had a tie to all of this.

They stepped outside into the warm sunshine, and she gazed

253

up at the blue sky. She'd seen so little of it as a kid—always living in one hotel or another, wherever her parents were performing. Though their illusionist act was simply that—an act, a cover for their criminal activities.

"Uber should be here soon," Grey said, rubbing her back.

An hour later, Greyson held the Uber door open for Riley, and she stepped out into the desert.

They thanked the driver and stood rooted in place as he drove away.

The whistling wind swirled the mesa in sandy waves, giving the sensation of the ground being in motion.

"Let's go inside," she said.

"What are we looking for?" he asked, following her up the path nearly buried by the mesa. The cacti were the only sign of life.

"Something that shows us where this all started, and I think it's here." She nodded toward the run-down house coming into view.

The wooden door stood ajar, and after they both slipped on gloves, Riley opened it fully with a rasping creak.

Sunlight beamed through the windows of the shadowed interior.

They walked through the house, its furniture still in place—sort of. Chairs tipped over, graffiti smattered across the walls. Beer cans on the floor. Clearly a teen hideout. "Kelly and Jared are tied to Claire," Riley said, "and she's tied to Ralph—or Lance or whatever his real name is."

They cleared the house and found nothing helpful.

With a frustrated sigh, Riley leaned against the paneled wall in the kitchen, then pressed off the wall. "I really thought we'd find—"

"Wait," he said, a crack in the wall catching his gaze.

"What?"

He stepped forward. "The wall has a crack."

"It is an older home."

"Hold on," he said, moving to lean across the table and run his fingers along the thin edge.

"Here," she said, behind him. "Let's move the table out of your way." They slid the dining set off to the right, giving him full access to the wall.

Slipping his fingers as far as they'd wedge into the crack, he pulled back. "It's stuck, but I feel cold air. There's something back there." His gaze followed the crack down to the floor. "There's a bar lock on it at the base." He unlocked it and pulled the wall-door open.

"That's odd," she said. "We don't usually have cellars out here."

She clicked on her phone's flashlight and started down the wooden steps. They creaked beneath her feet.

Grey pulled his gun and followed. The steps swayed beneath him, groaning with each movement.

A light pull dangled over Riley's head as she hit the floor, and she pulled it, illuminating the dank space. "What is this place?" She turned in a circle. Doors lined the perimeter.

She moved to open the door but the knob held firm. "I'm getting into this room," she said, pulling out her lockpicks. "There's a secret here to be discovered, and I'm viewing this as public property at this point."

"I'm with you." He turned with his back to the door, scanning the space and the stairs, before angling his body to cover their six and their twelve on a pivot.

She popped the lock, and the door squeaked open.

A lone bed with a ratty cover sat against the wall. What looked like a chamber pot stood in the corner.

"You think this could be—"

"Where he held them?" Greyson said.

The door creaked shut, and he moved to open it again but stopped in his tracks.

"What?" she said.

He followed the tracks with his fingers. "There are nail scratches on the back of the door."

"Oh . . ." Her hand flew to her stomach.

"Deep breath," he said, a wave of nausea roiling in his own gut.

"Why hold them prisoner? Cults usually brainwash people, and that's the vibe I got about Claire. That she bought his lies until one day she didn't."

"Maybe he held the ones that didn't buy in anymore down here instead of letting them go so they could tell people the truth of this place." Greyson strolled the perimeter of the room.

"There's got to be more here," she said.

"What do you mean?"

"Kimmy said he left in a hurry. There should be more here to tell the story."

They stepped out of the room and into the next two in turn, finding the same setup. But the third room held a desk, a chair, a locked file cabinet, and a picture on the wall.

Greyson strode toward the desk while Riley headed straight for the picture. She pulled it away from the wall to reveal a safe.

"Always behind the picture," she said. "I'll get to work opening it."

"I'll go through the desk," he said, opening the first drawer and moving for the second. He was almost through clearing them when she let out that satisfied yelp.

"I got it," she said, opening the safe door.

He glanced over to find it empty save for a couple of papers.

She pulled them out and scanned them. "A deed to the land in Lance Winslow's name and a deed to an adjacent two-hundred-acre property."

She shoved the papers into her new purse. "I thought there would be more."

"Maybe there is," Grey said, holding up a lone key from the final drawer.

"Does it go to the desk?"

He tried it in all the drawer locks. "Nope."

"So what does it go to?"

"Hang on." He knelt and scooted under the desk. "Sometimes there are—"

"Hidden slots."

"Right." He ran his hand along the bottom of the desk. "Anything?"

"Nada, except . . ." He shifted.

"What is it?"

"There's something under this rug." He crawled back out from under the desk. "Help me move the desk."

He took one side while she took the other. Moving the desk fully revealed an artisan rug. They each reached for an end of the rug.

"Okay," he said, and they flipped it back to discover another safe.

He smiled. "Better get to work."

She set to it, and in under a minute, she had opened the safe.

He peered over her shoulder.

Four small square wooden boxes were nestled inside.

They looked at each other.

She opened the first three boxes. Nothing. The fourth box held a gold-and-diamond tennis bracelet. She lifted it out so they could both examine it. *L. J.* was inscribed on the gold charm dangling from it. Underneath the bracelet was a lock of hair held together by a thin rubber band. She looked at him, her face pale. "Do you think . . . ?"

He hated to say it. "It looks like a curated collection to me . . . for the ones who didn't make it." He'd seen it before on the serial case he worked with Phillip.

Riley stiffened. "A killer's keepsakes. But why are the other boxes empty?"

"Maybe he hadn't filled them yet or—"

"He left in a hurry, and these got left behind."

Either way, Lance had started a collection, and Greyson had a feeling the cult was just the beginning.

FIFTY-FIVE

AN HOUR LATER, Detective Zane Carter, accompanied by two police officers, stood in the same spot they'd been in, looking at the same boxes. With gloves on, Carter went through the items, pausing at the tennis bracelet. "L. J. . . ." he said. "I'm trying to rack my brain for missing women. It would have been about six years ago that we visited this awful place."

"What happened back then?"

"When Claire Greaves escaped, she claimed she'd met Lance Winslow at a revival and had fallen for the guy."

Greyson's brows shot up. "She'd fallen for him?"

"Yeah. Said she'd fallen in love with the guy and moved in with him. Only she wasn't the only woman."

Riley's jaw slackened. "Ewww."

"She claimed, at the time, he wasn't romantic with the other women. That he was 'helping' them in their suffering."

"Suffering?" Riley asked.

"Yeah, he'd promised to help heal the women from whatever was plaguing them. Apparently all the women had health issues like hers."

"A waitress at the Argo who knew Claire said she had a kidney disease."

"Yeah, and the wacko said he'd heal her, and she believed him and went off her meds. I don't recall the full story offhand, but

I grabbed this on the way out of the office when you called." He pulled a notepad out of his jacket pocket. "I'm old-fashioned," the only-forty-years-old detective said. "I write everything down and date the books. Keep them in a box at the precinct. I looked up the case in the database and pulled the corresponding notebook."

He quickly flipped the pages up and over the spiral rings. Finally, he stopped. "Here we go. Lance Winslow." He scanned the page. "Right. Okay. Claire said she stopped her meds and felt good for a while until . . ." He scanned farther down. "Until her symptoms returned. That's how she realized he was conning her and the other women. She managed to get away, but by then she was really sick. Poor girl died days later."

"We heard that. It's awful."

"It gets worse," Carter said.

"Worse?" Greyson blinked, the arid air sucking the moisture from his eyes.

"Claire had recently inherited a decent amount of money from a relative, but she gave it all to Winslow. For the 'cause' to heal the hurting."

Riley covered her mouth to smother a cough. "Sorry. The room is—"

"Caked with dirt." Carter scuffed at it with the sole of his shoe. "No windows. Little air. Except what seeped through the floorboards."

Greyson studied the windowless room, the adobe walls, the door with the lock hanging from the handle they'd opened. "Looks like he kept some captive down here." *Please say they didn't stay locked up in cells by choice.*

"Claire didn't know anything about the cellar when we asked her about it."

"I imagine he kept it hidden."

"Hey, Zane," one of the officers said. "No missing women from Vegas with the initials L. J., but there's a missing woman from seven years ago from Scottsdale. Sounds like Winslow traveled."

The detective shook his head. "I'm afraid of what all we're going to find before this is over."

FIFTY-SIX

THE FOLLOWING MORNING, with new identities in hand, Jared smiled. "Our freedom," he said, tapping the two passports and IDs against his palm. "Thanks, Carl," he said to their friend.

"Of course. What happened to Claire was wrong. I'm glad you guys were able to make it right . . . in a way."

Kelly swallowed. It would never be right, but at least a solid portion of the money Lance Winslow stole from Claire was back with her family, who, by the looks of the decrepit ranch, desperately needed it.

"You heading out?" Carl asked.

"Not in daylight," Jared said. "I think we should lay low. Take a nap. We've hardly slept in days."

"You can use my place," Carl said.

"Thanks, man." Jared clapped him on the shoulder. "You're a true friend."

"Of course. I take care of my friends. You can use my spare car again when you leave tonight."

"Thanks a lot, but we've got other exit plans," Jared said.

Carl frowned. "Oh?"

"The tunnels," Kelly explained. "We've got a vehicle stashed a mile outside them."

Carl smiled. "You two have planned for everything."

Kelly took a calming inhale, trying to settle her fraying nerves. She prayed Carl was right but feared otherwise.

"How much do you think Kelly and Jared really know about Ralph?" Riley asked as Greyson strode across the plush carpeting in their hotel room.

"I don't know. I'm just glad Carter's on the case."

"I bet when that hair is tested, they'll be able to match it to that other missing woman."

"I fear you're right." His concern for Riley was off the charts. They were no longer hunting a con—one who had sent killers after them—they were dealing with what appeared to be a serial killer who kept women captive and then buried them in the desert. How many more women had he killed?

He paced back by Riley. It'd been his experience—a painful one—to learn killers didn't stop. They just bided their time.

"What's first today?" she asked.

"When we saw them last night, your brothers said they're still hunting down where Kelly grew up to see if they can track her that way. I say we start with the Vax International, where Jared worked."

"Sounds like a plan."

He ached to talk to her, to tell her how God was working on his heart, deep in his soul, but he knew it would be better to wait until the case was over, and they could have a deep conversation, one not interrupted with updates, clues, and, worse yet, a killer chasing them.

Grey frowned. Where was Kevin? Despite the gunshot wound, he should have caught up by now. Or was it as Grey feared and Kevin was hanging back, hoping they'd lead him and Brent to Kelly and Jared?

A half hour later, when it was time to hit the Vax, Grey stood and stretched. "You ready?" he asked.

Riley nodded, and he stretched once more before moving to the side of the hotel room door, keeping her at his six. He scanned the hallway. "Looks clear." He took a step out, fully on alert.

They tracked down the corridor and didn't relax at all until they were in the elevator alone.

Riley wrapped her arms around her waist, her hands shaking.

He stepped toward her and tipped up her chin. "We're going to get him."

She nodded.

"We will." They had to. He couldn't let another killer get away.

FIFTY-SEVEN

KELLY LAY BESIDE JARED in the bed, Carl's apartment silent save for the occasional flurry of daytime partying out on the street as people passed by the low-level apartment building.

Jared snored. Really snored. Poor man hadn't truly slept in days.

She hadn't either. But she had a mission.

She eased toward the edge of the mattress.

Jared's chest rose and fell in rhythm.

Please stay asleep.

She had to do this. No. She was *compelled* to do it.

She eased over more, nearly to the side of the bed.

He shifted, and she stilled, clinging to the edge of the mattress.

He blew out a breath and shifted again.

She waited.

Soon the snoring returned in force.

She rolled off the mattress, landing in a Black Widow pose, and held again.

No movement, other than his chest rising and falling.

She was clear.

Cracking open the apartment door, she glanced up and down the hallway. Her heart in her throat, she stepped into it, praying no one had found them.

She strode down the dim hallway—silently as she could. She rounded the corner and descended the stairwell for the outer door.

The 7-Eleven with the pay phone out front was a dozen blocks away. She'd walk fast, hoping with all her heart she'd return before Jared woke, but she had no choice. Kathryn's family deserved to lay their daughter to rest, and Lance had to pay for what he'd done.

Reaching the pay phone, she turned her back to any onlookers and fished the quarters from her pocket. One by one, she slipped them into the slot. The coins clanged as they plopped into the metal box.

Taking a deep breath, she gathered what remained of her frayed courage and dialed the local precinct's non-emergency number. All 911 calls were recorded and would only signal more alarm. The non-emergency number was probably monitored, too, but with a less ready-for-action operator on the line.

"Vegas Police Department," a woman answered.

"I need to make a report," Kelly whispered.

"I can hardly hear you. Can you speak up?"

"No, I can't." She placed her hand over the receiver, trying to muffle her voice. "I just need to report that Lance Winslow killed Kathryn Buford."

"Who is this?"

"There's proof, but I can't send it now. Just tell them to look into Lance Winslow and his alias Ralph Masters. He ran a cult at a house thirty miles northeast of downtown Vegas. The police checked it out six years ago. Tell them we know he killed her, and I'll send the proof in once I'm safe."

"Safe? Are you in danger? Do you need an officer?"

"I need to go. Just tell them."

"Miss—"

She hung up the phone and stepped back into something hard. She squeezed her eyes shut. *No.*

FIFTY-EIGHT

KELLY WOKE, her head hammering, her eyes hazy. The last thing she remembered was bumping into Brent and having their off-grid location beaten out of her.

She blinked. Darkness surrounded her.

She tried to move, but her hands and feet were bound, the raw rope cutting into her wrists. She screamed, but the duct tape over her mouth muffled it and tore at her skin when she moved her mouth. She wiggled, kicking something over with her feet.

Where was she?

Small. Cramped. Low ceiling. No. Roof. No. Hood. She was in the trunk of a car. A moving car by the motion under her and the hum of an engine.

Panic shot through her. Did he have Jared somewhere too?

Her stomach flipped. Was Brent going to beat her more? Torture her for the location of the locket? Nausea from what she might be facing rushed over her again as the car sped down an unknown road.

The Vax casino was no different from any other on the strip. Loud. Flashy. Secluded from the outside world. A frustrating hour of unanswered questions later, Riley and Greyson headed for the exit, and they couldn't reach it fast enough for her.

Greyson held it open, and she stepped through, nearly slamming into a man.

"Oh, excuse me," she said, then she glanced up at him. *Jared?*

He didn't run. Didn't move. Just stood there.

His face ashen, his expression raw, he cleared his throat. "You're the PIs after us, right?" He looked at Riley. "Kelly's friend, right? She showed me a picture of you two on her phone."

"Yeah . . ." Riley said, still trying to figure out what was happening.

Grey's brow furrowed. "How'd you know we were here?"

"Simon and Kimmy gave me the heads-up. Look, I need your help." His voice cracked. "They have Kelly, and I don't know where she is. I've searched, but I'm not a tracker like you two. I didn't know where else to go."

"You want us to help you find Kelly?" Saying it out loud didn't make it sound any more reasonable. The man they'd been hunting had just walked up to them. That had certainly never happened in her career before.

"Yes. Please, I know they're going to hurt her."

"Trying to get the location of the money?" Greyson asked, his shoulders broad, a guarded wariness in his stormy gray eyes.

Jared swiped his nose. "The key is far more important than the money."

Grey frowned. "Isn't the key for where the money is stashed?"

"No." Jared shook his head. "We kept the money on us."

Ri frowned. "Why?" Why keep that much money on them?

"We had someplace to deliver it."

She put a pin in that and followed her curiosity to where the key led to. "Then what is in the locker?"

"There were papers in the safe we robbed that prove Ralph Masters owns the retreat, plus a handful of passports with different names but all with Lance Winslow's picture, and some jewelry."

"Jewelry." Ri meet Grey's gaze. "The empty boxes."

He nodded.

"Boxes?" Jared frowned. "I don't understand."

She explained.

"Any idea who the jewelry you have stashed belongs to?" Greyson asked.

"Yes. At least with the star locket. It belonged to Kathryn Buford," he said. "She was found dead last year, buried only a mile from the cult house. She always wore the locket and was wearing it when she disappeared. That's how Kel and I knew he'd killed her."

"I knew it was a sicko's collection." Grey's shoulders went rigid.

"Yeah." Jared exhaled. "He's a sicko all right."

"Is that why you robbed him?" Ri asked. "To punish him?"

"Yes. For what he did to our friend Claire."

"Kimmy told us about her."

"Oh." He shuffled his feet. "Lance killed her, and it's a long story, but the money went where it should have."

"What do you mean?"

"That's all I'm going to say. Now, can we please find Kelly?"

"We'll absolutely help you find her," Riley assured him. "But we're going to need your help to do so."

Tears misted in Jared's blue eyes. "I'll do anything to get her back. *Please.*"

"Where would she go?" Greyson asked.

"*She?* No. He took her. Brent. He's who Lance sent after us. I know he has her. She wouldn't leave."

"Okay," Greyson said. "Let's sit down and work our way through this knot."

"Kelly's missing, and you're talking about sitting around chatting?" Jared said, perspiration clinging to his brow, soaking the blond hair framing his face.

"Going off half-cocked isn't going to help us find her. If anything, we'll make mistakes," Greyson said, firmness in his tone.

A subtle smiled touched Riley's lips. Always so resolute and steady. She loved that about him, but thanks to their time alone, she was seeing more of his free, feeling side, too, and it was enticing.

"Fine." Jared ran a shaky hand through his hair. "Where do we do this?" His leg bounced, his stance shifting again and again. The constant swaying motion threatened to make her dizzy.

"Our hotel room." Riley led the way back to the Argo. "Can I just ask one question?" She looked over her shoulder at Jared.

"All right," he said, his voice uneven.

"Where does the key actually go? I feel like I've seen it before, but maybe that's because locker keys all look somewhat alike."

"The roller-skating rink in Jeopardy Falls."

"Of course." She'd recently stored stuff in those lockers while skating at Christian's birthday party that Andi threw him last month. "But wasn't it closed when you stashed it?" If her timeline was right.

"Yeah. Kelly picked the lock."

"Oh." Yet one more thing she didn't know about the woman she'd thought was becoming a friend.

"All right," Greyson said as they entered the hotel suite. "Take a seat." He gestured to the sofa.

"I'd rather stand," Jared said, pacing the oriental rug.

"It's best if you really settle and focus during this time." Greyson strode to one of the armchairs and took a seat. Riley took the other one.

Jared nodded and plunked down on the damask sofa, his leg bouncing so high she feared he'd nail himself in the chin.

"Okay, let's start with how you two got separated. Where were you? When did you realize she was missing?" Greyson lifted the small hotel notepad off the coffee table and grabbed the gold pen with the casino name engraved on it. "Spare no detail." He glanced at Riley. "The details matter."

So he'd adopted her saying. She bit back a smile, knowing now was not the time.

"Okay." Jared rubbed the back of his neck. "We were sleeping for a few hours at a friend's apartment."

"Which is where?" Greyson readied the pen to write.

"Three blocks off the strip on Flamingo. Anyway, I was asleep. We were both supposed to sleep until nightfall when we could head out through the tunnels to a car we have waiting not far from the other side."

"And then where to?"

"Our home."

"Home?" Greyson's brows arched.

"We built a home over the last year up in northern Nevada. Sort of an—"

"Off-grid location." Riley finished for him.

"Yeah." Confusion and a hint of admiration tinged his tone and blanketed his worried face. "How'd you know?"

"We put it together," Ri said, looking at Grey.

Jared swiped his stuffy nose. "Can we please go find her now? We're wasting time."

"We're making a plan for the best course of action. Now, let's stick to it." Greyson tapped the pad with the shiny pen.

Greyson holding a sparkly gold pen was amusing but adorable.

"Would Kelly have gone to your house on her own by any chance?" she asked.

"No." Jared shook his head. "She would have stuck to the plans."

"Which were? One more time, please." Grey continued tapping his pen on the notepad.

"I already told you." Jared's knee bounced higher until he nailed it with a thumping crack on the edge of the coffee table. Pain etched on his face, but he shook it off, scooting back on the sofa to avoid another collision. "We were sleeping for a handful of hours at our friend Carl's."

"And how do you know Carl?"

Jared looked sharply at Greyson. "Why does that matter?"

"We need to know everyone who may have talked."

"Carl didn't talk. He wouldn't betray us like that."

"All right." Greyson jotted down the name. "When did you realize Kelly was gone?"

"I woke up to use the facilities, and she was gone. I thought she was just in the bathroom since the door was closed, but after a while, I started to panic. Knocked on the door, searched the full apartment. She was gone. I ran out into the hall, searching the building, but she was nowhere."

Riley crossed her legs. "Did you look anyplace else?"

"Yes, the Argo, in case she came back to talk with someone, and then the Vax for the same reason, which is where I found you."

"Could she be waiting in the tunnels?" he asked.

"I don't see why she would." He nibbled his thumbnail. "I don't understand why she left the apartment in the first place. Oh, geez." He flopped back.

"What?" Riley scooched forward in her chair.

"Kelly had been fighting with me."

"Over what?" Riley propped her elbows on her knees.

"She wanted to call the cops about Kathryn Buford. Let them know she had proof that Lance killed her. I bet that's where she went. To find a phone." He rubbed his brow—hard. "I should have just let her call."

"Why not use her phone?" Grey asked.

"We ditched those way back when we figured out that's how Brent was tracking us. We got one burner cell, but I had it in my pocket when I napped. I should have let her call. If I had, she'd still be here." His face turned pale. "If I'd just let her, he . . ."

"We're going to get her back." Riley believed they would . . . one way or another.

Grey's expression turned grim. "Then I think I know where they took her."

"Where?" Jared straightened.

"To your off-grid location."

Smart man. It was an isolated place to get the information they needed out of Kelly, and they'd assume Jared would eventually head there, and then they'd have them both.

"If you're wrong and we drive all the way out there, we could be getting farther and farther from Kelly."

"You're welcome to stay here and look, but Riley and I are heading to the off-grid location. We'll need an address or coordinates to find it."

"No." Jared got to his wobbly feet. "Let's go."

"How long a drive we talking to the location?" Riley asked, getting to her feet as Greyson did the same.

"Nearly seven hours north."

Riley's cell rang as she headed to the bedroom to grab a few items. "Hey, bro," she said.

"Hey," Deck said. "I think we got a bead on the guy tracking Jared and Kelly. You aren't going to believe this, but we think he left town."

"Brent's got Kelly."

"Oh, man. That sucks. Any idea where?"

She caught him up to speed.

"Okay. We're north of the strip. Where are you?"

"Just about to leave the hotel."

"Okay. We'll be twenty minutes behind you."

"It's a plan. I'll send the directions once we have them."

"Roger that. And, kid—"

"Be safe." She smiled. As much as she wanted to prove she could handle herself, her brothers' love was a safe place to fall. They'd never let her down. Neither would Grey.

She just prayed they wouldn't let Kelly down.

Fifteen minutes later, they pulled out of the hotel valet line in their newly gotten rental, her nerves strung tighter than guitar strings.

Please, Lord, don't let Kevin find us. I know he's still out there. We know too much for them to let us live, but help us defy the odds and slip out of Vegas unnoticed. At least they'd lost him for a while. Either that, or he was watching and waiting. If so, they'd just led him to Jared. Or, rather, Jared had just walked straight into the crosshairs.

FIFTY-NINE

"OKAY, CAN YOU GIVE ME the address or coordinates?" Greyson asked as they headed away from Vegas.

Riley watched Vegas fade into the distance. She was leaving a very different person, with a very different life, surrounded by those who loved her. She really was no longer that terrified little girl. She shifted back around to look at the road ahead.

"Jared?" Grey asked again.

"I'll give you directions as we go," he said.

"Why? It's not like we're going in blindfolded," Grey said, draping his arm over the wheel.

"I'm not giving out coordinates. Getting there is one thing, but it's a twisty way to go. Coordinates are too easily shared."

Greyson exhaled. "Fine. Let's start."

Jared gave the first set of instructions, and Greyson followed them.

"My brothers are meeting us. We'll need to give them directions too."

"You can give them the same ones I give you," Jared said, looking over his shoulder at her.

"You aren't making this easy, Jared." Grey clamped the wheel.

Jared shifted his gaze back to Greyson. "Maybe not. But I'll get us there."

Riley sat back as they drove into the desert, heading for an unknown situation and destination.

Charley horses riddled Kelly's legs. She'd lost all track of time, but they'd been driving for hours on hours from the best she could guess.

Where were they taking her? What were they going to do to her?

She squeezed her eyes shut in the darkness, trying to will away the images of torture that lay ahead.

The car slowed, then stopped. The engine cut.

Please, Lord, I know I've sinned, but I was trying to make things right the only way I knew how. Please protect me in this moment. Let Jared come for me. Let someone come for me.

The trunk opened to reveal a blanket of darkness. A man silhouetted by the faint moon stood over her. All she could make out was his tall height and pronounced nose.

"Ready to have some fun?"

Her stomach dropped, and everything went black again.

Greyson checked the clock. According to Jared they still had an hour to go.

"From here, you follow the dirt road straight to it," he said.

"Okay, now that we've seen the way, could you please give us the address?" Riley asked again.

"Why? I can show you the rest of the way."

"We can't risk my brothers getting lost. We're going to need their backup."

"Okay, tell them to GPS Allister Road. Once they hit it, tell them to go south on Allister Road for twelve and a half miles, and then take Benton another five miles round about. It'll lead to this road we're on. Tell them to follow it to the end."

Riley tapped the directions into her phone.

Greyson hoped they weren't far behind. They'd need the numbers for whatever they were about to face. They needed Deck and Christian to have their six.

"I'm going to call local authorities." Riley lifted her phone.

"No!" Jared spun around to face her. "Please don't."

"Because you'll be arrested for theft?" she asked.

"No, because if they see cops, they're likely to kill Kelly. We have to do this on our own."

Greyson weighed the value of the assessment and glanced at Riley in the rearview mirror.

"I suppose he could take that tack," Riley said. "If they shot her and ran, the sheriff would stop to help Kelly, and they could get away. I imagine in the sparse county there's only a sheriff and possibly one deputy."

"Please," Jared pleaded.

Grey wrestled with the decision but kept coming back to the fact they needed the police there to arrest Brent and anyone else.

"I'm sorry, Jared. We need to call."

Riley dialed a number and put her phone on speaker.

"Sheriff's department. Sheriff Pearlman here."

"Hi, this is Riley MacLeod. I'm a private investigator. A woman's been kidnapped and is being held at an off-grid location north of Carver and south of Austin. That's your territory, correct?"

"Yes, ma'am."

She went on to explain the entire situation.

"Okay, give me the address, and I'll be there as soon as I can. I'm actually out of the office. I have my calls forwarded. I'm about half an hour away, but I'll head over as soon as I can make it."

"I'll text you directions. I'll notify you of the situation when we get there so you know what you're walking into."

"Thanks, and thanks for the call."

"You're welcome."

The call disconnected.

"So no police backup," Grey said.

Jared frowned. "He said he's coming, right?"

"They're at least a half hour behind. This thing could be all over by then."

Grey reached his hand back between the seats and took hold of hers, giving her a reassuring squeeze.

"Take that offshoot of the road," Jared said, leading them onto an angled road that looked more like a walking path. Tree branches swiped the truck as they drove down the path.

"Take it to the end, and then park behind the final copse of trees. It'll provide an overlook position."

Greyson did as instructed, and soon they were settled on the overlook. He gave Riley the night-vision binoculars her brothers had brought him, then he shifted to lay prone on the ground, his rifle set up, and stared through the night-vision scope.

A lone house, barely visible through the trees, sat a thousand yards away, down in a ravine. He scanned the area and noted what looked like three more paths that could be used as roads if needed. Smart location. And apparently self-sustaining from the solar panels on the roof and the water-collection system adjacent to the main building. A small outpost building sat on the opposite overlook site, again barely visible in the copse of trees surrounding it.

Near the house was Brent's black SUV that they'd seen in Amy and Gus's driveway, a dark Jaguar, and a white SUV. *Kevin.* But who did the Jaguar belong to? Was Lance taking a hands-on approach?

Grey shuddered to think so, then shifted his gaze to the small home. Lights illuminated a portion of the space. "I need the layout," he spoke low to Jared, who ran them through the floor plan.

"I'll take the living area," Grey said to Riley. "You take the kitchen."

She nodded and shifted her binoculars onto the room in question as he fixed his scope on the living room. It took time and a lot of patience, but soon a shadow passed in front of it. "I've got one," he said.

"I've got two," Riley said of her location. "And one is moving for the door. Got him," she said. "On the porch at two o'clock."

275

Grey panned back to the lit porch. Sure enough. Brent strode the width of it, his gaze on the hills, though he was staring into darkness, only the murky moonlight to see by. He pulled out a large flashlight and, turning it on, he scanned the perimeter.

"Still and low," Greyson said to Jared as Riley lay still beside him.

The light streaked over their location and kept going for a second, then it panned back. They were low enough in the tree cover that they should be almost indistinguishable from the foliage surrounding them.

Greyson held his breath, his torso pressed hard into the packed earth. Riley lay immobile beside him. Jared lay behind them, his head down on the ground—like a kid thinking if he couldn't see them, they couldn't see him.

Finally, after a breathless minute, the light moved on.

An engine sounded in the distance, running parallel to them on the main road they'd been on—if they could actually call it a "main" road. It was more like a narrow dirt path. The engine cut, and, barely audible from their position, doors shut.

They held.

Footsteps sounded in the brush.

He looked over at Riley, and she nodded.

They had company.

"It's the guys," she said in a whisper. "I gave them our location."

Relief swarmed Greyson's belly.

Soon Deckard and Christian lay prone beside them. Deck looked through the scope mounted on his AR-15. "How many do we got?" he asked.

"Brent's on the porch," Grey said. "The lights are in the kitchen and the main living area. We've got at least three hostiles—Kevin, Brent, and an unknown in the living room. Definitely a man based on build. And then Kelly, of course. So we've got four for sure."

"Could the unknown be Lance?" Deck asked.

"Jared?" Riley handed him her binoculars.

He stared through them. It took a minute, but then he nodded on an exhale. "That's Lance."

276

She took the binoculars back. "Kevin beat us here. I guess he knew we'd be coming."

Grey looked over at her. "That's what has me worried. They all know we're coming, and they're no doubt ready for us." But what choice did they have?

"What's the plan?" Christian asked, a rifle in hand.

"I'll go in," Grey said. "You three spread out and cover."

"I'm coming with you," Jared said.

"No." Greyson shook his head. "You'll just get yourself killed. Let us do our thing and handle it."

Jared remained silent, and Grey prayed he'd listen, though he feared his words were falling on deaf ears.

Riley shifted to her knees.

Greyson frowned. "What are you doing?"

She brushed the dusty earth off her pants. "You're not going in the front alone."

"Ri . . . It's decided. Deck can take twelve o'clock and Christian three and you six."

"No. You decided. I'm going in," Riley insisted. "I'm the one who knows Kelly. Besides, the sheriff should be here soon."

"Should we wait for him?" Christian asked.

"Every minute we wait is another minute Kelly could be killed," Jared said, his voice impassioned.

"Jared's right. We need to move." Greyson got to his feet as Brent fixed his light on the back side of the house, but it would be swinging back soon, he had no doubt.

Riley stood beside him.

"Ri, seriously."

"I've made up my mind."

Which meant there was no changing it. At least not in this case. He steeled himself. He'd always protect Riley with his life. Had always strived to protect her, but things were different now. This was the woman he deeply loved, and she was about to walk headlong into danger. There could be more men in the house than they were seeing, and the hostiles would definitely be armed. They had Kelly and the advantage. There was no covered way down to the house. All routes to the house from where Grey and Riley sat were visible to the porch.

Grey scanned the layout again, focusing on the boulders spread out along the back path. They'd have to time it right, and they'd be vulnerable between covers, but it was the best way he could see down.

"Riley, give Deck the sheriff's number so he can relay our location. Then turn your phone off," he said, and Riley nodded. She passed on the number to Deck and Christian.

"I'm on it," Christian said as Deck remained focused on Brent pacing the porch, his scope fixed on him. "Deck should stay here. I'll move to twelve." He lifted his long-range rifle.

"We need to go," Riley said. "Quick, the light's panning back."

Greyson grabbed his rifle in one hand and her hand in his other, and they ran back to the main road, holding to the tree line's edge. They were out of the line of sight from the porch, but once they moved from cover, they were sitting ducks until they hit the first boulder.

He turned to Riley. "I would feel so much better if you took position."

"And I'd feel better if you did." She racked her backup SIG, sliding a bullet into the chamber.

"Ri . . ."

"I appreciate you wanting to protect me, and I want to protect you in turn, but Kelly needs us in there."

He studied the firm line on her brow in the shifting moonlight as dark clouds passed over. Lightning lit the sky ablaze.

Great. A storm. That's all they needed. Light from heaven to give up their positions.

Please, Lord, provide us cover. Shelter us in your wings and help us to reach Kelly in time.

"All right," he relented, though he had no choice or say in the matter. Once Riley fixed her mind on something, she'd make it happen. "I suggest we go in that way." He pointed to the sliding hiking path sprinkled with boulders.

"Agreed," she said.

They moved around as the light from Brent's torch passed across the far side. Reaching the path, they both crouched low.

"One at a time," Greyson said. "Boulder to boulder."

"Got it."

Before he could blink, she was moving for the first one, twenty yards away. His throat squeezed, and he covered her.

Relief filled him as she made it. She gestured for him to come. He watched the light, waiting for the opportune moment, and took it, moving for the first boulder as she covered him.

The sky opened, and rain pelted down, coming too fast and furious for the dry, cracked earth to soak it up. A stream formed along the sloping path, creating the equivalent of a mudslide within minutes.

Riley moved for the next to last boulder and slid onto her butt ten yards from it. Brent's flashlight swung toward them, and Greyson readied his rifle.

His chest squeezed; the light was mere feet from Riley. The swift stream carried her nearly past the boulder, but she managed to grab hold and pull herself behind it before the light hit.

Momentary relief filled him, but they still had one boulder to go, and then they would walk into the real storm.

SIXTY

RILEY CAUGHT HER BREATH, her pulse throbbing in her ears. That was a close one. Too close.

The light swung away, and she covered Greyson as he moved for the boulder, which was just large enough to shield the both of them.

He slid to her position, and she grabbed his hand as he got close, helping to pull him behind the rock. Their chests resting against it, they peered over the top. Kevin joined Brent on the porch. *Great.* Two flashlights—sweeping in opposite directions. She prayed for her brothers to remain hidden and Jared to hold still.

She took a steeling breath, trying to settle the adrenaline shaking her limbs. "I'm going," she said.

Greyson tugged her arm, pulling her to him, and pressed a kiss to her lips. "I love you," he breathed.

"Now you tell me?"

"It seemed like a rather important time."

"I love you too." She pressed a kiss back. "Now, let's do this."

He nodded. "Please be as careful as you can."

She'd do her best. "You too." On that, she raced for the last boulder. She waited there, watching the two flashlight beams. Then she darted along the slippery earth for the sedan.

A splash sounded behind her. She looked over her shoulder to see Jared sliding unceremoniously down the mudslide. The flashlight beams converged, landing directly on him. She squeezed her eyes shut. They knew they were coming now.

Please let them think Jared came alone.

Reaching the sedan, she held, casting her gaze on the last boulder, hoping Greyson held there.

Kevin bolted up to greet Jared.

Brent remained on the porch, panning the light along the hill over and over. It hit the boulder as Jared landed at Kevin's feet.

Kevin hauled Jared to his feet.

Please don't let him look behind the boulder. Don't let him find Grey.

"Anyone with you?" Kevin hollered over the dousing rain. "I know they must be here."

She held her breath.

Jared shook his head.

Thank you, Lord.

"Why don't I believe you?" Kevin scanned the hill. Dragging Jared with him, he winced at the motion and switched arms, his injured shoulder taut and, based on his grimace, still painful. He moved for the boulder Greyson was positioned behind.

Her heart thwacking in her throat, she aimed her gun at Kevin's retreating back. He was giving her no choice—just like with Pete. She'd never wanted to be back in this position, but she was, and she'd protect Greyson with her life. She tracked Kevin until he was a mere foot from the rock when a shot hit the front of the boulder, shards of rock flying as the retort boomed in the night. *Deckard.*

Kevin turned and fired toward her brother's position.

He fired back, and Kevin ducked. "Come on," he hollered to Jared, traipsing through the sliding mud for the house.

Brent fired at Deck's position, and Deck fired back, the bullet hitting the man in the right shoulder. He screamed, and his gun slid from his right hand.

Kevin shoved Jared into the house, then fired at Deck.

A shot hit the porch rail with a loud ding from twelve o'clock. Christian covering his brother, their brother.

Greyson took the opportunity to race to the sedan, hunching beside her.

Lance positioned himself to be covered by the half-open door. At least from their and Deck's positions, but Christian had the shot if they needed it.

"What in tarnation is going on?" he yelled.

"We have company." Brent scrambled for the house, his hand covering the gunshot wound on his bleeding arm.

Lance cursed out a sarcastic comment, then stepped back into the house.

A fourth hostile stepped onto the porch, and gunshots rang in the night as Steve sprayed the hills with his semiautomatic.

Riley moved for the back side of the house, pressing her body against the cold, wet siding.

Greyson raced to join her.

The front door creaked open, and Riley peered around the side of the house but didn't have a view. She indicated her intended movement up the left side. Greyson nodded and indicated he'd move up the opposite side.

On three, they moved in tandem around the house.

"You want her to stay alive?" Steve hollered into the night, his voice echoing over the rain in the small canyon landscape. "Stop shooting, or I put one in her head."

Riley reached the edge of the house. Taking a steadying breath and saying a prayer, she peered around the corner.

Steve stood in the half-sheltered doorway, a gun to Kelly's head. Mascara-streaked tears lined her face, her eyes wide in horror.

"Please, don't." Jared's voice carried from inside the house.

"Shoot again," Steve yelled, "and she's dead."

Riley angled for a shot. If he'd just shift past the edge of the door, she'd have him. A hand wrapped around her neck, gripping her throat in a tight squeeze.

"Hello, lovely," Kevin said, a muzzle pushing against her temple. "One squeeze and you're dead. Now, we're going to walk into that house, and I don't want any trouble."

Sirens wailed in the near distance. The sheriff had arrived but certainly not subtly.

"The cops are here?" Lance roared, his voice emanating from inside the house. "Someone is going to die." A shot fired, and Kelly screamed.

Riley's chest squeezed harder than Kevin's grip on her neck. *Jared.*

Kelly wailed. "No. No. No."

Kevin shoved Riley around the edge of the house, and they came face-to-face with Greyson.

"The boyfriend come to save you?" Kevin said.

"You've got that right," Greyson said with conviction.

Kevin was positioned behind her, the muzzle to her temple. "Go for it, but you'll kill her in the process."

Deckard had the shot on Kevin's back, but with his semi-automatic, the bullet could go straight through him into her.

Greyson's gaze met hers. He was going to take the shot. She stilled and prayed.

"Now, be a good boy and lay down your weapon," Kevin said, his gun biting into her flesh, his other hand fixed around her waist, holding her tight against him like a human shield.

SIXTY-ONE

HIS MUSCLES COILED and heart racing, Greyson held up his hands and began to lower his weapon. He needed Kevin to shift just a little. No doubt his gaze would follow the lowering of the weapon, but he prayed his head would follow too. As slow as possible, he inched down, the weapon sideways but the muzzle still aimed at Kevin.

"Hurry up or she's dead," Kevin said.

Greyson nodded and shifted his stance. Kevin's head followed the movement. Praying, he fired. Nearly too scared to look, he forced himself to.

Kevin's body crashed to the deck, and Riley raced for Grey's arms. He moved to embrace her, but he was yanked back, a gun to his head. How? The man had come from around back. Had someone been in the shed?

"Didn't see me coming, did ya? I can hide in the trees just as easily as you can."

"Alvin?"

"Gotcha," he said, his voice low and with a bite of cruelty.

Riley's eyes welled with tears. She was a good shot, but not that good.

"In the house," Alvin ordered Riley. "Or lover boy is dead."

She did as instructed, and Alvin pushed him into the house, his gun fixed at his head.

He just needed to get Alvin to move by a window, giving Christian or Deckard a side shot.

"Well, hello," Lance said. "Welcome to the party."

Jared lay on the floor, his stomach seeping blood.

Kelly, bloodied and bruised, knelt beside him. She looked up. "Riley?"

"Hi, Kel."

Greyson calculated the window shot he needed to give Deckard.

"So you are the two causing all the problems," Lance said.

"We know what you did," Riley said, "and the police know too. You're not just a con; you're a murderer."

Lance's lips spread into a cold, thin smile. "Only when the occasion calls for it."

"The occasion?" Kelly yelled. "What occasion called for murdering Kathryn Buford?"

"She threatened to expose my empire," Lance spit out.

"Empire?" Riley frowned. "What empire? You're just a con at the base level."

"I built that con up beautifully. Alvin recruited the women for me, and I siphoned everything I could out of them. Murdering them, while it holds its own pleasure, was just a means to an end. Just like this."

Lance pointed his gun at Kelly and Jared. "Now the only proof of Kathryn's fate and my role in it is the locket. They took it, and the rest of my keepsakes, and they're going to tell me where they are, or they die."

"Keepsakes?" Kelly's face distorted in disgust.

"I even took one from that friend of yours, but after a while, I tossed it out. She wasn't a keepsake kill."

A red flush spread up Kelly's face. "A keepsake kill?"

"Your friend died from her disease. Not my hand."

"You killed her all the same," Kelly shot back.

"Fine." Lance shrugged. "I'll take that kill too. That's what this is all about, isn't it? Your stupid friend wasting away to nothing."

"You—" Kelly lunged for Lance, and he shot her in the thigh.

She screamed and grabbed her leg, stumbling back.

Greyson readied himself. It was now or never. He tripped over his own feet, lurching forward as they lined up with the window.

He heard the thwack before the loud report, Alvin's body slumping to the tan carpet as the shot rang through the night.

Greyson gathered his weapon and aimed it at Lance's head.

"So we're going to have a showdown?" Lance laughed.

"No need," Riley said, shooting him in the back of his knee, as he'd foolishly taken his eyes off her. He stumbled forward, firing his gun in the air as he fell.

Riley and Greyson ducked. She kicked Lance's gun away the minute it fell from his thick hands.

Greyson stood over him, putting the sole of his shoe on Lance's neck, his gun aimed at his head. "Move and you're dead."

Footsteps raced across the porch. *Steve.* Another gunshot rang out, and a thump sounded.

Soon Sheriff Pearlman raced through the door, followed by two more policemen he'd brought in.

"Looks like we've got a lot of injured here," he said.

"Self-defense," Riley and Greyson said in unison.

Pearlman smiled. "I don't doubt it one bit." He turned to one of the deputies—though the badge read a different county. He had called in reinforcements. Wise lawman. "Wanna call this in?" he said. "We're going to need at least four ambulances."

"On it," the deputy said.

Soon more sirens wailed in the night. Brent and Lance were handcuffed and placed on stretchers.

Kelly limped toward Lance, blood oozing from her thigh, but it looked like a through and through. "I'll see you rot in jail," she bit out.

"Keep wishing, honey. I'm a master manipulator. I can get myself out of this one."

"Not without the keepsakes, as you so disgustingly call them."

"I still have one man searching. He'll find them eventually."

"Not unless he has access to police evidence," Riley said, coming to stand by Kelly.

Kelly looked at her, and she nodded. She'd handed the key off to Deckard, instructing him to hand it to Sheriff Pearlman when he arrived.

Lance's brow rippled. "What?"

"Oh, did I forget to mention the locket is already in police custody as well as Lindsay Jacob's tennis bracelet and the chain and ring you stole from the other poor women?"

Once they knew the locker location, Joel had gotten a warrant to access it and take the items into police custody.

Lance's face blanched. "I'll figure a way out of this," he said, but his voice cracked. "I always do."

"Time to go," the EMT said.

"I'll see you at the trial," Kelly said as they rolled Lance by on the stretcher.

Lance looked piqued as the ambulance doors closed. The vehicle pulled away into the night, red lights swirling in the thinning rain, but no sirens this time.

Sheriff Pearlman saw Kelly and Jared to their ambulances and read them their rights. They'd be facing a number of charges, but Kelly appeared surprisingly serene. They'd accomplished their mission.

"You're going to be okay," Riley said, examining Kelly's injury. It was indeed a through and through, and it'd missed the femoral artery, thankfully.

"Thanks, Riley."

She nodded, and the EMT shut the ambulance doors.

Greyson, Riley, and her brothers filed back into the house to give statements, and the dead remained until the coroner arrived.

Hours later, they returned to their vehicles.

"So," Riley said, leaning into Grey. "What's this about you loving me?"

Deck cocked his head, then shot a confused look at Christian, who shrugged.

Grey smiled and brushed her hair back from her face. "I do with all my being. I only wish I'd told you sooner."

Deck's jaw tightened. "What is happening?"

Ignoring her brother, she bit her bottom lip. She hated to ask in this moment but needed to know. "And your future?"

"I want to spend every minute of it with you. I will trust God to take it one day at a time."

"Duuude," Deck said. "What is happening?"

Christian held up his hands. "I've got no clue."

Attempting to ignore her brothers, she gazed into Grey's eyes. "That sounds pretty wonderful to me."

Grey smiled, clearly oblivious to her steaming brothers behind him. He cupped her face and leaned in for a kiss.

"All right," Deck hollered, sliding up his sleeves.

Riley's eyes widened. Not fight mode.

"What on earth is happening here?" Deck moved to stand between them. "Tell me I did not see you almost kiss my sister."

"Deck," she said, trying to wedge between them as Christian moved to stand beside their brother.

"Stop," she said to Christian. "He doesn't need a wingman. There isn't going to be a fight."

Deck stiffened, his hand balling into a fist. "That remains to be seen."

"We love each other," she said.

Christian's jaw slackened. "Love each other as in . . . ?"

"I love your sister with everything in me," Greyson said.

"Way wrong answer." Deck raised his arm, pulling it back, and Riley shoved her way between them. Pressing her palms on Deck's chest, she pushed him back . . . well, the inch he'd let her.

"Whoa! Deck. Calm down," Grey said. "It's not what you think. . . . I mean, it is, but so much deeper."

Riley turned her gaze on Christian. "Talk to him. You're the rational one."

"He was about to kiss you," Christian said, like that explained everything.

"I understand. If I had a sister, I'd feel the same way," Grey said. "Go ahead." He waved Deck forward. "Take a shot."

"Don't encourage him!" Riley held her ground between them. "Deck, seriously, calm down."

Deck looked at her, and after a moment, lowered his fist. "Then explain quickly."

"We have loved each other for a long while but only just professed it."

"We're not fooling around," Grey said. "We want to be together."

"Together?" Deck grunted out. "As in date my—"

"*Our,*" Christian said, standing beside him.

Deck nodded. "Our sister?"

Before she could respond to something she and Grey hadn't even talked about, he cleared his throat.

"I want to be with your sister for always," Grey said. "It's not a casual date thing. It's serious."

"Serious?" Christian chuckled—that nervous laugh when he didn't know the best way to proceed. "You two try to kill each other."

"We're not that bad," Riley said. "But we're getting off course—"

"How? When?" Deck mumbled.

"The specifics don't matter," she said, moving beside Grey and wrapping her arm around him. "The fact is we love each other, and you two are going to have to learn to respect that."

Deck's gaze bounced between the two of them, then fixed on Grey. "You really love her?"

"I do, and I'm sorry you had to find out this way, but I love her."

Deck pinned his gaze on her. "And you . . . feel the same way?"

"I do, and I'm beyond happy."

Deck looked at Christian, who nodded and took a pronounced step back.

"Okay," Deck said. "I'm not saying I can wrap my head around this, but if you're happy, Cool Whip, then we're happy for you."

She stepped toward her brother. "Thank you. I know this isn't easy for you—"

"That's an understatement, but if you're both happy . . ."

"We are," she and Grey said in unison.

"Then that's that." Deck wrapped her in a hug and pressed a kiss to the top of her head, then pointed at Grey. "You take good care of her."

"I'll protect her with my life."

A hint of a smile graced Deck's lips. "I know you will."

Riley moved back to Grey's side, nuzzling into his embrace.

"Ugh, I don't want to see that," Deck said. "I'm out of here. See you back at the hotel."

"See you, guys," Christian said, shaking his head, a smile on his lips.

Eighties rock emanated from Deck and Christian's rental Jeep as they pulled away.

"So," she said, turning to face him head-on. "You said always."

Grey smiled. "I did, didn't I?"

"Always sounds pretty good," she murmured, snuggling against him.

"Then always it will be." He smiled before lowering his lips to hers.

SIXTY-TWO

"HEY, GUYS," Riley said, entering Deck's house, her and Greyson's arms overflowing with presents. "Present delivery number one."

Deck smiled and shook his head. "She did it again," he called into the next room.

A moment later, Andi and Christian appeared in the doorway.

Christian chuckled with a smile. "Of course she did."

"Oh my word," Andi said. "That's a lot of presents. I think I underbought."

"Nah. Riley is our Christmas elf. She loves giving others presents far more than getting her own."

"Oh, that's so sweet," Andi said.

"Except when it's a sweater with a bird on it," Deck murmured beneath his breath.

"Deckard Daniel, I heard that." Riley pinned her gaze on him as she passed. "And it was one sweater, and I thought it looked nice on you."

Deck looked at Andi and shook his head.

"And I saw that," Riley said, her back to him.

"I knew she had eyes in the back of her head," Deck said.

She smirked. She just knew her brothers very well.

291

"Drop them under the tree and come back," Deck said. "Chili's ready."

"Yum." She hurried into the living room and placed the gifts under the tree, instead of dropping them willy-nilly as Deck would. He still hadn't warmed up to celebrating the Christmas season. They'd been deprived of it for so long that she suspected it still didn't seem real or, rather, stable to him yet. Like he still anticipated it being ripped away again and was protecting his rugged, tender heart.

"Ready, luv?" Greyson asked, standing beside her after setting his armload of presents down and extending his hand. She placed her hand in his and stood still.

He arched a brow, studying her. "What's wrong?"

"How do you know—" She shook her head. "Never mind." The fact was he knew her well, nearly as well as she knew herself.

He caressed her hand. "Out with it, luv."

She exhaled and her taut shoulders eased. It was time. Time to share her greatest fears. "First, this investigation. The shoot-out . . ." She bit her bottom lip but continued, needing to get the muck out in the open. "It reminded me of . . ."

He clasped her hand tighter, intertwining his fingers with hers. "Of the shooting with Pete?"

She nodded. "I know I had no choice but the nightmares of it replay through my mind. Other than not going there to begin with, I don't know what else I could have done."

"Because there was nothing else you could have done. It was either him or you."

"I know that."

"In your mind. You need to know it in your heart. To fully accept that was your only choice or you'd be . . ." He took a stiff inhale and cleared his throat.

She narrowed her eyes. "You okay?"

"Just the thought of how close I came to losing you . . . all of us nearly losing you . . ."

"But you didn't." She stepped closer to him.

He swallowed and his gaze softened. "I think my heart stopped when the news came in."

She wrapped her hand around the back of his neck, running her fingers through his hair. "And you rushed to my side." She smiled, warming at the thought. "Along with my brothers," she added.

"Of course, we did." His gaze still soft and warm, he moved closer. His face mere inches from hers, he leaned in to look her in the eye. "You had no choice. You have to stop torturing yourself and let this one go or it'll eat you up as you continue to replay possible alternate outcomes when there were none."

"I know you're right. It was either him or me, but . . ."

"Surrender it to God, luv. Let Him work on the part of your heart that's still wrestling with it."

"You're right." She needed to go to her Savior with it all—the fear, the sorrow, the questioning. Only He could fully heal her. She trusted that without measure He'd meet her in that moment, in the place she dwelt, and He'd set her feet on the rock again— not on the shaky sand where she'd been standing ever since Pete.

Hope sprung in her heart that this *would* come to an end, and she'd be free to move forward, the heavy burden she'd insisted on carrying lifted from her shoulders—her soul.

She gazed into his beautiful eyes and smiled. "Thank you."

He quirked a brow. "For?"

She moved her hand to cup his face. "For being you."

Their gazes interlocked, the silence speaking volumes of the love emanating between them.

He tilted his head.

"What is it?"

He brushed her hair over her shoulder, inadvertently caressing the side of her neck in the process, giving her goose bumps.

"You started with *first*. So what's second?"

"Oh. Just the whole tangled investigation." Which seeing Big Max was part of.

"Well, you can rest easy in the knowledge that Ralph Masters is facing charges, and he'll be locked away for a long time."

"True." Based on the charges filed against him. She took solace in that.

Sheriffs Pearlman and Gaines had paired up on the investigation and discovered the awful man's real name—Trent Gregory. His cons and aliases went further back than they realized. The man was a chameleon, changing names and identities, his dark heart seeking to devour anyone he could profit from. Thankfully, Greyson was right, and he'd be going away for a long time.

She took a stiff inhale and released it.

Kelly and Jared were facing charges too, for robbery, but they were getting leniency for helping bring closure to many of the grieving families Ralph had hurt. Still, it looked like they'd serve some time. Riley struggled to see the friend she knew in the woman who'd been handcuffed and put in the back of a police car.

"I know she was your friend," Grey said.

How did he always do that? Read her mind? "She was, but I wonder if that part of her life was all an act. If she was a chameleon too—playing a role until she and Jared got what they wanted."

He rubbed her arms. "What they did was wrong. There's no way around that, but they did it for altruistic reasons—to give money to Claire's family."

"That doesn't make it right."

"Not at all, but they aren't the typical criminals just in it for themselves."

"True."

"This case has shades. Not just black and white. Outside of stealing being wrong, which is clear as day, the motives and layers to this case make the waters murky."

"I'm still trying to wrap my head around it."

"I didn't know Kelly, and I am too." He slipped his arms around her, resting his hands on the small of her back. "But we'll let the courts handle their case and shift our focus to what comes next."

"Which is?"

"This." He lowered his lips oh-so-softly to hers.

Following a family supper, Greyson and Riley exited to the empty living room. She snuggled into him on the couch. He warmed at her touch and wrapped his arm around her as *The Santa Clause* played on Deck's TV.

He chuckled as Tim Allen got sucked down the chimney pipe, but Riley tensed in his arms.

Odd. She'd been so relaxed before the movie started.

It happened again when Tim Allen went down the chimney and through the fireplace, stopping to fill the stockings.

He cocked his head. "What's wrong?"

"Nothing."

He tipped her chin up with his fingers, making her look up at him.

"We both know I know you far better than that."

She pursed her lips and gave a deep sigh, then shifted one knee up to her chest. "It's just, I love seeing the fireplace all decorated for Christmas and the stockings hanging on it."

"But?" he nudged.

She shrugged, her lips pursing again. She hugged her knee tighter.

"We never got that."

He frowned. "Got what?"

"Stockings," she said, the words almost a whisper.

"I'm so sorry," he said. "That's awful." His dad had been horrible when it came to Christmas. But at least he'd had his loving mom and lots of Christmas traditions. He couldn't imagine growing up with none.

"It wasn't my parents' type of thing to . . . you know, parent in general. I mean, I love Christmas and celebrating it, but at the same time, it kind of sucks to have never gotten the surprise of Santa Claus or stockings waiting by the fire."

He covered her hand with his. "I wish I had the power to go back and make it different for you." He'd give practically anything to do so.

She gave a sorrow-tinged smile. "That would be nice, but it's just the way things were." She cast her gaze down.

"But"—he nudged her chin back up—"they aren't that way anymore."

"True." She smiled, really smiled this time. "I have *you* this Christmas. I couldn't ask for a better present."

He nudged her nose with his. "You most certainly have me."

"Certainly, huh?"

"You have *all* of me"—he pressed a kiss to her lips and nuzzled her nose—"for as long as you'll have me."

"You sure?"

"Positive. God showed me it's still a daily choice of surrender and trust, but I see that now, thanks to you too."

"Me?"

"Yes. Without your hope and faith in me . . . I don't know that I'd ever have found this joy."

"Joy, huh?" She tickled him, and he tickled back, then he engulfed her in one fell swoop, sliding her onto his lap and kissing her with soft, slow tenderness.

"Ugh," Deck grunted. "Again with the kissy stuff. I thought we decided you'd restrain yourself in front of Christian and me."

She leaned her head over the back of the sofa. "You're the one who came into the room."

"Just restrain yourself when you're near us, period," Deck said. "We're happy for you, we really are. But we don't want to see that."

"We're together seventy-five percent of the time," Ri said. "You're going to see it sooner or later."

"Let me live in my own little world. I'm still not there yet. I'm not a fan of surprises, and this one threw me for a massive loop."

The doorbell rang, and Riley smiled. "You better get ready for another surprise."

"Agghhh. Please tell me you didn't hire a Christmasgram again? I don't like people singing at me, and it was flat-out embarrassing at the office."

"It's not a Christmasgram, but I beg to differ. It was hilarious watching your face."

"I got it," Andi said, her heels clicking along the terra-cotta tiles in the foyer entrance. The door creaked open and all went silent.

Deckard frowned. "Who is it?" he called.

No answer.

"Andi?"

No answer.

He pulled his gun at their visitor's silence and moved for the foyer.

Riley hopped up to follow him, pressing her lips together to simmer the smirk he knew was fighting to come out.

He rounded the arched adobe wall, slipping through the wide opening, then he stopped short. "Harper?" She looked nothing like the strong, driven woman he'd known. Instead she had the same haunting look in her eyes as Riley had after the shootout with Pete. And her frame was that of a slip.

She brushed her hair behind her ear.

Deck narrowed his eyes. Were her hands trembling?

"Hi, Deckard," she said, her voice weak.

"You okay?" he asked, striding to her.

She swallowed, then nodded, but he wasn't buying it.

"I thought your deployment was extended?" he asked, wondering why she was back so early and so bedraggled.

"I left early," she managed, her poor lips cracked and scabbed.

"Oh?" He let his gaze track over her. Bruises covered her collarbone and her forearms, but he feared more were covered by her evergreen sweater.

She shuffled her feet. "Can I come in?"

"Right. Of course." He stepped back, allowing her passage.

"Can I give you a welcome-home hug?"

"Of course." Her words came out dry.

He wrapped his arms around her, and she stiffened. What on earth had happened?

SIXTY-THREE

DINNER WRAPPED UP, and Riley forced each person to open one present because she couldn't stand the anticipation. Grey smiled. He found it absolutely adorable.

"Let's go in the front room," Riley whispered in his ear, her breath sweet and warm.

Greyson couldn't get there and out of sight fast enough. They were trying to be considerate of her brothers, but it was only getting harder as the day wore on.

They hadn't even reached the couch when she slipped a finger through his button-down shirt and tugged him to her. She didn't even speak, just pulled his lips to hers.

"Oh, come on," Deck said.

"You were in the kitchen," Ri said.

"I'm not now."

"Okay, we'll go to my place." She looked up at Greyson. "That work okay?"

Better than okay, he mouthed.

"Thank you," Deck said.

"At some point you're going to have to get used to this," she said, the words trailing behind her to the door.

"Agreed, but today is not that day."

298

Riley just shook her head as Greyson helped her into her coat. At only thirty degrees and with snowfall on the horizon, he wanted her bundled up.

He slid on his coat and then stepped from the warm house into the frigid air.

"It's snowing," she said of the first flakes fluttering down, but it didn't take long to intensify.

"It's so beautiful," she said, stretching out her arms and twirling around.

"*You're* so beautiful."

She smiled as he approached, tugging her winter stocking cap down. He tried nudging her toward her house, but she was having too much fun in the freshly falling snow.

"I hope enough falls to make snow angels and a snowman."

"I hope it falls enough to strand me here."

"I thought you were already staying in Deck's guest room for Christmas morning?"

"I am, but I wouldn't mind staying longer. I got used to waking up with you on the road. Seeing you looking even more stunning than the sunrise."

She stepped toward him, leaving boot prints in the thin layer of accumulated snow.

"Well," she said, wrapping her arms around his neck, "maybe one day we can wake up beside each other."

He wanted nothing more. "That sounds perfect."

"It does?"

He nodded and took her hand in his. "Your hand is so cold. You should have worn gloves."

"You can warm me," she said, stepping up on her tiptoes and kissing him with boldness, love, and fervor.

Deckard grunted. "I thought you'd be at your place by now."

They turned to find the whole gang standing there.

"What are you guys doing out here?" Riley asked.

"Just waiting," Andi said.

"For what?" she asked, confused.

Greyson slipped a strand of errant hair behind her ear. "Your present is waiting at your house. I think they want to see it after you do."

"It is? When did you . . . ?" She narrowed her eyes. "Is that why Andi had me out shopping all day and then practically shoved me into your house?" she said, pointing at Deck.

"Hey," he said, holding up his hands. "I had nothing to do with this."

"Other than totally helping." Greyson smirked.

Deck shrugged.

"Can we go?" she asked, a twinkle in her eye.

"Absolutely."

"After you two," Deck said, gesturing her and Greyson forward with the sweep of his hand.

Christian and Andi followed, Harper trailing along, her arms wrapped tight about her waist.

Riley wrapped her hand around the doorknob and paused, looking over her shoulder. "Is it necessary we all come?"

Greyson shrugged. "They helped."

"All right, already," Deck said. "I'm freezing out here. Let's hurry this up."

"You should have worn a co—" she started as she opened the door, but trailed off as she paused in the entryway.

A fireplace sat where her TV stand used to—the TV now mounted above it.

"I took the liberty of getting us each one." Greyson rubbed circles on her back. "I hope that's okay."

"It's better than okay. I can't believe you guys installed a kiva fireplace for me." She stepped toward it.

"Do you like it?" Greyson asked, moving with her.

"I love it." Tears tumbled from her eyes. "And I love you," she said, pressing a kiss to his lips.

"On that note, I'm outta here," Deck said.

"I'm with you," Christian said.

Andi chuckled. "Come on, Harper. Let's leave these two alone."

The door shut, and Greyson opened his eyes to find them blissfully alone. "There's another gift."

"For Christmas Eve?" she asked.

"Yes, ma'am. But there will still be plenty tomorrow morning." He handed her the large red-and-white snowflake-patterned gift bag.

She pulled the tissue paper out of the bag, and a combination of a smile and tears covered her face. "Christmas movies."

"All the good ones," he said. "I thought we could have a Christmas movie marathon tonight and hang those stockings"—he indicated two lying on the coffee table, one with his name and one with hers—"on the mantel shelf. You don't have to put mine up, I just thought . . ."

She stopped him, tears still misting in her eyes. "It's perfect."

Greyson smiled and wrapped his arms snug around her.

Thank you, Lord, for this treasure. May I always cherish her as she deserves.

An hour later, they were back up at Deck's house, the whole gang watching *Noelle* and sipping hot cocoa.

A knock sounded at the door.

"I wonder who it is this time," Deck said.

"I'll get it." Riley popped up, but Deck had already beat her to it.

Deck opened the door and reared back. "Dad?"

"No time for chitchat. Your sister is in grave danger."

Dear Reader Friends,

Thank you for picking up my book. I hope you enjoyed Riley and Greyson's adventure. However, *Two Seconds Too Late* touched on deeper topics, such as depression. The reality of depression is very close to my heart as my depression can be debilitating, but there is hope, and it's found in our Savior. It doesn't make the dips any easier, but trusting that He'll carry me through the deepest waters and walk beside me through all the sorrow keeps hope in my heart. I pray for anyone with depression that our Savior's hope would infuse your heart, and if you need help, please talk to someone in your community, like Greyson does through counseling and trusted friends.

The other reality that I wrote about is veteran suicide, something that is near to my heart. As a veteran spouse and having served this nation by my husband's side during his years in the United States Navy, I resonate with our military families and veterans as the statistics have increased in our nation. Twenty-two veterans commit suicide every *day*. Every single day. If you know a struggling veteran, please visit your state Veterans Administration services or dial the 988 Suicide & Crisis Lifeline. Let us pray as veteran Desmond Doss did, "Lord, help me save one more."

Blessings,
Dani

Acknowledgments

Thank you to my Lord and Savior, without whom this book would not exist. May I glorify you in every story you place on my heart and soul.

To my hubby—I couldn't do this without your support. Thank you for brainstorming when you have zero context for what I'm trying to explain. For your patience, constant motivation, and encouragement. Thank you, luv.

To Kayla—Thank you for always encouraging me, for brainstorming ways to kill characters with me, and, most importantly, for bringing me Starbucks while I'm in deadline craze. And a ginormous thanks for coming up with the title for this book.

To Ty—Thank you for jumping in and researching ideas for me and my crazy plots. And for always cheering me on. And giving me two amazing grandsons doesn't hurt. LOL!

To my awesome grandsons—For fun without measure. You bring such joy to my life. I love talking story ideas with you two! And thank you for coming up with the title for book three. I love it!

To Joy, Renee, Lori, Lisa, and Carrie—For your incredible feedback. It was beyond helpful in shaping this story. I appreciate you all so much.

To Crissy and Amy—For being there every step of the way

through this story. For all your generosity, hospitality in opening your home, and, most importantly, for your tremendous help with our flooded house. We couldn't have started to recover without you. Thank you from the bottom of my heart.

To Lisa—For twenty-seven years of wonderful friendship and counting. Thank you for all your help with the flood and for salvaging as many family photographs as you could. I would have lost them all without you.

To Jill Kemerer—For your amazing friendship. I'm beyond blessed to have you in my life. And deepest thanks for your help with our flood recovery.

To Dave—Thank you for all the years together, for signing me in the first place and championing me over the years, and for being an all-around amazing editor. I'm going to miss plotting my crazy storylines with you. I wish you the very best. I'm a better writer because of you and the time you invested in me.

Tricia Goyer—For your friendship over the last year and all your help during the flood. I so appreciate you!

To my entire team at Bethany House—Thank you for all your hard work and creativity and for getting my books into the hands of my readers. And, last but not least, for championing my stories.

FOR MORE FROM DANI PETTREY,

read on for an excerpt from

ONE WRONG MOVE

Making amends for his criminal past, Christian O'Brady has become one of the country's top security experts. But a string of heists brings attention from Andi Forester, an insurance investigator with her own checkered past. The two of them are drawn into a dangerous game with an opponent bent on revenge, and one wrong move could be the death of them both.

Available now wherever books are sold.

ONE

"WAIT HERE," Cyrus ordered.

"Why?" Casey asked—though pawn suited him better. As much as it galled him, Cyrus needed the insipid man. Needed his skills. For now. But when they were done, so was he. "Why?" he asked again.

Cyrus gritted his teeth. So incessant. He shook out his fists. Only a handful of locations to go and the questions would cease. *He* would cease. "It doesn't take two of us to get what we came for," he said, hoping Casey would accept the answer and let it drop, but he doubted it. "I've got this. Two of us will only draw more attention."

"Fine." Casey slumped back against the van's passenger seat.

The imbecile was pouting like a girl. And, that knee. Cyrus wanted to break it. Always bouncing in that annoying, jittery way. The seat squeaked with the rapid, persistent motion. He shook his head on a grunted exhale. If Casey didn't settle . . . if he blew their plans. Cyrus squeezed his fists tight, blood throbbing through his fingers. Too much was at stake. His own neck was on the line.

He turned his attention to the task at hand. "I won't be long," he said, surveying the space one last time before opening the van door. The lot behind them was dead, the building still. He climbed out, his breath a vapor in the cold night air. He glanced back at their van, barely visible in the pitch-black alley.

Shockingly, Casey remained in the passenger seat, his knee still bouncing high.

He shut the van door as eagerness coursed through him. The thrill and rush of the score mere minutes away. Just one quick job and then it was finally time.

He slipped his gloved hands into his pockets. A deeper rush nestled hot inside him, adrenaline searing his limbs. His fervency was for the kill.

He moved toward the rear of the restaurant, where the rental rooms' entrance sat. His gloved fingers brushed the garrote in his right pocket, and he shifted his other hand to rest on the hilt of his gun. Which way would it go? Garrote or gun? Anticipation shot through him. Rounding the back of the building, he hung in the shadows and then stepped to the door and picked the lock—so simple a child could have done it. But what had he expected of a rent-by-the-hour-or-day establishment?

Opening the door, he stepped inside the minuscule foyer and studied the two doors on the ground level. Nothing but silence. He found the light switch and flipped off the ceiling bulb illuminating the stairwell, then crept up the stairs, pausing as one creaked. He held still, his back flush with the wall, once again shadowed in darkness. Nothing stirred.

Reaching her room, he picked the lock, stepped inside, and shut the door, locking it behind him.

She was asleep on the shoddy sofa, a ratty blanket draped across her. Getting rid of her now might be easier, but what fun was it killing someone while they slept? And he needed to make sure she had the items.

He stood a moment, watching her chest rise and fall with what would be her final breaths, then he knocked her feet with his elbow.

Her eyes flashed open as she lurched to a seated position. She rubbed her eyes. "You're late."

Less chance of witnesses.

"You have the items?"

She nodded.

"Get them. We're in a hurry."

She got to her feet and headed for the bedroom.

He followed.

To his surprise, she climbed up on the dresser and reached for the heating vent.

Huh. She was smarter than he'd expected, yet not bright enough to know what was coming.

Pulling the dingy grate back, she retrieved a black velvet pouch and a bundle of letters held in place by a thick rubber band.

"Hand them over," he said.

She hopped down and hesitated. "I get my cut, right?" She clutched the items to her pale chest.

"You'll get your cut," he said, wrapping his hands around the garrote.

She released her hold. Taking the bag first, he slid it into his upper jacket pocket, then slipped the letters into his pant pocket. "Good job."

She brushed a strand of hair behind her ear, revealing her creamy neck. "Thanks."

Restless energy pulsed through him.

"Are we done here?" she asked, shifting her stance, her arms wrapped around her slender waist.

"Just about."

"What's left to do?" she asked, her head cocked, and then she stilled. She took a step back. So she'd finally figured it out.

"No." She shook her head, backing into the paneled wall. In one movement, left hand to right shoulder, he spun her around and slipped the garrote over her head.

He'd intended to give her the option—the easy way with a gunshot to the head or the hard way with the garrote. But the hard way was far more pleasurable, giving him the best elated high.

It really was a shame. She was a pretty thing.

Five minutes later, he was back in the van, leaving the body behind.

"You got everything?" Casey asked as they pulled onto the street, their headlights off.

Cyrus smiled and handed both items to him. They were a go. The appetite for what was to come gnawed at Cyrus's gut, but in a good way. It was time to feed the anticipation that had been growing in him for nigh on a year. It was time to scratch that itch.

Dani Pettrey is the bestselling author of the COASTAL GUARDIANS series, the CHESAPEAKE VALOR series, and the ALASKAN COURAGE series with nearly a million copies sold. A three-time Christy Award finalist, Dani has won the National Readers' Choice Award, Daphne du Maurier Award, HOLT Medallion, and Christian Retailing's Best Award for Suspense. She plots murder and mayhem from her home in the Washington, DC, metro area. She can be found online at DaniPettrey.com.

Sign Up for Dani's Newsletter

Keep up to date with Dani's latest news on book releases and events by signing up for her email list at the website below.

DaniPettrey.com

FOLLOW DANI ON SOCIAL MEDIA

Dani Pettrey   @AuthorDaniPettrey   @DaniPettrey

More from Dani Pettrey

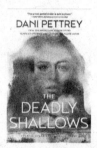